A
NEW FOREST
WITCH

≈

Siobhan Searle

In loving memory of my father.

Prologue

"Give sorrow words; the grief that does not speak knits up the over wrought heart and bids it break." William Shakespeare

It feels as if there is a hole inside of me. An emptiness, which makes it hard to breathe, Anabel Weststar reflected (most people called her Nan) as her father's wake wound down. Nan clutched the metal handle of the locked wooden box, which contained her father's ashes, as she mechanically thanked his few friends and neighbours for their heartfelt condolences. Unrecognizable faces, none of which she could claim as family, for Houston Weststar had been Nan's only relation and the one person dearest to her in the entire world.

What am I going to do without him? Nan grieved. A drowning sensation of abandonment sucked the air out of her lungs and replaced it with an engulfing loneliness.

She looked down at her father's cubicle coffin and felt a blinding rage of despair build up inside her at the cruel injustice, which had snatched this haloed idol from her life. It had been less than a week since Nan had seen her father, happy and healthy, before the unexpected heart attack ripped his life away. Nan wished she had savoured his smiling face, his laughter, his common scolding, and their farewell embrace.

However, what haunted Nan most was the knowledge she had known, sensed, something was amiss that dreadful night. She had ignored her unexplained power only to be punished later by the devastating phone call from the hospital stating her sole parent was dead. A death she might have prevented if she had only trusted her instincts, but now would never know.

With the last of the mourners out the door, a comforted smile spread across Nan's lips, when Rory's face appeared. "How are you holding up, Chickipoo?" Rory asked. Chickipoo being the pet name Rory had adorned her university friend with the first day the pair met on campus four years prior.

"I'm still alive, I guess," responded Nan.

"What do you say we get out of here then?" ventured Rory, Nan's chauffeur for the day's sorrowful event and life-saviour, keeping her afloat.

"Sounds perfect," Nan sighed in relief. She couldn't wait to be back within the peaceful walls of her nineteenth century farmhouse. Her father's beloved home and place where he belonged, even now.

"Great, all set then?" Rory gave Nan a reassuring smile.

Her father's cold lifeless remains in her hands, nothing but a small plastic bag full of bone chips and ashes, Nan breathed in a shaky breath and gave an affirmative "Yes".

Leaving the rented hall with her trusted friend, Nan wondered—unable to come to terms with it all—how he could be gone? Unaware that from his death loomed her own.

Chapter 1
"Philosophy is really nostalgia, the desire to be at home."
Novalis

As they drove back to the farm in Rory's beat-up old, lime green Volkswagen Bug, Nan tried to take her mind off her loss and find peace in the Ontario landscape. The wooden box set safely on her lap. Normally, she would be white knuckling it the whole ride due to Rory's inventive driving skills, but today Nan took no notice.

They turned onto the dusty, old dirt concession road, which led to her father's Myrtle farm. The place Nan called home. A hard worker all his life, Mr. Weststar had bought the property before Nan had been born, attracted to the place's remote peaceful setting, a private man by nature. The sixty acres of land was never farmed nor housed livestock in its barns, apart from a couple of chickens and a horse Nan received one birthday, but Mr. Weststar had made it a comfortable home and great atmosphere for a young girl to grow up in.

Nan saw the familiar rustic yet classic red brick, Victorian house appear from behind the trees as they continued down the country road. Unique with bay windows, wrap-around porch, black peaked shingled roof, and dual chimneys, it sat high atop its own little private mountain—the closest neighbour fifteen minutes away. A pair of weeping willows framed it in like a painting, the house a perfect memory of a time past. The gravel driveway, equipped with water beaten potholes and edged with boulders Nan's father had placed himself, wound up the tiny hill to the house's side.

The car came to an exuberant stop. Nan was almost launched out of her seat as Rory announced, "We're here," when she unbuckled her seat belt.

"No really." Nan exclaimed, a bit dishevelled. She adjusted her grip a little tighter on the chest.

"What?" Rory smirked in mock innocence. "I was just making sure you were awake."

"If you had tried any harder you would have delivered me right through the door." Nan exited the car, chest in hand.

"I never thought of that, maybe next time." Rory laughed and followed Nan to the house's side door.

Nan unlocked the door and stepped aside to allow the awkwardly burdened Rory, who carried platters of unwanted food from the wake, to go ahead of her. Meanwhile, Nan braced herself for the sadness the familiar surroundings were about to plague her with. Once inside, Nan heard the horrifying sound of frantic nails on hardwood and cringed.

Unable to get the warning from her lips, Nan watched in disbelieve as a large pair of white paws slammed down hard on Rory's chest and threw her to the floor, hurling the food trays into the air. The blue/grey and white furry owner of the paws stood over Rory's prostrate body and covered her face in slobbery kisses.

"Blue, you maniac!" screamed Rory, trying to shield her face from the dog's saliva.

Nan placed her father's ashes on the sideboard by the door and hurried into action. She grabbed the old pit bull's collar and hauled her muscular body off Rory's torpid, sprawled frame. The victim cursed the beast as she got to her feet. Satisfied her friend was unharmed, Nan took in the mass of displaced food and empty platters scattered all over the entryway. Relief washed over her, thankful for the touch of normality after such a gruelling day, laughter burst out of Nan.

"What are you laughing at?" exclaimed Rory in ill-humoured astonishment, not seeing the joviality of the situation.

"I'm sorry," Nan apologized and tried to suppress a giggle. "But it was just so funny."

"I'm glad my possible paralyzing misfortune, thanks to your unruly mutt, is funny to you," scowled Rory, She gave the canine villain a disapproving stare, as the animal sniffed around the mislaid food.

Nan attempted to wipe the broad smile from her face, as her eyes followed Rory's menacing gaze and quickly knelt down to save the jeopardized vegetable bits and sandwich triangles. Blue turned in her master's direction and licked Nan's cheek. "I missed you too," cooed Nan to the slobbery beast and held up one of the righted platters to Rory. Nan smiled wider as Rory shook her head and marched down the hall towards the kitchen.

After the other two trays were collected, Nan got to her feet and placed them on the sideboard, then reclaimed the wooden coffer. She looked around the memory-filled space. Nan's father, a workaholic, had little time over the years for updates to the place and much of its original décor remained. Nan scanned the walls as she stood solemn in the hallway and was flabbergasted at just how out-dated and neglected they looked.

The long narrow hall, with hardwood floors, aged white wooden wainscoting and doorframes, still had the old ornate, floral patterned wallpaper, which looked as if it was hundreds of years old. To the right of the entrance was the opening for the living room, which contained one of the house's unique bay windows. The stairwell to the upper floor hugged the living room's entry wall and across the hall was a beautiful pair of sliding mahogany doors, which led to Nan's father's den. Down the hall was the usual array of rooms; dining room, bath, kitchen, and what once had been the cold storage, now a general mudroom.

As nostalgia washed over her, Nan headed into the living room with Blue close at her heels and flopped with a huff onto the couch. Rory soon joined her, a glass of water in hand and eyed the discarded platters disapprovingly before she too reclined on the lazy-boy chair near the room's entrance.

"Well, despite my pummelling in the doorway when we got here, things didn't go to bad today," stated Rory, as she rested her arms behind her head.

"I'm just glad it's over." Nan gave a half-hearted smile. She tried to take her mind off the day as she patted the big oaf of a dog at her side. Then, struck with a jolt of recognition she said, "I should go check on Poe in the loft."

"Oh I'm sure he's fine," reassured Rory. "You know him; he's probably curled up on one of our beds."

"True." However, upon second thought, Nan added, "But I really should go get him and bring him to the house for the night."

A couple of years earlier, Nan had made it one of her missions in life to tame and domesticate the big steel grey barn cat, with white nose and paws, who wandered about the farm. It didn't take her long and after a month of coaxing him with food, she finally won the battle of wills and he had been her lazy, fat house companion ever since.

"So are you sleeping here tonight then?" Rory asked, worried the removal of the cat from their joint living space signified Nan's as well.

For the past couple of years the two girls had shared a loft Nan's father had fashioned them out of the old haymow in the barn. Despite its odd location and agrarian attributes, he had managed to turn it into quite a nice little apartment for them.

"Yeah, I think I'll stay at the house for a while," answered Nan, not catching the slight concern in Rory's tone.

"Suit yourself," Rory shrugged. She tried to resist the premature urge to get upset at the aspect of losing her roommate. "That just means you'll miss out on one of my famous popcorn movie nights."

"I'm sure I can survive this once," Nan smirked, as she got to her feet. "Well then, I should go get him."

Rory jumped up at the same time and headed for the door. "Yup, I better hit the hay as well. Have to work tomorrow."

"I'm pretty sure dad cleared out all the hay, Rory, but I can get you more if you like," Nan joked, the first time since getting the life changing call from the hospital.

"Oh aren't we the comedian tonight." Rory turned back to Nan at the door and smirked, "If you get scared in this big old house all by yourself tonight, you know where to find me."

"I'm sure I will manage. The ghosts and I are old friends. Besides I've got Blue to protect me." Nan looked down at the dog's happy, salivating face.

"Sure, she could always tackle anybody that comes through the door," grumbled Rory. She glared at her earlier assailant with doubt.

As she opened the door and turned to leave, Rory caught a glimpse of Nan's tired appearance, as she got ready to follow her to retrieve the cat. "Don't worry about getting Poe tonight, just try, and get some sleep. He can keep me company for the night and I'll bring him over in the morning before work."

"Really?" exclaimed Nan, "You don't mind? Oh that would be awesome."

"Yeah, no problem." Rory looked at Nan and then gave her a timid smile. "But promise me you will put that down at some point tonight."

Puzzled for a moment, Nan followed Rory's gaze to her hands and realized, not cognizant, she still clutched her father's ash box. Awe struck at the fact she had carried the rather heavy chest all this time, unaware, as if it was another limb.

With a saddened sigh, Nan replied, "Yes, I promise I'll put him down soon."

"Good," said Rory. "Okay well, I'll see you tomorrow then." She walked out the door.

"See you tomorrow," called Nan behind her, before she closed the door.

Nan rested her head on the door's hard surface for a while and listened to the quiet of the house. She felt as if at any minute her father would jump out and yell "Gotcha", as if the whole terrible event was just a bad joke. However, as she looked down at the object in her hands, she knew that would never happen.

She headed back into the living room toward the mantelpiece over the large brick fireplace and placed the precious urn on top of it. Satisfied her father would be safe for the time being, Nan let her attention be drawn away to the whimpering dog at her side.

"I'm sorry girl. You've probably had your legs crossed for hours. Come on, want to go outside?" They headed out of the living room and down the hall to the kitchen's back door. Nan grabbed the food platters on the way.

After she shut the porch door behind Blue, Nan turned back to the kitchen's immaculate surfaces and decided she should try to locate the dog's food. A truck driver by trade and backyard mechanic at leisure, both of which being dirty jobs, surprisingly Nan's father had been an obsessive, compulsive housekeeper. An aspect of his character, Nan now cursed while she opened every cupboard in search of a simple bag of canine chow. Finally, she unearthed a Rubbermaid tote of Purina in the mudroom and the dog's bowls on the linoleum floor at the counter's end. She filled them up and let in the ravenous mutt.

With Blue tended to, Nan considered making herself something to eat, but listened to her better judgement and decided against it. Well aware that in times of crisis or intense stress, her appetite always failed her. Instead, she headed back to the living room to retrieve her father and opted to go upstairs to the room of her youth, to change and shower. Though black was Nan's usual shade, the whole dress and heels thing screamed "Not her".

Almost an hour later—having placed her father's urn on top of her old mahogany tallboy—Nan had showered and changed into pyjama pants and a spaghetti strapped T-shirt. Nan returned downstairs refreshed and much more content. She plopped herself back down on the couch and settled to kill some time channel surfing, the idea of sleep not yet feasible.

Nan's eyes continuously wandered over the room's yellowed wallpaper as she flipped through the satellite's guide flip. *Boy is it in need of a facelift,* she thought. Plagued with an anal-retentive nature to fix things amiss, Nan jumped to her feet, remembering how her father use to keep left over paint cans in the dirt floor basement and went to investigate.

Chapter 2
"Nothing is as painful to the human mind as a great and sudden change." Mary Shelley

The next morning, Rory gave a half-hearted knock out of politeness on the house's side door before letting herself in, with Poe held firmly under her arm. She had learned from yesterday's ordeal and braced herself when she heard the familiar sound of rushing nails on floorboards, as Blue rounded the corner at full speed, charging for the open door. Poe cringed, alarmed, in Rory's arms at the sight of the undignified brute.

With a huff she called the stupid dog back inside and closed the door. Rory was about to summon Nan, as she tried to keep the curious pit bull at bay and the annoyed cat from leaping to safety, when a voice from the living room beckoned her, "I'm in here, Rory."

Blue at her heels and Poe hissing in her arms, Rory entered the living room and froze. "What the hell are you doing?" she shrieked horrified. The struggling feline dropped to the floor as Rory took in the scene of Nan balancing precariously on a ladder, paint roller in one hand and tray in the other. Newspaper littered the room's floor and furniture to shield them from globs of forest green paint and empty cans scattered everywhere.

"Don't you like it?" exhaled Nan, shocked by her friend's disapproving expression and the rough bite of her words.

"Yes, it looks great," answered Rory in a kinder tone. She entered further into the room, side stepping cans in the process. "But why are you doing it now and why didn't you ask me for help? You're supposed to be resting...grieving."

"I know," acknowledged Nan sombrely, "I just got looking at the walls last night and at how in need they were of modernization and couldn't help myself. Besides, dad always said it was better to keep busy and come on, don't you think the green looks better than that tacky wallpaper?"

"Yes it is fantastic," Rory had to admit, but with a more serious tone, added, "I just think you should have waited and I could have helped you."

Nan beamed with self-satisfied pleasure at the sight of the room's transformation and shrugged, "Oh that's okay. I found it refreshing. I was thinking of tackling the hall next. The paper out there is hideous."

Rory stared at Nan's eagerness in disbelief, worried her energizer-bunny routine and complete oblivion to the dramatic events of the last week, was unhealthy. With a slight scowl, she inquired, "Did you sleep at all last night?"

Oblivious of Rory's concerned gaze, Nan answered, "No, I got started on the walls and I guess I kind of lost myself in it all." She looked down from her perch on the ladder and saw her friend's serious expression. "What?" asked Nan.

Like a mother hen, Rory rebuked, "And I suppose you haven't eaten anything either have you?"

"No," Nan confirmed, like a scolded child.

"You know you don't have to take on the world all at once, Chickipoo. Give yourself time to grieve, rest, to figure things out. You've just had a bomb dropped on you. It's okay to do nothing for a while."

Silence followed, as Nan digested Rory's words and found her voice to say, "I do hear you and you're right, but I just feel so lost when I'm doing nothing. Keeping busy makes me not have to admit to myself that it's real and how much I miss him."

"I know. I just don't want you to burn yourself out." Rory sympathized and decided there was nothing more she could say. Instead, she gave her friend a pleasant grin and said, "Now how about we go find you some breakfast?"

"Sounds like a plan," Nan smiled. She came down the ladder, put down the roller and tray, then trailed after Rory into the kitchen. Blue trotted along behind.

"Oh by the way I brought Poe with me," stated Rory as she walked down the hallway. "He leapt out of my arms though, when that menace of a dog appeared and I'm not sure where he..." She trailed off, when she caught sight of the dining room as they passed and abruptly stopped and screeched, "You did this room too?"

Nan almost collided into the back of her. After she regrouped, Nan recollected she had not mentioned the exact extent of her evening remodel. "Oh yeah, I just figured while I was waiting for the paint to dry in the living room, I might as well spruce things up in here too. Not that anyone really uses it though."

13

Frustration bubbled within and with a shake of her head; Rory marched on down the hall towards the kitchen, not knowing where to start. Once in the room, she clapped her hands together, looked around and exclaimed, "Now let's see what we have in here. Do you have any coffee?"

"Um, I'm not sure," Nan frowned, as she walked past her to let Blue outside. "But there's tea in the black canister over there on the counter by the kettle."

"Seriously," vociferated Rory in disgust.

"Dad and I happened to prefer tea, thank you." Nan smirked as she went over to the counter and turned on the electric kettle.

"Oh yes I forgot, Lady Diana." Rory scoured the cupboards, climbing on the counter to reach the top ones. "We less sophisticated mortals would rather drink our cup of mud in the morning," she bantered.

"I think I'm more like Kate Middleton actually. Anyways if you want mud the garden is right outside, help yourself," Nan joked.

"Oh ha-ha," Rory grunted and continued her search.

"Okay well, while you're climbing the cabinetry how about I make us some toast?" Nan chuckled.

A muffled "Okay" came from one of the cupboards in agreement. Nan put some bread into the toaster and made her tea. A few minutes later just as the toast popped up, Nan heard an exuberant shriek of success from the person covert inside the cupboard over the stove. Rory retracted her dishevelled chestnut coloured head with a broad smile, as she triumphantly brandished an old tin of instant coffee. As Rory jumped down from the stove, she yelled "Eureka" before heading to the already hot kettle.

Nan simpered and asked doubtfully, "Are you sure that coffee is still good? It looks like it is a hundred years past its expiration date."

Rory waved off Nan's pessimism with an insouciant raise of her shoulder and unconcerned wrinkled brow. "Sure it is. Coffee never goes bad it just solidifies over time. Haven't you ever been told that things get better with age?" She then grabbed a butter knife from the cutlery drawer and thrust it at the dense rocklike contents of the tin.

Nan shrugged, finished buttering their toast and let Blue back in, then placed the plates down on a little circular table in the small breakfast nook near the porch door. It was framed in on all sides by large windows, which overlooked the eastern fields and forestry. In the summer, Nan found it quite a pleasant location to sit and read, with its view of the small creek that ran across the property and great oak, elm, and pine trees guarding it. Closer to the house one enjoyed the sight of wild flowers along with the two stately willows and few forsythia bushes lorded over the back lawn.

Nan's train of thought was broken then, when after she dropped a lump of coffee in a cup, Rory asked, "So how long did your boss give you off work?"

"We didn't really determine a specific time limit," explained Nan, "He just said to take as long as I needed."

"Hey now, you can't beat that," smiled Rory and came over to join her at the table, where she set down her coffee and took a bite of toast.

"I guess," but then in a more serious tone, "I probably shouldn't take too long though."

"Oh come on, it's not like you've got the most important job in the world you need to rush back to," Rory smirked, as she tried to discourage Nan's sudden sense of responsibility.

"True," admitted Nan, not being able to counter for when in reality Rory was right. After she had graduated from university, her major being ancient history, Nan landed a job as a research assistant at the Lucy Maud Montgomery Heritage Society and though it was not her ideal job, she had hoped it would prove advantageous in the long run. Unfortunately, her luck had not panned out and as of late, Nan had spent most of her time working as a tour guide at the society's manse house in Leaksdale, just 34.8 km from Myrtle.

Rory let her mind fall once again on her night's lonesome loft stay and asked, "So what do you think you will do now? Since things have changed and all?"

Nan had tried to avoid thinking of matters much and replied with a puzzled expression, "I'm not sure actually. Dad had everything in order regarding the house and his assets, which I've already seen to at the lawyers before his wake, so really there's not much left for me to tend to."

"What do you plan to do with the farm?" prompted Rory. She hoped her anxiety didn't show.

"Oh I'll keep it of course," said Nan, as if it was ridiculous to assume otherwise. All at once, Nan clued into the context of their discussion and grasped its purpose. She looked up at Rory and added, "You don't have to worry, Rory, you can stay in the loft. I'm not going to kick you out."

With a nonchalant air, Rory replied, "I'm not worried, I was just thinking of you and your financial state, that's all."

"Yeah, okay! I'm sure that was your top priority." Nan gave Rory a knowing grin. "The mortgage was paid off a year ago and dad's insurance money was enough to cover his debt, so really all that's left to maintain is the utility bills and taxes, which between my income and the rent from Mr. Watson for leasing the cow pastures, I should have no problem keeping on top of things."

"Plus my rent for the loft," Rory reminded.

"That too," acknowledged Nan, surprised she had forgotten.

Rory continued to wonder what was processing in Nan's head. Finally, she found enough courage and asked, "So I guess you will be moving back into the house then?"

"Yeah I might as well. There's no point in leaving it empty. Besides it might sound stupid, but I feel closer to my dad here," replied Nan.

"That doesn't sound stupid at all," smiled Rory compassionately.

More at ease now her fears were out in the open, Rory relaxed back into her cream coloured, upholstered wooden chair. A long silence passed between them before a light bulb clicked on in Nan's head and she looked up at Rory in glee. "You know you could always move in here with me."

Speechless, Rory gaped at Nan in shock. When her frozen vocal cords relaxed, she shrieked, "Really, are you serious?"

Nan smiled at her friend's elated expression and confirmed her offer with a slight giggle. "Sure, why not. We lived together in the loft anyways, why not here?"

"Oh this is going to be so fantastic. We can be just like Laverne and Shirley," beamed Rory. Like an excited schoolgirl she clapped her hands together and stomped her feet. With the jubilance in the air and breakfast over, Rory's excitement could not be contained and she sprang to her feet, looked down at Nan, and said, "Let's go move our stuff."

Nan laughed, stood, and headed to the sink to put their dishes down. "Don't you have to work today?"

"Not till this afternoon, that gives us lots of time to move our stuff from the loft."

"You might want to pick your room first," Nan smirked.

"Oh awesome," and Rory bounded out of the room for the stairs.

Nan exited the kitchen for the stairs and called up, "Just don't pick the master, I'm going to move my stuff into it," but Rory did not hear her, already on the hunt.

Every now and then as she leaned on the banister, Nan would hear an excited expression of "Wow" or "Oh awesome" float down from the second floor. She waited for what felt like a lifetime, before she headed upstairs to see how the adventurer was making out.

Half way up the stairs, she was met by Rory's irrepressible face peering over the railing at her. "Holy crap, this place is huge! It has five bedrooms."

"Yes, I'm quite sure I grew up here," laughed Nan, as she climbed the rest of the stairs. "Have you figured out which room you want?"

"It was a hard choice, but if it's okay with you I'd like your old room," Rory grinned. She had heard what Nan had said after all.

"Sure."

"Amazing. So what do we do first?"

"Well, we'll need to move my furniture out of my old room so you can move in of course, but first I'll have to empty dad's stuff out of the master," explained Nan, a game plan in mind. She looked at Rory's eager face and asked, "Could you run downstairs to the little door on the stair's side and get me some boxes? They're right on the basement landing of the stairs."

"Sure," and off she went, while Nan headed to the master suite.

As Nan looked through drawers, Rory reappeared with an armful of boxes of different shapes and sizes. She placed them on the floor. "So what's in the basement anyways? I've always found basements intriguing."

"Just when I thought you couldn't get any weirder." Nan shook her head at Rory's quirkiness, as she assembled boxes. "It's just your typical run of the mill basement. No dead bodies, hidden treasure, or dark family secrets, unless you find furnaces and water heaters interesting?"

"Oh that sucks," Rory moped. "Here I thought this old house was full of secrets and ghosts."

"Oh don't worry the house is haunted, you won't be disappointed there," reassured Nan. She opened one of her father's dresser drawers and began to empty it.

"Sure, sure," laughed Rory. "You're just trying to scare me." Headed back downstairs, she added, "I'm going to get my stuff from the loft."

Chapter 3
"Never fear quarrels but seek hazardous adventures."
Alexandre Dumas

The rest of the morning and early afternoon was spent moving furniture and removing unwanted items. The job was easy since the majority of the work was moving things from one room to the other. Nan had opted to use most of her old bedroom belongings, which resulted in only Rory's possessions being brought over from the loft.

They placed Nan's father's furnishings in one of the spare rooms, which did not take long since there was little, her father spent minimal time at home, always traveling, driving trucks. Once accomplished, the girls initiated moving Nan into the room and then the stuff Rory had hauled over from the loft into her new abode.

When the heavy lifting and assembling was said and done, the pair separated. Rory had a bit of time before work in which she could personalize her space and Nan decided to try to bring some order into her new disorganized chamber. However, as she stood in her father's former room, with its bay window seat, tiny white painted brick fireplace, and en-suite, Nan found it hard not to envision him standing in front of her.

However, before Nan had a chance to uproot herself and claim the room as her own, there came a knock from downstairs. *Saved by the bell*, she smiled in relief, exited the room, and rushed down to answer the door.

Upon opening it, Nan discovered her old reliable high school chum, Parker. "Hey you," she greeted, pleased by his unexpected appearance.

Nan had first met Parker in her third year of high school. He had dated one of her former good friends, now out of touch. Though he had been three years older than her, a high school drop-out and had an incriminating reputation, the pair had instantly hit it off and remained devoted friends ever since.

It was bitterly obvious however, that Parker's heart belonged to Nan, no matter whom he was dating. He had hinted many times about them becoming a couple and on one or two occasions had asked Nan out, but to no avail. As much as Nan liked Parker and found herself giddy in his company, the answer was always "No". Some unforeseen force always held her back, though the chemistry was undoubtedly there. May be it was his bad boy demeanour or immature ways, Nan didn't know, but self-preservation always stepped in.

As she looked at his smiling face all the mixed emotions Nan had harboured for years came back to her. Parker had made a brief appearance at the wake the day before, but left early due to work. He felt horrid and upon seeing her asked, "Hey you, how are you doing?"

"Okay I guess," answered Nan with a shrug. She changed the topic as she moved away from the door to let Parker inside. "How are things with you?"

"Not too bad."

Just then, Rory jogged down the stairs, curious to see who their visitor was. Her face fell at the site of Parker's muscular form standing in the hallway, the downfall of humanity as far as she was concerned and a regrettable member of Nan's life. "Oh it's you," she groaned.

Not wanting to give her the satisfaction of knowing he had noted her coldness, Parker grinned politely at Rory's iceberg face and replied, "Yup it's me. How are you doing Rory?"

Rory remained on the bottom step where she had halted at the sight of him, arms crossed and a pungent scowl. "Fine," she grumbled.

Nan still stood by the door. She gave Rory a disapproving glower. Parker smirked, then turned his attention back to Nan and said, "I told you I'd drop in to check up on you and figured there was no time like the present."

"She's fine. She has me here," Rory burst forth, cutting any chance Nan had to respond off before the words formed on her tongue.

Nan glared at Rory more incensed and quickly stated, "Well I'm happy you're here. Come on let's go into the living room." She motioned with a tilt of her head for them to enter the living room, then offered Parker coffee or something to drink.

Parker accepted her offer for some refreshment and headed through the opening to the living room, patting Blue on the way, while Rory trailed behind. With an exaggerated whistle, he said upon entering the room, "I love what you've done with the place."

Suddenly, Nan realized she hadn't cleaned up yet, the room still littered with newspaper and empty paint cans. She rushed past him, embarrassed, and quickly tried mending the situation, saying mortified,

"Oh I completely forgot about this mess." As she ripped paper off the couch, added, "Here have a seat if you can find your way around the mayhem."

Parker laughed as he walked through the maze to the now revealed couch, "Ah no worries. You've obviously been busy. It looks good."

Nan glowed, her anxiety instantly melting away as it always did in his company.

Soon the three of them were all reclined comfortably with nice hot beverages in hand. Nan and Parker on the couch, side by side, with little space between them, and Blue at their feet, while Rory sulked on the lazy-boy near the entrance, secretly hoping some unforeseen catastrophe would drag Parker away or perhaps an anvil would drop from the ceiling on his head like they did in cartoons.

"So everything's been going good then? You've been keeping busy since I saw you yesterday," commented Parker casually, giving Nan his typical James Dean smirk.

Rory abruptly got to her feet, having come to the conclusion Parker wasn't going to leave any time soon, and cut into Nan's reply once again, "Well I have to get ready for work." Then, she stomped off up the stairs and left the two friends staring in surprise.

"Yes, things have been okay," replied Nan. She shook her head in bewilderment at Rory's gruff displace.

"Well that's good."

"It's hard, but everything's been taken care of so there's not much for me to do except give the house a makeover and eventually deal with dad's business."

Puzzled, Parker looked at her and questioned, "I thought your dad was retired?"

"For the most part," Nan explained, "But you know dad, he couldn't be idle long. He bought a flatbed and started his own towing business."

"Oh okay," he nodded, "So what are you going to do, run it yourself?"

With a sarcastic expression on her face, Nan laughed, "Oh yeah totally. I'll just give up my career and become a flatbed driver." The sentence ended with the impression there should have been a "Duh" at its finish.

Amused by her feisty mien, one of the many unique qualities which had attracted him to her in the first place, Parker shared her laughter and said, "Well no, but you could hire someone to drive it for you."

The wheels of thought and opportunity spun in her head, Nan deliberated for a bit over what he had said, before saying, "No it would be too much of a hassle, and I wouldn't know where to begin."

"Aw come on, it wouldn't be that hard for a smart girl like you. I could give you a hand if you want." Parker saw the moment of opportunity flash before his eyes and seized it. "Actually I could drive it for you."

Blindsided by his last statement, Nan stared at him in disbelief. "What about the job you already have?"

For as long as Nan had known Parker, he had been either between jobs or in short-lived positions. This being one of the reasons she had never brought herself to see them having any future together as a couple. A construction labourer, Parker was a strong, capable young man. Not the dress up, meet the parents type of guy. A lot like her father when she thought about it, who had met Parker on several occasions and from what Nan could tell, had liked him.

Nan nonchalantly studied Parker's tanned, brawny features and thought it over. His tattooed arms, cropped off dark brown hair, and alluring hazel eyes sent little sparks of attraction up her spine.

"It's seasonal, so I'm pretty much going to be unemployed soon anyways," he replied.

Still sceptical at the idea of upgrading their relationship to an even more intimate one, Nan objected, "Yeah, but the towing business can be pretty demanding and besides I don't even know how successful dad had gotten it."

"Knowing your dad he was probably making a good buck," Parker smirked.

"True." When it came to her father, Nan knew he was never the type to do something half-hearted and could do just about anything mechanical. Not to mention he could drive anything with wheels and would go like a bat out of hell.

Parker gave Nan a coaxing smile, which produced a smile in return. Then he leaned in a little closer and purred, "Come on, Nan. I know it will be great and besides you will get a kick out of bossing me around."

Her resolve yielded to his enticing ways and before she could truly consider what she was saying, Nan laughed and agreed, "Well okay, but let's be partners instead."

He stared at her in thrilled, but stunned amazement, his mind whirling at all the possibilities. "Are you sure? Being business partners is a big step," he asked.

"Of course I'm sure. It's not like we're going to bed together or anything. We're just business partners. Besides with me working for the heritage society, you'll basically be running the show all on your own."

Nan was too excited over their new business venture to notice the longing gaze her last comment had made in Parker's eyes and as she talked on, the echoes of the phrase "In bed together" hung in his thoughts. He couldn't help but envision her smooth, ivory skin pressed up against his and their heaving breaths mingled in passionate lust and exhausted pleasure. Perhaps this new arrangement might bring that image closer to reality, he hoped.

"Awesome," finished Nan. She took Parker's mechanical nod for agreement. Then adrenalized, she jumped to her feet and exclaimed, "Well let's get started. Um, do you want to see the shop?"

He eyed Nan's chiselled, enthusiastic face with amusement and followed her example. Once on his feet, he smiled, shrugged and replied, "Sure."

Nan grabbed her fall jacket off the newel post before going out. She gave Parker's bare arms a disapproving look and muttered, "I don't know how you're not cold."

"I'm hot stuff!" Both burst out laughing.

Rory, bounded down the stairs in her waitress uniform, which consisted of black pants and a black T-shirt with green stripes down the sides—the restaurant's name, Appetito, emblazoned over her left breast—asked with a frown, "What's so funny?"

"Oh nothing," dismissed Nan with a casual shrug.

"Going somewhere?" Rory snooped further, taking in Nan's jacket and the open door, giving Parker a pointed stare.

Not thinking of the outcome due to her eagerness, Nan replied, "We're just heading out to see dad's shop. We're going into business together."

Rory's eyes widen as big as saucers, full of shocked horror. Her mouth opened and closed like a fish, not trusting what she might say next. Once over the initial surprise, but still too consumed with rage, she huffed, "I'm going to work," and stormed past them out the door, to her car, never giving them a second look.

Nan's jubilation abated as she tried to digest Rory's less than impressed mannerism, unable to grasp what her issue was.

Parker ignored the little histrionic scene as if it had never occurred and smiled at Nan. "Well, shall we go?"

Not allowing Rory's abrupt negativity spoil the rest of her day, Nan renewed her twinkle and walked out the door with an ebullient "For sure."

****

The two walked down the gravel laneway towards the barn, to one of the two large outbuildings. Nan's father had converted the old machinery shed into a giant garage, not long after moving in. He had torn most of the sidewall down, leaving the rest of the exterior original, and installed two large garage doors for working on his transports.

Parker and Nan went over the tools, truck, books, and were fairly confident in the end their joint venture would turn out to be a good investment. When the shop talk was said and done, both in agreement to start right away, the two fell silent for a bit and let it all sink in.

"The only downside is that it's going to be a real pain to drive out here from my sister's, to get the truck every time there's a call. I'll have to look into renting a place closer," mused Parker.

"Oh yeah, I never thought of that." Nan frowned, before a light bulb went off in her head and she added, "You know the loft is empty now that Rory and I are staying in the house. You could always rent it."

He couldn't have planned it better if he had tried, Parker thought. Not wanting to show his elation, he shrugged, "Yeah that would work."

"Great. It has some furniture in it to, if you want to use it."

"Perfect, I don't have much except for a couple of garbage bags full of clothes and my tools, at my sister's," he grinned.

"You're such a hobo," Nan laughed, "When do you want to move in?"

"How about tomorrow?"

Surprised by his promptness, all Nan could say was "Oh okay."

24

All the details hashed out, they closed up shop and headed back to the house on the pretext Parker was leaving. "So what are your plans for the rest of the day?" he inquired, looking for any excuse to hang around.

"Well since I've spruced up most of the downstairs I was thinking of tackling the hall and stairwell next."

"I can give you a hand if you want," he shrewdly offered.

"Awesome," replied Nan, happy for the help and enjoying his company.

Back in the house, Parker assessed the situation of the hallway while Nan moved the paint supplies out from the living room. "You know it would look a lot better if we removed the paper before painting the walls," Parker stated in a professional tone.

"Why? I just painted over the wallpaper in the living room and dining room, and they look fine," Nan frowned.

Parker smirked and nodded his head. "It's okay, but you can see the seam lines of the paper underneath."

"Well I wasn't expecting it to go in *Homes & Gardens* magazine," Nan balked, indignantly. "I was just trying to freshen it up."

"I know, but if you're going to do something you might as well do it right. Right?" Parker's smirk grew wider at Nan's obvious annoyance.

Nan couldn't count the number of times she had heard those exact words come out of her father's mouth. "Fine. So how do you want to do it then, *Holmes on Homes*?"

"Do you have a wallpaper steamer?"

A little puzzled, not a question she was asked every day, Nan gave it much thought before she ventured to reply, "I think I might have seen one once in the attic."

"Great, let's go look." They headed up the stairs, both grabbing one of the boxes of Nan's father's discarded possessions on the way to the attic.

Chapter 4
"Nothing weighs on us so heavily as a secret."
Jean de la Fontaine

It had been years since Nan had gone up into the attic. As a little girl, she had decided to play pirate and sought booty amongst the many chests and boxes stored away in the space. However, her pilgrimage was short lived when her father discovered her and was less than impressed. He scolded her severely and banned her from ever entering the attic again, which she had obeyed, until now.

As she walked up the steep narrow steps, Nan smelt the faint odour of century's worth of mould, mothballs, and stale air. At the door crowning the staircase, Parker pushed against it with his broad shoulder and tried to budge the thick old wood on its stiff unyielding hinges. After applying a great deal of pressure, the door opened and they found themselves in a dull, dimly lit, dust filled room, with low peaked rafters and a single beam of light that emanated through a solitary octagon window at the room's end.

The atmosphere was ominous. Cobwebs hung everywhere and there was an eminent sense that at any minute a bat was going to swoop down and accost their heads. Nan had once encountered a bat and she remembered it well. The room itself from floor to rafters was piled full of boxes, trunks, suitcases, unwanted furniture, and years' worth of knickknacks—once someone's treasured possessions, now forgotten relics.

As Nan looked around at the dismissed objects, an odd chill ran down her spine. She gave a little shiver and spun around as if she expected to find someone standing behind her. No one was there.

"It's a lot smaller than I would have figured it was from looking at it outside," Parker observed. He wandered through the cramped space in search of a spare inch to set the box Nan had laden him with, down and locate the paper steamer. Nan inched behind him, stopping every couple of seconds to look over her shoulder. The strange sensation of being watched continued to tickle her neck.

Parker set his box down in front of a stack of others and began rummaging through them. "It's almost as if your dad kept everything he ever owned."

Nan laughed despite the eerie surroundings and put the box she carried on top of Parker's. "He did. Dad was a genuine pack rat."

She turned in the opposite direction as if someone had just called her name. Nan stared into the unoccupied space, unnerved. *Something's not right,* she shivered. *Could it be one of the ghosts in the house?*

It had been a well-known fact between Nan and her father, that their comfortable country home was haunted. In the night, it was a regular occurrence to hear footsteps on the stairs, doors closing, piano music, and most commonly the sound of a radio. Nan was sure she had even seen an apparition once, as if it was trying to communicate with her.

As a child, Nan's father had explained to her they were not alone in the house, but were in no harm, the former occupants simply unready to leave. This helped Nan not to fear the lost souls sharing their home and since then had never been bothered by them. Until now that is. Even having grown up in a haunted house, Nan could find no explanation for the unsettled feeling upon her.

Curiosity getting the best of her, Nan wandered to the other side of the room and left Parker to his search. As she rounded another stack of boxes, her steps froze in astonishment. There, staring her straight in the face was a small rectangular door, almost unnoticeable due to the never-ending heap of items in front of it.

Startled, Nan yelled to Parker, "Hey look at this."

Within seconds, Parker appeared beside her and looked around at the desolate mess. "What?" he asked, not spotting the door.

"Look," exclaimed Nan as she pointed to the cluttered entrance.

"Wow, now that's weird." Parker strolled forward to get a better look. Nan still cemented to the spot.

Not wasting any time, Parker robustly erupted into action and began moving the pile of junk, which barricaded the door. "I knew this attic seemed too small. I never would have spotted it, how did you see it?" he grinned with self-satisfaction.

Nan watched him nervously. "It was like something was drawing me to it."

All she received in response was a sarcastic grunt. Again, Nan felt the odd ripple run down her back. A bit queasy, she looked around and anxiously said, "Maybe we should just forget about it and go find the paper steamer so we can get out of here."

Parker paused, looked at her in a contemptuous manner and laughed, "Don't tell me you're scared. Afraid a ghost is going to jump out at you?"

Nan scowled and huffed, "No, I just think we're wasting time that's all and for your information smarty pants the house is haunted."

"Yeah okay, Nan, and bats turn into vampires at night, right?" he mocked.

Like a spoiled child with a pout on, Nan all but stomped her foot before muttering, "It's true! I've heard them myself."

She got no reply. Nan thought back to all the times she had heard the unexplainable noises and seen the shadow play on the walls out of the corner of her eye. She knew the ghosts were real, but what were they trying to tell her?

With everything out from in front of the door, Parker grabbed its metal latch to open it. Nan shrieked, "No wait!"

Caught off guard by her outburst, Parker looked back at her over his shoulder and asked, "What?" When she couldn't come up with a logical reply, he shook his head irritated and sighed, "Oh will you stop." Reaching for the knob once more, Parker gave it one good pull and the door creaked open. A small room was revealed.

"See nothing happened," Parker said sarcastically.

For fear of what might come out, Nan had closed her eyes. She opened them upon hearing Parker's triumphant words and was relieved to see that all the door had concealed was the other half of the house's attic. She followed Parker's lead and stepped inside. Nan was shocked to find the space practically empty, apart from an antique wooden bedroom set—consisting of a dresser, nightstands, vanity, and headboard and footboard—a floral fabric straight back chair and a couple of boxes, all neatly piled to the left of the door.

Parker knelt down to examine one or two of the boxes. "There's nothing spooky in here except a bunch of tacky girl's clothes."

A little ashamed of her wimpy behaviour, Nan looked down at him and with a tiny smile and said, "Yeah, I guess I got all worked up for nothing."

"I'd say."

Anabel, a whisper floated through the air. Nan went numb. "Did you hear that?" she asked with a shiver.

"Hear what?" Parker's slightly muffled reply came from the box his head was in.

Nan turned and looked around the bare room, a gnawing feeling chewed at her gut. *It had been a voice, I know it,* she thought, *someone had called my name.* Something was wrong she could feel it. They never should have opened the door.

Then, her eyes fell upon it. At the back of the room, under another octagon window, apart from the rest of the stored items, was an old tin steamer trunk. Floods of light from the outside world setting it aglow like a prophetic alter. *Why is it set apart from everything else?* Nan contemplated*, almost as if dad didn't want anything to touch it.*

"That's strange," vocalized Nan, transfixed by the mysterious trunk.

"What's weird?" Parker looked in the direction Nan indicated. "What that old trunk?"

"Yeah, don't you think it's weird how it's placed over there away from everything else?"

"So what?" he frowned, unable to grasp the unusualness of the situation. "You read way too much into things, you know that?"

Nan shook her head at his narrow-mindedness and huffed, "So, why isn't it with the rest of the stuff then, huh? It's almost like dad was trying to hide it or something."

Parker chuckled. With a mischievous wink, he said, "Oh yes, maybe it's a ghost trunk or better yet, maybe there's the dead corpse of one of your dad's secret lovers in it."

"Oh shut up!" barked Nan, less than impressed at his jest. "My dad didn't have any lovers."

However, Nan couldn't deny something about Parker's theory caused alarm bells to ring off inside her head. The joys of the secret curse she had been plagued with all her life, an ability to know or sense things for no explainable reason, told her so now. The closed, barracked door, the half-empty room, and isolated trunk, it all smelled disastrous to Nan.

She mustered up her courage and inched her way over to the trunk to check it out for herself, leaving Parker and his jokes behind. An overwhelmed dread engulfed her. At the trunk, Nan knelt down before it and ran a hand over its aged wood—the battle of indecision wreaked havoc inside her. Slowly she lifted one brass latch of the trunk's face and then the other. With a deep breath in preparation for what she might find, Nan placed both hands on the lid and pushed up.

An ear piercing "bang" rang throughout the silent room. Nan screamed and jumped to her feet. Parker was also visibly alarmed as they both whirled around towards the room's entrance. In the doorway stood the fury innocent, puppy eyed face of Blue, with her smiling mouth and wagging tail. Upon searching for her master, the dog had nudged the narrow door with her snout and caused it to fly back and hit the wall, giving both Nan and Parker a heart attack as a result.

"Really, Blue?" Nan bellowed upon seeing the hapless animal and placed a hand over her palpating chest.

Parker bent down, petted his knee and called the dog over, "Come here you silly girl," at which Blue perked up and pranced toward him happily.

Her pulse settled a bit, the expected danger having passed, and Nan knelt back down in front of the trunk and once again attempted to lift the lid. It wouldn't open. Stunned, Nan let her hands fall to her knees and looking over her shoulder at Parker—still patting the attention-loving canine—moaned, "It won't open."

Parker got to his feet to come and investigate. He soon detected her issue after he looked the trunk over thoroughly and with an impish grin, said, "That's why, it's locked," and showed her the locked padlock on the trunk's side.

Nan scowled at this new anomaly. "That's weird," she whispered.

"Looks like your dad didn't want anyone getting inside," Parker shrugged, released the lock and walked away from the trunk.

"Yeah, but why?" agonized Nan.

He headed for the door with Blue at his heels, bored with the unsolvable mystery. "I don't know, but let's find that paper steamer and get back to work."

Nan sighed and continued to stare at the trunk. She had the sickening feeling something sinister was hidden within its bowels. *What was dad trying to hide, and from whom?* Not sure, she really wanted to find out, but with intrigue gnawing at her gut, Nan reluctantly got to her feet and left the room.

****

Not long after they exited the strange room, the two found the wallpaper steamer and headed back down to the main floor to commence their task. It had become late by the time they tackled the hall, but with Parker masterfully stripping the walls and Nan painting them, they soon had made great progress. They ordered a pizza and plugged along, unaware of the time until Rory walked through the front door, signalling it was well past ten o'clock.

"Wow," Rory exclaimed as her eyes swept over the freshly painted, ivory walls. She spotted Nan on the stairs, paintbrush in hand and said as she shut the door, "You've been busy."

Nan smiled with satisfaction. "Yes it's been a very productive day, thanks to Parker." Rory's gaze followed as Nan nodded her head in his direction further up the stairs.

Rory's expression changed in an instant from pleasant to that of a rabid dog. Completely ignoring Parker's presence, as if he was an unpleasant hallucination, Rory snarled, "He's still here?"

Parker took no notice of her tactlessness and continued working away, but Nan glowered and in a sharp disgruntled tone, fired back, "Yes he is. He's been helping me and as a matter-of-fact, he's going to be here a lot more from now on. I've rented him the loft."

"What?" hissed Rory, invisible flames spewed from her dilated nostrils.

"We're going to be working together anyways, so I might as well rent it to him instead of letting it sit there empty."

"Sure, but not to him!" Rory tartly opposed.

Surprised by Rory's blatant churlish manner and lack of decorum in Parker's presence, Nan stared at her in stunned silence. Nan narrowed her eyes and with an authoritative stance, replied, "I can rent it to whomever I choose. It is my property and no concern of yours."

Astounded at Nan's imperious attitude and mad at herself for lashing out like she had, Rory shrank down within herself. "Of course you can. I didn't mean…" She didn't finish her sentence, but instead walked down the hall to the kitchen without another word.

Nan watched Rory's retreat with a repentant heart. She looked back up at Parker who gave an unsure shrug, but then returned to work. There was nothing to be done about it now she thought and she followed his example and resumed her paintbrush.

Within another hour, the stretch of wall going up the stairwell was finished and the pair stepped back to admire their work. It was time to call it a night they decided. Parker helped Nan clean up sombrely, knowing there was no point in prolonging things, and then headed for the door. "Well I guess I should be hitting the asphalt."

Nan followed him and said appreciatively, "Thanks again for all your help."

"Glad to be of service," he smiled, giving her a theatrical bow.

"Oh get out of here, you," laughed Nan and playfully pushed him on the shoulder.

Parker yearned to grab Nan and wrap her in his embrace. Drawing their bodies tight together and kiss her succulent, warm, perfectly formed lips. Nevertheless, he knew it wouldn't happen. Instead, he headed out the door and yelled back over his shoulder, "Be good and I'll see you tomorrow."

"Always," Nan giggled as she watched him get into his black Dodge Ram.

He laughed, "Yeah right," before he closed the door, started the accelerator, and drove away.

Nan glanced into the living room after she shut the door. Rory had been hiding there since her reappearance from the kitchen, where she pretended to be oblivious to everything but the rerun of *Gilmore Girls* she watched on the television. Too tired to deal with any extra drama tonight, Nan tended to Poe and Blue and then trekked upstairs to her room.

She changed into her pyjamas and climbed under the covers, the bed being the one thing she had managed to organize in her new room before

Parker's arrival. Her aching muscles rejoiced at the feel of the soft mattress. Blue curled up comfortable on the floor and Poe stretched out at her feet all ready for the night's slumbers. Not plagued by thoughts of her father due to tiredness, Nan soon found herself in a deep comfortable sleep.

****

It was dark, a black blindness. Nan felt her breath catch in her larynx as she searched her ebony surroundings, trying to figure out where she was. She stretched her arms out and pivoted in all directions, hoping to find a surface or something with mass in the dense stillness. There was nothing.

Panic brimmed inside her. Nan tried to call out, but uttered no sound. She was mute, as the darkness around her. Nan froze to the spot, not knowing what to do next, engulfed in the shaded silent abyss.

What is going on? Where am I? The thoughts whirled through her mind, as desperation traveled up every nerve in her body.

Far off in the distance a dim, red glow appeared, like a lighthouse's beacon against a stormy sea. Hope sprang to Nan's chest as she willed her fear paralysed legs towards it. One foot in front of the other, she neared the cerise beam. It illuminated more around her as a steady mist began to grow.

She neared the source of the light and looked down. Alarmed, Nan realized she wore some sort of medieval gown, not the string strapped T-shirt and fuzzy shorts she had gone to bed in.

Finally, she reached her target. Nan found to her horror that the scarlet glowing orb sat above a large golden steamer trunk. Flustered and disconcerted beyond logic, Nan stared as mist poured forth from the trunk's seams and grew dense and eerie against the red hue.

Let thy out, Anabel, a voice whispered in the night.

The sound of her name made Nan's blood run cold. She spun around and scanned the dark surroundings for the voice's owner. She was alone.

Let thy out, Anabel, she heard again.

Nan stared down at the trunk and realized the voice came from inside.

Be true to thou self, Anabel. Let thee out, it urged desperately from the seams.

33

With a pensive step forward, Nan reached down, fear still thudding in her heart, and unlatched the clasps. The trunk opened. As if by the speed of light, two great skeletal hands burst forth from the mist, grabbed her arms and pulled her down into the belly of the beast. Nan screamed for dear life, flailing in vain. But the lid slammed shut behind her.

Chapter 5
"Why, sometimes I've believed as many as six impossible things before breakfast." Lewis Carroll

Nan listened to the harmonious songs of the blue jays and cardinals singing in the trees outside her bedroom windows, as she lounged in bed. The night's dream temporarily erased from her thoughts by the gentle beam of light, which illuminated the room's area rug and deposited her into a state of tranquility. In no particular hurry to rise from the warm bed, Nan stretched and pondered what she should do today.

Poe yawned and stretched at the bottom of the bed, having claimed it once he realized the house was his new domain. He reached out with his front paws then slowly travelled up the length of the bed to Nan's head, where he fluffed his furry tail in her face to remind her of his presence.

"Good morning to you too," Nan laughed. She swatted the cat's tail out from under her nose then stroked his sleek grey fur. Blue soon observed her competition reaping all the attention and rose from her spot on the cerulean rug. She plopped her snout on the bed near Nan's hand to get her due acknowledgement.

Reclined, daydreaming as usual, with the two rivals competing for her sole awareness, Nan suddenly detected the faint odour of burnt toast. *Oh boy, Rory's in the kitchen again.* She smiled as she thought to herself. Though her present occupation was waitressing, Rory was by far no cook and every time she tried her hand at it, it was catastrophic.

The smell soon evolved into a cloud of real smoke. A tad concerned, Nan reluctantly got out of bed to go and investigate the situation further. An ear piercing sound suddenly emanated from out in the hall. Nan shrunk back a bit due to the effects of the hall's smoke alarm, then covered her ears and headed for the door. Poe dove for the safety of the closest, while Blue howled in pain.

Out in the hall, Nan found herself engulfed in a veil of smog, which trailed down the stairs. She made her way through the marked path to the kitchen—opening every window she passed on the way. There, as she had expected, Nan found a frantic Rory. Desperate to silence the kitchen alarm, she waved a huge smoke cloud, which billowed from the stove, out the window above the sink.

Nan tried not to burst out laughing at the spectacle in front of her and instead fetched the broom from the hall closet and the dishtowel from the stove handle and went to Rory's aid. She turned the stove off and removed the frying pan, which contained bits of charcoaled food, in the process. Once the overt alarm was mastered and the rest of the windows opened to clear out the smoke, Nan gave Rory a mocking grin, "Trying out your culinary skills again I see."

Still a little frazzled, Rory apologized, "I'm so sorry if I woke you. I just thought I'd surprise you with a nice breakfast for once." It was to be her attempt to make amends for the unpleasant affairs of the night before.

Nan smiled at her friend's helpless expression and turned on the kettle. "Don't worry about it, I was already up." Nan raised an eyebrow as she caught another glimpse of the burnt contents in the frying pan. "What were you trying to cook anyways?"

"Bacon and eggs," Rory sighed.

Nan stared at the frays of burnt ash in the pan in shock. The curled up pieces of debris must have been the bacon she guessed. "Where are the eggs?" she laughed.

"I hadn't gotten that far yet," Rory huffed, putting her hands on her hips with a slight scowl. She snatched the skillet from Nan's examining eyes and dumped the contents in the trash. "I was just about to start them when that stupid malfunctioning smoke alarm started screeching at me."

Nan smiled and backed away from the stove with her hands up in mock surrender. Rory watched Nan's forswearing gesture, and then bellowed in sulky desperation, "Well if that damn stove didn't cook so high, then it wouldn't have burnt."

"Okay, Rory, relax. I'm sure it is entirely the stove's fault." Nan smirked as she made herself a cup of tea and Rory a coffee. After handing Rory the mug, she retreated to the oval table with her tea and said, "Though it has worked successfully for everyone else for years."

Rory burst out into a fit of laughter as she joined Nan at the table. "Oh shut up," she retorted after she caught her breath.

Soon the whole kitchen sang with gayety as the two girls laughed and joked on about the misfortunate blowout event. Once the convivial mood had abated and the two sat quietly, Rory inquired, "So would you actually like some breakfast?"

Nan almost exploded again, but struggled to control herself. "Thanks, but I'm pretty sure charcoal is bad for the digestion and I'm not sure it would go with my tea and smoke inhalation."

"Suit yourself, but I think I'll have some toast," Rory grinned and rose.

"Try not to burn it this time."

After Rory got her toast and Nan, having risen to make a second cup of tea, had fed the hungry duo of animals, they both returned to the table and resumed their conversation. "So what is on your agenda for today?" asked Rory.

"I'm not really sure," replied Nan, as she sipped her tea.

"No doubt thanks to your lack of sleep," nagged Rory in concern.

"Oh now don't start. It's normal for me, I've always had problems sleeping, ever since I was a baby," huffed Nan, annoyed she had to explain it again for the thousandth time.

"Well it can't be good for you. Maybe you should go have it checked out."

"I have," answered Nan tiredly. "I went to one of those sleep clinics a couple of years back and they said there was nothing wrong with me."

"Really?" exclaimed Rory in disbelieve, "That's weird."

Nan sighed and placed her elbow on the table, resting her head on her hand (something her father had hated). "I know. Dad said even as a baby he had a horrible time getting me to sleep and that as I got older I constantly had bad dreams and would sleep walk. Now I just don't sleep at all, but still have nightmares when I do."

"Hmmm," mused Rory meditatively. "Well at least you don't sleep walk any more or I'd have to chain you to your bed." she smirked, lightening the mood in the room.

Once they had caught their breaths after another bout of laughter, Rory asked while she sipped her coffee, "What do you dream about anyways?"

Nan's thoughts fluttered back to the dream she'd had the night before and she proceeded to relate all the bizarre details to Rory; the horrible darkness, the silence, the eerie red glow, the trunk, the mysterious voice, and the hideous hands, which drug her into the trunk's depths.

More alert now, Rory exclaimed dramatically, "Wow, that is bizarre." Nan nodded her head in agreement, the dream's images playing over in her mind as if on a projector.

"Maybe it's trying to tell you something," suggested Rory, as she tried to refrain the drooling dog who had taken it upon herself to come over and get some attention by slobbering all over Rory's housecoat.

Nan grinned at the exhibition then snapped her fingers for Blue to come away and desist in her pestering pursuit of Rory. "I doubt it. I've always had weird dreams," she answered dismissively.

"It just seems strange to me. Most people don't have constant insomnia and continuous bad dreams," observed Rory.

"Sure they do, what about people who suffer from night terrors or dream anxiety disorder?" Nan pointed out. "Besides I went for that test and they said I was fine," She hoped this would end the conversation.

Rory frowned, but let the topic drop for a moment while a silence built between them. Then, she added, "You know some people believe dreams tell us things or are sort of messages."

"Come on, Rory, you don't believe that hog wash do you?" scuffed Nan, worried her friend was serious. She would hate to think Rory thought she was even weirder then Nan already felt deep down.

"Well you never know. It might be true," challenged Rory, "Aren't you always telling me that your instincts guide you or speak to you in some way?"

"Well yeah I guess," admitted Nan in defeat, unable to deny it.

"Then maybe it's not such a stretch to think that your intuition might be trying to talk to you while you sleep." A small triumphant smile crossed Rory's lips.

"I suppose it could be possible," agreed Nan. Nan couldn't deny it. Ever since she was young, she had had an uncanny ability to predict things based on her gut. Be it the weather, outcomes of events, sickness, and so on. Her hunches never let her down.

So then, why couldn't my dreams be telling me something? She considered. Nan let her thoughts play around with Rory's suggestion as she returned and asked, "Okay, so if you're right, then what was the dream trying to tell me?"

"That I can't figure out," replied Rory, puzzled. "I wonder what the whole spooky trunk thing is supposed to represent."

Realization sprung to mind and Nan remembered she hadn't told Rory about yesterday's adventures in the attic due to their fight and quickly acquainted her with all the outré details.

Once Nan had finished her recital, Rory clasped her hands together, like someone who had just solved a mystery and exclaimed, "Well then that's what the dream's trying to tell you. You need to go look in the trunk."

"I can't, it's locked remember?" replied Nan exasperated, having just explained that to Rory seconds earlier. "I don't even know where the key is."

"When in doubt use bolt cutters, Chickipoo," Rory grinned.

Unable to help herself, Nan smirked at her friend's optimism and replied, "It's a disc lock, so unfortunately that wouldn't work, but thanks for the advice."

"Well it was a good plan while it lasted," Rory sighed.

Their morning beverages finished and having exhausted all conversation of the mysterious dream for the time being, the girls talked about their plans for the day and how after work Rory was going to visit her mother (her father deceased) for the night and wouldn't be back till after work the next day.

Nan didn't want to rekindle the flames of the episode the night before, but thought she should at least mention it. She gave Rory a sideways glance and with slight hesitation, said, "Oh yeah, Parker will be around this afternoon. He's going to start moving his stuff into the loft."

She got no response and for what seemed an eternity, the two girls sat in silence. Rory gave Nan a scrutinizing look and said, "He's still in love with you, you know that right?"

Shocked by Rory's proclamation, Nan gave a false laugh, "No he's not."

With a serious expression on her face, Rory exclaimed, exasperated, "It's brutally obvious, Nan. You'd have to be a complete dunce not to see it." Then, shaking her head at Nan's stunned look, she added, "I just think your opening a can of worms that's all and that is all I'm going to say about it." She rose from her chair and left the table, heading for the hall.

Nan desperately tried to think of something to smooth the situation over again and was about to follow Rory, when she whirled around and said, "Oh by the way, would you mind keeping the radio down at night? It kept waking me up."

"I didn't have the radio on last night," Nan frowned, puzzled.

"But I heard it clear as a bell," protested Rory.

"Sorry, but I don't know what to tell you," said Nan with a shrug. "Maybe you were dreaming."

"No," Rory answered firmly, "I'm sure it was a radio." Then looking at Nan's innocent expression one last time, she turned and walked away bewildered.

Nan heaved a sigh of relief, glad Rory hadn't pushed the inquisition further. She would hate to try and explain to Rory that the sounds she had heard were not of this world, but the ghosts who inhabited the house with them.

Chapter 6
"I've dreamt in life dreams that have stayed with me ever after, and changed my ideas; they've gone through and through me, like wine through water, and altered the colour of my mind."
Jane Austen

That afternoon, after she had tidied the house up and threw a load of laundry into the washer, Nan found herself lost, with nothing more to occupy her mind. Rory had gone to work and Parker was busy moving into the loft. The house was quiet. Nan couldn't help, but reflect on how utterly alone she was.

No stranger to the blights of solitude, being teased and isolated by her peers throughout high school and then university for her aloof nature—thanks to her advanced maturity and intelligence—Nan had always had one person who didn't ostracize her, her father. She now discovered even her years of sequestration couldn't comfort or appease the sting of her unadulterated forsakenness.

Nan tried to block out the pain and searched around for something to do. With a defeated huff, she laid back on the couch. Blue came and curled up on the floor by her side. Nan closed her eyes for a couple of minutes, while she thought of the day ahead and soon fell asleep.

****

Darkness crept in like an eclipse. Nan tried not to let fear get the best of her. She stood alone in the pitch black, not a sound to be heard, not a shape to be distinguished. *Not again*, Nan thought. An eerie dread welled up inside her. Rooted to the spot as if some unforeseen force gripped her, Nan's heart raced while she tried to make sense of the cold dark prison she was once again submerged in.

It's only a dream, she told herself. The memory of the similar occurrence the night before sprung to mind.

The icy chill of the air bit at the nape of her neck. The faint rush of wind whistled through the invisible space. Nan looked down and found she wore the same period style dress from her prior nightmare. *What is going on? Why am I dressed this way?*

She urged her steadfast form to move for fear of the unknown and stepped forward, reaching out into the abyss. Her hands connected with a stone edifice. *I'm in some sort of cave*, she registered. She felt her way along the rock wall through her dark surroundings. Suddenly the darkness began to lift and the bare stone became visible under Nan's hands.

A hand gripped Nan from behind. She screamed for help and fought to free herself, but to no avail. The mysterious being's hold was too tight.

Nan squinted into the lingering darkness. She could discern a hooded figure in front of her, the one who held her, but could not see their face. "Who are you?" Nan shrieked. "What do you want with me?"

The wraith pulled Nan deeper into the bowels of the cave. Nan struggled, but the demon's grasp was iron hard. Nan's shin struck a large unmoving mass, which caused her to come to a halt. A crimson mist grew up from the ground all around her.

Nan looked down to see what barred her path. Fear sweated from her pores as Nan gave a little yelp when she saw the trunk. Her head pivoted in all directions searching for an escape, but the cloaked phantom still held her arm. Then Nan noticed another figure behind the trunk, deeper into the grotto. An old hag, clad in earth woven rags with strange blue markings all over her skin.

Terror stricken, Nan yelled out to her, "Help me please."The woman looked up then, eyeing Nan calmly, but uttered no reply nor came to her aid.

Let her out, Anabel. Accept her. A voice said from some unforeseen force.

The hooded jailor thrust Nan up against the trunk, which caused her knees to buckle. Nan gave one last frantic look to the woman for help, but she had returned her gaze to her bits of leaves she toiled with.

The trunk lid flew opened. Nan screamed and reached out for help to the hooded figure who loomed over her. The empty face watched her fall, before the lid closed sharply down and locked Nan in the darkness forever.

✳✳✳✳

Nan woke with a lurch, heart racing. Blue jumped to her feet in alarm. Relieved to see the familiar sights of her living room, Nan flopped back down on the couch and sighed, "It was only a dream."

She took a deep breath and thought of her earlier conversation with Rory. *What if she is right, what if the dreams are trying to tell me something?*

There was no harm in investigating the possibility further, Nan decided and got to her feet and headed upstairs. Once in her room, she made a beeline for her laptop, which awaited new discovery on top of the antique secretary desk in the bedroom's corner. Within seconds after she turned it on, Nan had brought up the web browser and an array of options under dream interpretation.

She scrolled down the list of sites from guides on interpreting dreams to dream analysis. Nan clicked on this one and that, not sure what she was actually looking for. Lost in her studies as always, Nan spent the rest of the afternoon and early evening learning all she could about the study of dreams and how the urge to make sense of one's dreams was an age-old practice that dated back to the time of the Babylonians.

Intrigued, Nan proceeded and learned how some people actually kept dream journals to record all the details of their dreams in, in order to decipher them later. Online dream dictionaries were available for such endeavours, making it possible to look up and identify meanings of places, objects, colours, sounds, and so on.

Curious, Nan clicked on such a site and soon came across the word 'darkness'. The site said 'darkness' was synonymous with ignorance, evil, death, and fear, and that being consumed by darkness meant one was desperate, depressed, insecure, or searched without enough information. *All food for thought,* Nan concluded, as she leaned back in her desk chair and pondered what significance the information had to the dreams she'd been having of late.

It was now dark; Nan turned her eyes to the clock on the bottom of the laptop screen, which read eight forty five. She decided that was enough research for one day, she closed the browser, and shut off the computer.

Nan sat in the chair more unsure than ever. She tried to make sense of everything. Her dreams were trying to tell her something. But what?

The answer lied in the trunk like Rory had said, Nan was sure of it. Nevertheless, where was the key? She saw the unusual lock in her mind and wondered where her father might have kept its key.

Her mind lighted on the night her father had his heart attack and how the hospital had given Nan his immediate effects, which included a rather large ring of keys. *May be the key for the trunk is on that ring*? Eyes shining at the possibility, Nan jumped to her feet and lunged across the room to her nightstand where she had placed her father's hospital possessions. In her haste, she ripped the drawer open, grabbed the keys and bolted from the bedroom (leaving the nightstand drawer dangling) for the attic.

Excitement brimmed in her gut. The cold November chill and late hour made her endeavour seem ominous as Nan mounted the creaking narrow stairs to the eerie attic. She took a deep breath, biting back her nerves at proceeding alone—especially at night—Nan opened the attic door and walked inside.

Toughen up and stop being such a scaredy-cat, Nan told herself as she entered the shadow-filled room. Her tension deepened as Nan continued through the maze of clutter. Forgetting to bring a flashlight in her haste, Nan left the door to the stairwell open, which provided a dim light, while she searched for an alternative light source to illuminate the room.

With a jolt, Nan jumped back, her breath caught in her throat and almost landed in a pile of boxes. An unearthly, black silhouette stood in front of her. Nan's first instincts were to run from the room screaming, but fear froze her to the spot. She closed her eyes tight and shook her head in the vain attempt to make the figure dematerialize. Nan tried to collect herself. However, when she opened her eyes she found it was still there.

Nan removed her gaze from the chilling shadow and nervously looked around for some sort of aid in the battle against the night. She glanced up towards the rafters and to her surprise saw a pull string for a single, unshaded light bulb. Nan pulled the string in relief and the room was illuminated.

She looked back in the apparition's direction, but found there was no one there. Instead, there stood an oval framed, stand-up full-length mirror, in which her reflection stared back at her. *Oh you idiot,* Nan sighed. She mentally reprimanded herself for such silliness, though she would have sworn she had seen a human shadow and not just her own image.

With the light bulb lighting the way, Nan could see where she was going and it didn't take her long to locate the forgotten door and other half of the attic. She halted in front of the odd shaped door, every muscle in her body told her not to go any farther. A sickening feeling someone watched her once again tingled up her spine.

Nan whirled around, half expecting to be confronted by the mysterious figure she had seen upon entering the attic. No one was there. Unnerved, Nan scanned every nook and cranny before she turned her attention back to the door. Nan felt the ring of keys firmly in her grasp. All her worries thrown aside, she opened the door and walked inside.

Nan looked to the rafters for a light bulb as in the room's twin chamber, but found none. There was a dim glow of moonlight through the room's window and sliver of light from the adjacent room. Once her eyes had adjusted, Nan spotted the trunk, strode over to it, and knelt down.

Nan grasped the lock in one hand and fumbled with the ring of keys for her first attempt. She chose one, reached out and tried it in the lock. As the key entered the hole, someone grabbed Nan's shoulder from behind.

Startled, Nan screamed, bolted to her feet, dropped the keys, and almost hurtled over the troublesome trunk in the process. She groped at her back in panic, her body shaking all over. Nan looked around the room in petrified terror, but there was no one there.

Almost too scared to move, but not wanting to remain in the blackened room, Nan shook herself and said into the haunted space, "Oh will you get a grip." She knelt back down, searched for the missing keys, then chose another from the ring and tried again.

Nan tried every key in the lock with no success. She sat defeated in front of the allusive trunk and wondered what to do next. Downcast at her failure and not wanting to stay another minute in the eerie room, Nan got to her feet and left the attic.

Chapter 7
"The truth is rarely pure and never simple." Oscar Wilde

Safe back on the home's main floor and out of the creepy attic, Nan walked in a daze to the kitchen. She popped a frozen dinner into the microwave, figuring she should eat, and then leaned on the counter in deep contemplation. *What is the big secret about the trunk and where did dad put the key? I have to find out what's inside.* A horrible possibility struck her. *What if dad disposed of the key after locking the trunk, to forever keep its contents a secret?*

Nan's heart sank at the prospect. She felt a nudge on her thigh and looked down to see the devoted eyes of the old pit bull staring up at her. "I know, you miss him too don't you?" Nan sighed.

Nan continued to stand at the counter, while she mechanically ate her pathetic excuse of a meal. Once finished, she decided as there was nothing else to do, she might as well go to bed. Nan turned to leave the kitchen when she was struck with an epiphany. "The den!" She sprinted down the hallway like a mad woman, to the mahogany doors of her father's study.

The room was in great need of a dusting, Nan thought as she looked around at the wood panelled room, with its large walnut desk and leather chair, floor to ceiling glass door bookcases, and oil paintings of classic cars. Nostalgia washed over her and she smirked as she ran a hand over one of the bookshelves' glass doors.

So many times Nan had argued with her father about housing books on their shelves instead of using them for extra storage. "If they were mine," she would start, but he would always counter by saying, "Not all of us collect wasted paper like you do," and that would be the end of it. The memory floated in Nan's head while she gazed around the masculine room and sighed mournfully, "I miss you dad."

Reminded of her mission, Nan sauntered around the room and wondered where to begin. After her eyes swept over the desk, she began to rummage through its drawers in no particular order, carefully putting everything back in its proper place, as if her father might discover her intrusion. The drawers consisted of the usual things one assumes to find in a desk: paper, envelopes, paperclips, tacks, a letter opener, stapler, and so on. However, being her father's, Nan also found maps, trucking logbooks, and vehicle repair manuals, but no key.

Nan sunk back in the leather chair, disappointed, and stared at the grand desk. *I was sure the key would be in one of the drawers.*

Nan looked harder at the bottom right drawer of the desk and perked up when something struck her as odd. She leaned forward, reopened the drawer and dumped its entirety onto the desk's top. The drawer was inches shallower on the inside then out. Nan ran her fingers along its seams and found a tiny brown leather strap wedged into the drawers back crevice.

Astonished, Nan grasped the bit of hide in her fingers and pulled. It didn't budge. Nan pulled harder and soon the entire bottom of the drawer dangled from the strap in her hands.

"It's a false bottom," Nan whispered in disbelief. Nan's heart sank as she peered inside, expecting to find all sorts of mysterious items, and found that the drawer was practically empty, containing only some bits of paper and a small jeweller's case.

As Nan lifted the scraps of paper to put them on top of the desk, a straggler came loose and fluttered to the floor. She huffed with irritation as she retrieved it off the floor. However, flipping it over, Nan was shocked to discover it to be an old faded colour photograph.

The photo was of a young woman, about Nan's age of twenty-one. So proud and majestic the unknown woman stood in a wheat field, her long flaming mountainous red hair and simple floral print dress blew in the wind as she stared off into the distance, as if she was lord of it all. Her eyes were bold and lively, but at the same time sad. *It's my mother,* Nan breathed in awe.

Nan never knew her mother or seen her in a picture, but never the less she was certain the woman she now gazed upon was she. As a child, Nan had asked about her mother and was quickly told by her father that she had died after Nan's birth, from what he had never said. Consumed by grief Nan's father rarely spoke of her, which left Nan to guess what type of a person she was, what she had looked like, and if she would have been proud to call Nan her daughter.

Though she could sit there and stare at her mother's picture forever, Nan thought back to her goals and reluctantly placed the photo aside and forced her eyes back to the contents of the drawer.

Next, she opened the jeweller's box. Inside was a locket on a long sterling silver chain with a crescent moon engraved on its cover. The initials *R.R.* were engraved on the back of it. Nan frowned, her mother's name had been Rhiannon, which explained the first *R*, but their family name was Weststar, meaning the second initial should have been a *W*. So then, why was it an *R*? *Perhaps it's for my mother's maiden name,* Nan pondered.

Inside the locket were two oval photographs, one of a baby and the other a man. Nan immediately recognized the infant as herself, having seen the same picture in her father's wallet a million times. She had no doubt the handsome young man was her father, which proved the locket had once belonged to her mother.

Elated to finally have proof of her lost parent's existence, who had been nothing but a figureless ghost for so many years, Nan placed the locket down next to the photo and sifted through the rest of the papers for more.

Amongst them was an envelope with her father's name etched in feminine script on the front. Nan lifted the yellowed envelope. It was aged and maimed as if it had been opened many times. Nan removed the single piece of paper from within, penned in an elegant, steadfast hand, and read.

My Dear Houston,

I have no illusions what I'm about to do is not treacherous or that this scrap of paper will bring you comfort, but I could not just abandon you without a word. I love you too much to do that, though no doubt you think otherwise now.

There are not enough ways to express how truly sorry I am. I can't pretend anymore. I don't belong here and it was selfish of me to try. I should have walked away that fateful day we met, but I loved you too much. Now I'm paying the price. In the end, this is for the best and I hope someday you will forgive me.

I know none of this makes sense to you now and I'm sorry, but I can say no more. All I can tell you is I was meant for a different life and strayed from that path when I met you. I'm a prisoner of misfortune like so many before me.

Know this, no matter what my future holds I will always love you and our gorgeous little girl. Watch over our darling Anabel.

Forever and always,
Rhiannon

Nan stared in shocked stupefaction. *Does this mean my mother is still alive? That she didn't die, but left? But why did dad lie to me all these years?*

All this time Nan had thought she was an unfortunate child who'd lost her mother, when in fact she had abandoned them. *Why did she leave?*

Swamped with every emotion in the book, hurt, confusion, sadness, anger, regret; Nan sat on the leather chair, unmoved, oblivious to everything around her, including the unsolved mystery of the trunk and hidden key.

Like a zombie straight out of the grave, Nan got to her feet, grabbed the photo and locket from the desk's top, the letter still clutched in hand, and exited the room. Blue pranced in front of her trying to get her attention, but Nan paid the poor beast no heed, walking past her and up the stairs to her room. Nan entered the room and closed the door, nearly hitting the helpless, locked out dog's nose in the process.

Nan turned off the bedroom's light and climbed into bed, clothes and all, curled up in the fetal position under the covers and clutched her newfound treasures, shutting out the world around her.

My mother may still be alive.

Chapter 8
"We need never be ashamed of our tears." Charles Dickens

Parker could see Nan's red Dakota parked by the side of the house from the loft's living room window. Woken by a ringing telephone, an unsettled Rory on the line, Parker had listened groggily as she rambled about how Nan hadn't answered any of her calls or text messages. His first thought was that Rory was overreacting or that maybe Nan had finally smartened up and was ignoring her, but as he looked out the window at the house, he decided not to pass up an opportunity to see Nan and turned to head out the door.

Parker knocked casually and waited for Nan's alluring, happy face to appear as the door opened. She never came. He frowned, puzzled, then gazed over his shoulder once again at the truck and knocked louder. *She's got to be home,* he thought, trying the door to see if it was locked. It wasn't.

"Okay," Parker uttered suspiciously. He knew Nan was a stickler for locking the door, unless she was up. As he opened the door and stepped inside, Parker's alarm was heightened by the deafening silence, which hung in the semi-darkened house.

A fury of nails on the flooring suddenly echoed off the walls and out of nowhere Blue came flying down the hall like a bat out of hell and out through the still open door. Parker sprang back to escape the charging bull and whirled around after her in surprised confusion. To his relief the loose canine went as far as the nearest patch of grass, where she hurriedly relieved her bladder and then trotted obediently back to him.

That's weird, thought Parker and petted Blue on the head. *Nan never neglects the animals*.

Back inside, Parker called Nan's name multiple times, but came up dry. He began to share Rory's concern and looked down at the happy dog by his side. Suddenly he remembered a game Nan use to play with the dog. He knelt down, petted the mutt's strong head, and asked in an enthusiastic tone, "Where's mommy, Blue? Where is she?"

Overjoyed at the game, in an instant the dog raced up the stairs. An amazed Parker stayed knelt on the floor, until he got to his feet and chased after her. Parker soon reached the landing and found a grinning Blue, wagging her tail in front of Nan's closed bedroom door.

He praised the dog, then gently knocked on Nan's door and called her name. Again, he got no answer. Agitated at the stillness from within the room, Parker opened the door and sprang inside. He immediately sighed in relief when he saw a sleeping Nan, curled up safe in her bed.

Surprised at how sound Nan slept for a girl who didn't normally sleep, Parker crept over to the side of the bed and gently touched her shoulder, giving it a little shake, and said her name.

As if electrocuted, Nan's eyes shot open and looked at him. "Hey sleepy head," Parker smiled.

"Hey," Nan mumbled in return as she stirred a bit and rubbed her eyes to look around her room and gain perspective. "What are you doing in my room?"

"Rory called and asked me to check on you. I guess you haven't been answering your phone or cell."

"Wow, she called you?" Nan smirked, as she propped herself up higher on her pillows.

"Yeah, that's what I thought, but I guess I was her only option," Parker chuckled. "Since when do you sleep so well anyways?"

Nan put her hand on her forehead, still groggy and confused. "I guess I was more tired than I thought."

"I'd say. You didn't even hear me calling you." Parker looked harder at Nan's ghostly pale face and raccoon eyes and asked in concern, "Are you okay?"

"Yes," answered Nan instinctively, but then gave it a second thought. "No...Well...oh I don't know."

Parker sat down on the edge of the bed next to her and leaned forward to place a comforting hand on Nan's shoulder. "What's wrong?"

Nan sighed, then ruffled through the bedding until she located her mother's picture, locket, and the detrimental letter from the night before. She handed them to Parker to examine and told him of the previous night's event.

"So your mom is still alive?" he asked, stunned.

"Maybe, I'm not sure. But dad lied to me my whole life. He told me she was dead. I just can't believe he would do that," Nan said sadly, as she hugged her knees insecurely.

"I'm sure he had a good reason," soothed Parker, not knowing what else to say, sensitivity not being his strong suit.

"Well I'm never going to know now am I, because he's dead. Everything he told me was a lie and now he's gone and he's never coming back and I'm all alone," Nan burst out in anger. On the brink of hysterics, she collapsed her head onto her lap.

"Hey, hey now, it's going to be alright," Parker cooed and wrapped his warm, muscular arm around her.

"No it's not. He's dead, he's really dead, and I miss him so much," Nan whimpered. Not able to hold back the emotion any longer, she burst into tears—the first time since she had watched the life drain from her father's body, as he lay helpless in the hospital bed.

Parker squeezed Nan tighter and then pulled her against his broad chest. As he rocked her gently, he said, "It's okay. He loved you, you know that."

Nan cried until she had nothing left. Nuzzled against Parker, safe and warm, Nan could feel a sense of calm come over her. She laid there and breathed softly, while he rubbed her back and rocked her slowly.

It felt good to be in Parker's arms, Nan thought, but then the realization of her break down hit her. Nan was mortified at letting anyone, especially Parker, see her in such a state, normally so composed, keeping things bottled up inside until she was alone and unobserved. Nan realized she clung to Parker's chest, on what used to be a dry T-shirt. She straightened, red eyed and runny nose, and looked up at him sheepishly.

"Feel better?" Parker smiled.

"I'm sorry, I don't know what came over me," Nan apologized and pulled away from him into a sitting position.

Parker cupped her chin in his hand and turned Nan's face back to him to stare deep into her sea grey eyes. "It really is okay. I understand."

Solace washed over her and with a half-hearted smile, Nan nodded back at him knowing he truly meant what he said. Nan realized for the first time in that moment, just how much Parker honestly cared for her, but more surprising, that she cared for him. Nan couldn't explain it, but she almost felt as if she belonged in his arms.

"Come on, let's go downstairs and I'll find a way to cheer you up," and getting to his feet, Parker held out a hand for Nan to grasp and let him lead her downstairs.

Downstairs, Parker sat Nan on the couch and turned on the television. He soon found an old episode of *Ghost Hunters*. After he went into the kitchen to find them something to drink and perhaps to nibble on, and then the pair relaxed with a glass of pop on the suede couch.

Nan hadn't allowed herself to get too close to Parker in the past for fear of leading him on, but she decided to throw caution to the wind and let him comfort her and placed her head on his lap. Her head cradled, Parker tenderly ran his fingers through Nan's thick, dark brunette hair. Nan gave a peaceful sigh; the strokes of his fingers caused a warm, comforting sensation to well up inside her. It sent little tingles down her arms, causing goose bumps, and made her wonder what it would be like to feel his strong, capable hands on her skin.

I could get use to this, thought Nan, the situation felt so natural and right.

"This show is so fake, I don't know how you watch it," Parker sneered, which woke Nan from her alluring dream state.

"Haven't you ever seen a ghost or been in a haunted house before?" Nan laughed.

"No."

"Well maybe someday you will," Nan smiled, still enjoying her head massage.

"Yeah okay," Parker snorted. Changing the subject, he asked, "Hey, do you want me to order a pizza or something?"

"Sure," Nan replied. Absentmindedly she rose, reached over to the end table for the cordless phone, and handed it to him, then nestled back onto his lap. "Oh I suppose you'll need the number," she laughed, getting ready to get up again.

"No that's okay, I've got it saved in my phone," as he gently pushed Nan back down onto his lap and pulled out his cell phone and hit speed dial.

"Order a lot of pizza, do you?" she mocked.

"Yeah, yeah," Parker chuckled, "I'm a guy, we're too lazy to cook."

Nan giggled at his jest. Once Parker had ordered the pizza, he resumed running his fingers through her hair and continued to make derogatory comments about the show, while Nan lulled back into a state of serene euphoria and tried once more to make sense of the situation the *Ghost Hunters* crew investigated.

After a bit, Nan shot bolt upright as if bitten by a bug and shrieked, "The key!" She hurtled herself across the room and sprinted across the hall into her father's den, while Parked sat stunned on the couch.

With a puzzled expression, Parker soon appeared in the den's doorway. He stared at Nan in confusion and secretly wished they could return to their cuddle session on the couch. "What are you looking for?" he asked, as he watched Nan rustle through a bunch of papers on the desk.

"The key," Nan exclaimed, not looking up from her task. "I forgot all about it. It has to be here."

"What key?" queried Parker, still lost.

"The one for the trunk," she huffed. "It must be…" but before Nan could finish her sentence, she lifted the false bottom of the drawer and there, taped to the backside of it was a single bronze key.

"Ah ha!" Nan shouted. She peeled the tape off the key and brandished it triumphantly. Just then, there was a knock at the door.

"I'll get it. It's probably the pizza," said Parker, as he turned to answer the door.

Elated beyond comprehension, Nan rushed out of the den and bounded up the stairs. Parker shook his head as Nan flashed past him, as he paid the delivery boy and got the pizza.

Nan reached the trunk in no time flat, due to her excitement. Nan breathed a calming breath. *It's the moment of truth.*

Nan looked behind her to make sure no phantom hands would grab her this time. As she eyed the boxes and furniture near the entrance it dawned on her, *they belonged to my mother.* Locked away by Nan's father after her mother had left, unable to bring himself to dispose of the stuff, but not wanting to look at it ever again.

This in mind, Nan slowly turned back to the trunk. Her heart raced as she lifted the key to the lock, took a deep breath and inserted it. With her eyes closed, Nan turned the key in the lock, and heard the telltale click.

Chapter 9
"The real voyage of discovery consists not in seeking new landscapes, but in having new eyes." Marcel Proust

Parker sauntered through the door of the formerly concealed room, pizza in hand and Blue close behind hoping he would slip and the cheese and pepperoni covered dough would be hers. It was like déjà vu, he thought when he found Nan cross-legged in front of the closed trunk. He rolled his eyes and proceeded forward.

Nan whirled around with a big smile when she heard his approach and said, "The key worked. The trunk's open."

"Then why is it still closed?" Parker grinned, coming up beside her.

"I don't know," Nan sighed, "What if you're right? What if there is something horrible inside? Maybe I don't want to know after all."

With a huff, Parker put the pizza down on the floor next to Nan, out of Blue's reach, and grabbed the trunk's lid with both hands, lifted it, and said in exasperation, "Oh come on, Nan, stop being so ridiculous."

The trunk was finally open. Stunned at Parker's mannerism and a little disappointed the mystery was over; Nan peered over the side of the trunk to see what hidden gems it concealed.

"Great, more women's clothing," snorted Parker.

Sometimes Parker's smugness is downright infuriating, huffed Nan, as she stared at the out of style women's ware—obviously her mother's. "Well there must be something in here. Why else would dad have locked it up?"

Parker shook his head and muttered, "I don't know, but you wouldn't think it would be to hide some dresses."

"I don't know either," she groaned, confused. "Want to help me look through it anyways?"

"Sure, why not," Parker shrugged and sat down beside Nan. He opened the pizza box, grabbed a slice and said, "Dig in," referring to both the food and trunk.

****

When Rory pulled up to the house, it was dusk. She hadn't heard back from Parker or Nan, therefore she was a bit surprised to find both their trucks in the driveway. She gazed at both the house and loft, but couldn't see a single light on in the darkened windows.

New alarm bells rang in her head as she got out of the car. What if her ultimate fear had finally occurred and Nan had weakened and fell prey to Parker's seductive ways? Maybe he had bewitched Nan into ignoring her all day. Infuriated by the ideas, Rory marched to the door, prepared to give the culprits a good tongue-lashing.

The house was in complete darkness when she walked through the unlocked door. Not even the dog could be seen. *That's weird,* Rory frowned, *oh no, maybe they're in Parker's loft, together*?

She searched all the rooms on the main level, but found nothing. Rory decided to head upstairs to investigate further. As she approached the second floor landing, Rory noticed out of the corner of her eye that the door to the attic stairwell stood open. She ignored the other rooms and headed straight up the stairs.

Rory ducked cobwebs and side stepped piles of junk, while she surveyed the desolate space for any signs of life. After she had pulled the string, which dangled from the rafters to turn on the light, and walked around a couple more stacks of boxes, she noticed the odd door that led to the attic's other half.

Rory poked her head into the semi dim space and scowled, she had found the fugitives she sought. Blue jumped to her feet and trotted happily over to Rory as she stepped inside the room, which caused both Nan and Parker to turn and look her way. Rory took in the strange scene with irritated frustration. The pair were together as she had expected, but sat in front of an old trunk with a pizza box between them and women's clothes scattered all over the floor.

Though no obvious disaster had occurred, Rory glared at them and blared, "I've been worried sick! Why haven't you been answering the phone?" Then turned from Nan to Parker, added, "And you were supposed to get back to me when you found her."

Nan sat in stunned silence. Parker, who found Rory's outrage comical, gave a condescending smirk and said, "I checked on her, see? She's fine. There I just got back to you."

Rory's face went from red to purple in two seconds flat. Nan decided she better jump in before her attic became a crime scene and smiled apologetically. "I'm so sorry, Rory, I got caught up in something and forgot all about my phone. Parker did tell me you had called."

Rory stared at Nan's remorseful face and her anger began to defuse. "Fine then, but you have to start realizing people worry about you."

"I will from now on, I promise," agreed Nan. She solidified her oath with a poor example of a Girl Guide salute.

"Nan, you were never in Girl Guide's," teased Parker.

Nan gave him a playful shove and they all burst out laughing. With the tense reunion over and as the jovialness died down, Rory looked at the mess and asked, "So what are you guys doing anyways?"

"Well," began Nan and then gave her a brief play-by-play of what had happened up until she had stormed in the room. Parker knew Rory was in for a long story and wordlessly held up the pizza box to her as she took a seat beside him—Blue laid not far away and watched the food with longing.

When Nan had finished and the room was once again silent, Rory shook her head in astonishment. "So your mom is alive?"

"Possibly," replied Nan, she still found it all hard to believe, "All the evidence points that way."

"Wow," Rory sighed. She looked from Parker to Nan and then back again, not knowing what else to say. Finally, her eyes rested on the open trunk. "Find anything helpful in there?"

"Not unless you consider a bunch of old dresses helpful," replied Parker.

"We were just about to lift the shelf out when you came in." Nan gave Parker an expression of mock annoyance before she asked, "Want to help?"

"Sure," exclaimed Rory, always eager to explore through forgotten things or just other peoples stuff.

Parker got to his feet and carefully lifted the brittle, ancient cardboard shelf out of the trunk, and set it down on the floor in the corner, while Nan watched with baited breath. With the shelf removed, the three immediately turned and peered into the trunk, but it was almost bare.

"Seriously?" growled Parker in annoyance, "What a joke. Why would your dad even lock up this crap?"

Nan's heart sank as she looked at the meagre contents and heard Parker's words. Had this all been a waste of time?

"Maybe he didn't?" All heads turned to Rory in that instant, which made her cringe self-consciously.

"What do you mean?" Nan frowned. Parker scowled in confusion beside her.

"I just mean, maybe your dad wasn't the one who locked it. Maybe it was already locked?"

"But this is clearly one of her dad's locks," objected Parker. He reached down and displayed the disc lock for Rory to see. "Women don't usually use locks like this."

"Maybe he gave Nan's mom the lock to use."

"Besides," added Nan, after a brief pause, "I found the key in dad's desk."

"Okay, it was just a suggestion," replied Rory and she put her hands up in surrender. "Anyways, we don't really know what all this stuff is. Let's take a look at it first before you go dismissing it, okay?"

"Okay." Nan perked up at her friend's wisdom and they all reached into the trunk. The contents of the trunk were indeed scarce. It consisted of a couple of hardcover books, a photo album, a small wooden box, a sketchpad, a huge leather bound book, and a little ring case.

Nan retrieved the small ring box first. Inside she found a beautiful ring. She marvelled at its dazzling gems, as she lifted it out of the case to get a better look at it. The ring was extremely old, with a bronze band, intricately engraved, and a square cut ebony stone in the centre, encircled with a mass of tiny diamonds entwined in the shape of a serpent.

Nan's eyes were glued to it. She turned it over and over in her hand to glimpse its beauty from every angle. A strange sense of calm came over her. She lifted the ring higher, unable to deny its draw, then slipped it onto her finger. It fit perfectly, like it had been made for her.

Nan started and looked up from the enchanting stone when Parker's voice asked, "What is all this stuff?"

He held the small wooden box with artful carvings on its surfaces. Nan leaned over to examine it. She frowned as she peered into the rectangular box and saw it contained nothing, but a lock of raven black hair wrapped in a silk handkerchief, a little cork topped glass bottle with some kind of herb in it, and a handful of coloured rocks all etched with runes.

"Well I know that these markings are called runes," stated Nan as she reached inside the box and lifted one of the stones out."But I have no idea what the hair and vial of plant stuff is or what it's used for."

"It's pretty weird if you ask me," replied Parker. He closed the box's lid after Nan returned the rock.

"Even the carvings are a bit eerie," pointed out Rory, as she looked closer at the box. Upon better inspection, one could distinguish morbid scenes of death, skulls, skeletal figures and raging battles between the living and the dead, carved on its sides and lid.

"Maybe your mom was one of those Satan worshipping type people," teased Parker.

"She was definitely strange that's for sure," added Rory. "Look at these drawings I found." She held out an open sketchbook she had been perusing for the others to inspect. All the drawings were done in charcoal and depicted glum scenes, such as graveyards, abandoned decrepit buildings, formidable animals, dreary landscapes, and faceless figures.

"Maybe they're not my mother's," dismissed Nan. She didn't like the mental image she was getting of her unknown parent so far.

"Whose would they be then?" inquired Rory. She put the sketchpad aside and reached back into the trunk for the hardcover books."They were all signed *R.R.* and the wooden box had an *R* carved on its cover amongst the drawings. What was your mother's name?"

"Rhiannon," uttered Nan disappointedly. She knew there was no denying they were her mother's, as she flipped through the photo album, which contained black and white pictures of faces she had never seen before.

"Then they must be hers," determined Rory, as she put down the books having lost interest.

"Maybe she was just crazy," Parker exclaimed, deciding to throw his two cents into the conversation as he patted Blue. He missed the glower Rory gave him.

"That would explain why she abandoned her daughter," responded Nan, downhearted. Parker instantly regretted his own words.

All was silent after that, the three friends not knowing what to say and instead turned back to look through the stranger's things once more. Nan looked back into the trunk of discarded items and suddenly felt as discarded as they were. *Maybe my mother left because she didn't want a child, a husband, or just a family in general.*

The only item left in the big old steamer trunk was a massive leather bound book, with brass clasps on the side, which kept it shut. Nan stared with curiosity at the strange archaic volume as she lifted it out with both hands, for it was quite heavy. Its leather was tart and the clasps tarnished. Upon closer inspection, Nan could see a faint stamp in the aged hide, which appeared to be an entwined snake in the form of a five-point star in a circle, a pentagram. *The serpent resembles the one on the ring*, thought Nan, glancing down at her finger were the ring remained.

The whole thing a bit uncanny, Nan released the book's clasps and opened it. The pages were yellowed and crisp. Nan flipped the aged pages and was stunned to discover different textures and parchments, evidence that the book had been added to many times over the years, possibly centuries, and was penned, not printed, in different hands. No expert on languages, she was fascinated at how with every addition to the book the text varied in dialect, the last pages of the book being the only ones in English and an old version at that.

She scanned what appeared to be an Old English rhyme or perhaps recipe at the book's end. Nan was in the process of deciphering it, when her attention was drawn away when Parker waved his hand in front of her face and said, "Hey, earth to the bookworm."

"Yeah?" answered Nan, as she blinked out of her trance.

"I asked you a question," he smirked.

"Oh sorry, I didn't hear you. What did you say?"

"Obviously. What's in that book that's so great anyways, nude pictures or something?" Parker laughed.

"Don't be so crude," barked Rory, appalled.

"Anyways, do you want us to put all this junk back in the trunk?" he shrugged innocently at Rory's chiding.

"No, I want to keep some of it out to look at later," answered Nan. She got to her feet, book in hand, to gather the items she wanted left out. "Basically this book and perhaps the sketchpad. Oh and maybe those hardcovers as well, they look interesting," she added and pointed to the stack of three books by Rory's feet.

"Okay," Parker and Rory said together as they began to stuff all the clothes and everything haphazardly back into the trunk's bottom, before the shelf was put back in and the lid closed.

With everything clean, the three each grabbed one of the items Nan wanted left out, before they headed back downstairs and called it a night. "We never did find anything that was worth locking the trunk up over," observed Rory, as she picked the sketchpad up off the floor.

"Yeah, it's strange. I don't get why...," Nan didn't finish her train of thought, but instead reached down to pick up a drawing, which had come loose and fallen to the floor when Rory picked the book up.

The charcoal sketch was of a cloaked, hooded woman in a medieval tunic style gown with hooped sleeves. The cloak shadowed her face, as she retreated, as if pursued, into a thick wall of dense trees with only a narrow treacherous hoof trodden path to guide her. Nan stared at the ominous maiden, transfixed, her sketched eyes enchanting orbs, which stared back at her. There was something about the mysterious maiden, especially her eyes, Nan couldn't help but feel as if she had seen before. *It's as if I know her,* mused Nan.

"Wow, that one sure is creepy!" said Rory, when she looked over Nan's shoulder at the drawing.

"Ha, she's got your eyes," added Parker.

"Really, you think so?" Nan frowned.

"Oh totally," mocked Rory. "Now come on, let's get out of this dingy place."

****

Out of the attic, the three carried their loot downstairs to Nan's room, where they unloaded it onto her desk and turned to leave. Rory exited ahead of the rest, which allowed Parker to reach out and catch Nan's elbow before she could follow. "What, what it is?" inquired Nan, alarmed.

"I found these at the very bottom of the trunk before I started putting stuff away and thought you might like to check them out without Rory's prying eyes," he explained, as he pulled a bundle of three letters wrapped in a red ribbon from his sweater pocket and handed them to Nan.

"Oh," exclaimed Nan in surprise. She took the offered bundle and stared down at the top envelope. "They're addressed to my mother."

"Maybe they will have some of the answers you've been looking for," smiled Parker, then he walked around Nan and left the room.

Words failed her as she stared at the handful of letters, itching to open one and reveal its truths. Instead, she decided to look at them later and placed the letters on her nightstand, before she went to re-join her friends downstairs.

The group past the rest of the evening with some brief, pleasant chatter before they said their goodnights. Parker retreated to the loft and Rory sought the solace of a warm bath, while Nan headed back upstairs to her new reading material.

She donned her pyjamas, then curled up in bed and reached for the bundle of letters. After she untied the red satin ribbon, which bound them, Nan sifted through the envelopes. All were addressed to one Rhiannon Ravenwood, the second *R* on the locket now made sense.

Why wasn't mom's last name the same as my father's? Hadn't they gotten married? Nan wondered, as a whirl of questions swirled through her head.

Two of the letters were postmarked before Nan was born, but the third was dated 1989, the year Nan was born. The return address on the letters' back read, D. Greenwick from New Forest, Hampshire, England.

Intrigued, never knowing her parents had connections in England, Nan picked the letter with the oldest postmark, opened it, and read.

Dearest Rhiannon,

I am grieved that circumstances have come to this and you determined flight to be your only salvation. I wish you had sought me out first; you would have been safe here. However, what has past has past and I desire that you find all the happiness in your new life, that you've yearned for, for so long.

But remember, a woman's heart holds a great many secrets, which may be her undoing, guard them well.

I fear distance shall not dismiss your trials of old and the past will hunt you no matter where you land. Our foe is an unshakable menace, who leaves no liability or loose end neglected. The ocean's mass may not prove wide enough of a barrier to protect you.

Always remember who you are and the great lineage you arise from. Know I will continue to be here if you need me and that England is your home.

Blessed Be,

Aunt D.

Nan's mind swam with new query. *My mother emigrated from England; left her life, her family all behind. But why? Who was the unnamed foe this D. Greenwick referred to?*

Nan rubbed her temples, more confused than ever. Her father having lied to her about her mother's death, the truth that her mother had abandoned them, the unexplainable locked trunk, and now the knowledge her mother had fled from her home once before, all crowded Nan's subconscious.

None of it makes sense. What does it all mean? Had her mother left them because the person she was running from had found her and had her father lied in an attempt to keep Nan safe?

Nan sank down under the covers and nestled her head into the pillows. *What kind of a family is this? Who is this Aunt D?*

She tried to decipher the clues as she closed her eyes, but the ache in her head prevented any conclusion from coming. After she pondered the many new questions, which assaulted her psyche, Nan's eyes grew reluctant to open and right before she drifted off to sleep, the image of the hooded woman's eyes passed before her lidded view.

Chapter 10
"Even if she be not harmed, her heart may fail her in so much and so many horrors, and hereafter she may suffer – both in waking, from her nerves, and in sleep from her dreams."
Bram Stoker

Anabel. Anabel, whispered the mysterious haunt. Nan stirred at the sound of her name. Panicked, she sat up in bed and peered into the night-blackened room, scanning for the echo's source. She saw nothing.

Anabel, it hissed out again.

Then, she saw it. At the foot of her bed a glowing white transparent form, with cold dead inky pits for eyes, stood, motionless. Its feminine features, cascading hair, and curved dress, were barely distinguishable.

Anabel, her name floated down to her again. But the ghostly image's lips never moved.

In the darkness, it shone like a bonfire against the blackened night sky. The figure turned from the bottom of the bed and floated to the door. Nan watched intently as it reached the threshold. It stopped and turned back to her.

Come Anabel, Nan heard in her mind, before the apparition turned and disappeared through the closed door.

Numbed by what she had just witnessed, Nan didn't know whether to follow or have herself committed. Cursed with a cat's curiosity, she launched to her feet and apprehensively approached her bedroom door, grabbed the handle and opened it.

The hallway of her childhood home was gone. Nan now stood on a great limestone terrace, which overlooked an immense, thick, dark forest, spreading as far as her eyes could see down a steep cliff face. *Oh boy,* Nan's mind raced, *where am I?*

Not a fan of heights, Nan urged her legs to step away from the platform's wall, but they wouldn't move. Panicked, Nan attempted to look down, but her eyes remained fixed to the view.

O.M.G. what is going on? Nan said, but then realized no sound had left her lips nor did they part.

Her gaze involuntarily dropped to the ground where she caught a glimpse of her reflection in a rain puddle upon the aged stones. Nan started for the image that stared back at her wasn't her own.

Her pyjamas and simple shoulder length brown hair had vanished, instead the woman looking back at Nan was dressed in a smock style cambric gown (commonly seen in the early middle-ages) with long sweeping sleeves and low squared off neckline, bordered in a silver braid, and flared skirt, accented down the centre with rich damask. Thick mountainous raven black hair was pleated down her back, crowned with a circlet. The only resemblance to Nan could be found in the woman's sea grey eyes.

Astonished, Nan tried to run her hands over the lightweight cotton fabric, but couldn't. *What am I going to do, this isn't me,* she thought, frantic. But the eyes that stared back at her said otherwise.

Why am I frozen in another person's body? Her mind screamed silently, as Nan fought to gain control over the foreign body and find her way back to reality.

Nan's possessed form suddenly turned and Nan saw with horror a formidable cliff top fortress towering in front of her. A shiver ran down her host's spine, as if in response to her own fears. Nan hastily committed all she saw to memory, in hopes she'd find a way to escape, though she had no idea how she would get the unyielding body to comply once she did. Instead of an escape, Nan saw a chilling, sinister figure in the shadows.

Aware he had been spotted, the mass approached. Nan could feel her host stiffen at the man's movements. Soon the ominous brooding eyes of the tall gruesome man, dressed in a blood red tunic with the loose cloak of a noble clasped at the shoulder, and long dark brown hair hanging down his back, burrowed into hers.

"*Ble mae ti ddianc i?*" he seethed through clenched teeth, in a language Nan did not understand. But her shadow self did.

Nan wanted to tell him she was not who he believed her to be, but the words were trapped in her throat, as she was in another's body. Her avatar gave no reply, but shrank back from the man's penetrating stare.

Nan's sympathetic nervous system was now on full alert. *We need to get out of here, run,* she urged her host. As if in response to Nan's desires, her alien self dodged to the left and ran past the menacing man towards the castle's terrace entrance.

A rough, pinching grasp clutched their arm from behind and Nan's possessed form was thrust back towards the terrace wall with great speed, as if in hopes to be thrown over it. The arm the man gripped burned and Nan's double's breath came out panicked, as the man pressed their lower back tight up against the stonewall, his unoccupied hand closing firmly around their throat.

"*Nid yw yr amser hwn, dy llances bach,*" the man hissed. He leaned so close Nan could feel his breath on her host's ear. The grip on their neck tightened even harder. Nan gasped with her host for breath as she felt the life drain from their body.

"*Ni fydd Ti ddianc ti, dim hyd yn oed at farwolaeth,*" he threatened. Soon all was black, as Nan's possessed lungs squeezed out the last bit of oxygen they had left in them.

****

Rory was already up and on her second cup of coffee when Nan entered the kitchen. "Wow, ouch, rough night?" She winced upon the sight of Nan's tired, drawn face.

"You could say that," Nan smirked. She let Blue out the porch door and turned to make herself a cup of tea.

"Let me guess, you had another nightmare, didn't you?" reckoned Rory.

"Yes and it was the strangest dream ever," answered Nan. Cup in hand, Nan joined Rory at the round table and told her all the bizarre details.

"This dream thing sounds like it is beginning to get really serious," Rory frowned, concerned, when Nan had finished describing the odd scenario. "I mean, look at your neck," and she pointed to the hand print bruise on Nan's throat, which Nan had seen that morning in her bathroom mirror. "How could a dream leave physical marks?"

"I don't know, but I have to get to the bottom of it, before something worse happens," replied Nan in earnest.

"Maybe I'll find more out in the letters," Nan muttered, but then saw the puzzled expression on Rory's face and quickly acquainted her with the news of the letters Parker had found the night before in the trunk.

"Why didn't he want me to be there when he gave them to you? What doesn't he trust me?" vented Rory, once Nan had finished.

"I don't know," replied Nan noncommittally. She didn't want to explain how Parker thought Rory stuck her nose into Nan's business too much. "Anyways, it appears my mom came here to escape someone pursuing her in England."

"Interesting," Rory mused. "Do you think that's who you're dreaming about?"

"Not unless my mom grew up in some kind of a Renaissance Fair culture. Besides my mother was a redhead," answered Nan sarcastically.

"True," Rory acknowledged. "Well anyways, maybe your mom went back to England?"

"Maybe, I only read one letter last night, but I'm hoping to find more out in the rest."

Rory looked up at the clock above the kitchen window over the sink and started. "Well, I'd love to stay and help you, Chickipoo, but I'm going to be late for work," she exclaimed as she jumped to her feet.

"Ah, that's okay," Nan shrugged unconcerned.

Rory came back down from upstairs moments later dressed in her waitressing uniform. She paused and glanced into the living room where Nan was now aimlessly tidying, and said, "You know, there's this woman in town who runs a little pagan shop, maybe she could help you understand these dreams better."

Nan snorted and replied in a caustic tone, "I thought you were a Christian, how do you know where pagan shops are? Dabbling in the occult are you?"

"No, I am a steadfast Christian, thank you. But I've seen it on the drive home and just thought possibly you might find help there," Rory smirked.

"Ah, okay," agreed Nan to appease her, before Rory disappeared out the door.

****

With no obligations on her plate, once Rory left, Nan made herself another cup of tea and bolted upstairs to read another letter. She adjusted the pillows on the bed to prop herself up comfortably, then reached for the next envelope from the pile, opened it and read.

Dearest Rhiannon,

It distresses me that my intent on writing to you is to acquaint you with the grievous news of your mother's untimely death. The event was sudden and as of yet undetermined. One of the upper maids found her lifeless corpse one morning in your former bedchambers, in your father's house.

It has been speculated that due to your impromptu flight, she killed herself from the wretchedness of despair. But as you may suspect, I have no doubt that fowl play is at hand. In your father's London house, none of you were safe. It was our family home were you all belonged, protected.

However, your uncle is martyring himself as an inconsolable figure, with his brother's widow gone and her eldest daughter lost. He is not ignorant of the suspicion I have thrown his way though. With your mother's death, he now more than ever seeks you out, under the claim of wanting to restore you, his beloved niece, to your proper place in society and within the family.

With the last of our numbers dwindling, this misfortune has put you in even greater peril. Though you have chosen to forsake the path of our ancestors and the traditions of old, the book you stole in the night might be all that is left of us. Guard it well. In the wrong hands, it could prove a dangerous weapon.

Keep safe my dear and watch over your shoulders. May the spirits protect you.

Blessed Be,

Aunt D.

With a heavy heart, Nan rested her head back on the pillows and let the words of the letter sink in. *How sad, mom really did lose everything, her home, her mother, her whole family. So then, why did she leave us too? We were her second chance.*

The plot of the story thickened, getting graver with every turn. Nan was beginning to grow reluctant to dig any deeper. *It all sounds like something out of an Ann Radcliffe novel. Mysterious deaths, formidable foes, suspicious uncles, fleeing in the night, no wonder dad kept me in the dark all these years. Or did he even know?* Nan wondered grimly.

Her mind swarmed like a hive of bees as she tried to process it all. A single piece of information suddenly jumped out at her. *The letter said mom stole a book. What book?*

Then the possibility leapt to mind and Nan got up and strode across the room to her secretary desk where the handcrafted leather bound book sat. *Could this be the book?* Nan ran her hand over the volume's stiff leather cover. *No, that would be too simple,* she laughed doubtfully, but a whispering voice inside told her it was. *I have to find out what it says.*

Nan moved everything else off the desk, out of her way, and laid the book open on her left, with her laptop positioned on the right in preparation to translate the historic text. Not quite sure where to start, still ignorant to the origins of most of the dialects, but determined to succeed, Nan flipped to a random page and began Googling similar looking script.

Enthralled in her research, Nan became oblivious to the time. On a whim, she glanced at the bottom of her computer screen. "Oh shit," Nan lamented, when she saw the time. She jumped to her feet, banged her knee off the desk's edge in the process, and rushed from the room. The previously forgotten two o'clock meeting with the L.M. Montgomery Heritage Society director re-registered in her mind.

"Oh boy, I'm going to be late," she whimpered. As she burst out the door to her truck, she dialled her boss's number on her cell, to give him some flimsy excuse for her tardiness.

Chapter 11
"Magic is believing in yourself, if you can do that, you can make anything happen," Johann Wolfgang von Goethe

Nan arrived at the Leaksdale manse house for her meeting with the director, her boss, almost an hour late. The appointment was brief and reproachful, but successful. Too engulfed in the mystery she had uncovered about her mother and her family to be able to focus on work yet, Nan stated she was still stressed and had much to attend to (though not entirely untrue) and wasn't yet capable to resume her duties. In the end, the director was sympathetic and permitted her a while longer on the assurance Nan would do her utmost best to make it a speedy return.

Satisfied with the outcome of her afternoon endeavours, on the drive home Nan suddenly realized she was famished and decided to stop by the restaurant Rory worked at to get something to eat.

Surprised by Nan's unexpected appearance in her section, Rory walked over all aglow and said, "Hey, what brings you to my neck of the woods?"

"I missed your smiling face," Nan joked. "No, I had a meeting with the boss today, which I completely forgot about and damn near missed."

"Tsk, tsk, bad girl," laughed Rory, as she sat down on the opposite side of the booth. "How did it go?"

"Not bad," shrugged Nan, "He doesn't like my absence, but agreed to give me more time off, as long as it's not too long."

"Cool, but I thought you wanted to go back to work?"

"Well, I did, but now with everything that's going on, you know with my mom and that; I'm not ready to throw in the towel yet. I want to find out what really happened and I can't do that when I'm working," explained Nan. She secretly reproached herself for being so irresponsible. Never being the type to shirk her duties or slack off at anything.

"Sounds reasonable," Rory nodded in agreement. "So, where are you going to start?"

At this Nan told Rory about the research project, which had made Nan late for her meeting in the first place. About how she had read another letter, which mentioned a book and she guessed it was the one they had found in the attic the night before and tried to decipher its cryptic texts.

Rory forgot all about the other patrons in the restaurant she was supposed to serve as she listened intently.

"So did you manage to translate any of it?" inquired Rory in fascination when Nan was finished her tale.

"No, not really," Nan sulked, "I did find out that most of the writing is in some sort of Brythonic dialect, but don't know what it says yet."

"Well that's a start at least," encouraged Rory.

Just then, a gruff call came for Rory from the kitchens. "Uh oh, I better get back to work," Rory smirked and rose from the booth.

"Yeah, sorry if I got you in trouble," said Nan with a wince as another disgruntled shout came their way.

"Ah, no worries, Pierre grumbles, but he thinks I'm cute so it's all good," Rory replied with a playful wink. "What did you want to eat anyways?"

"Just bring me a B.L.T."

"Gotcha," smirked Rory and she turned and headed off for the kitchen.

****

After finishing her late lunch, Nan headed home. She stopped for the town's only light and watched a couple of teens cross the street. Nan noticed a peculiar little shop on the corner. She hadn't spotted it before and stared at its single window with a white pentacle painted on it. There were lights on inside, the hour still being relatively early, which demonstrated it was open, but Nan didn't observe any customers coming and going.

I bet that's the store Rory was talking about, she pondered, as the light turned green and she drove away. However, as Nan continued down the road in the direction of home, she couldn't get the shop's image out of her head and before she knew what she was doing, she had made a U-turn and headed back.

A bell tinkled as Nan entered the store. *It is definitely an asthmatic's nightmare*, she thought (knowing from experience) being instantly assaulted by a thick over powering wall of fragrance. To her surprise though the incense were kind of tranquil and gave Nan the allure of being in a fairy story. No one was at the cash register, which was unusual and not a customer in sight.

Nan tried to navigate her way through the treacherously tiny, cluttered shop aisles, afraid of knocking something over. Every square inch had some kind of unusual or exotic item on display. There were shelves of books, art, jewellery, statues, herbs in plastic pouches, tiny coloured rocks, incense, and much, much more. None of which Nan had any idea the purpose for.

As Nan perused a buffet of gemstones, she was startled by a female voice behind her that appeared from thin air and asked, "Can I help you with anything? Are you here for a reading?"

Nan spun around so quick she almost knocked over a display of tarot cards. A middle-aged woman stood in front of her, with long tumbling blonde hair, in a brightly patterned black dress, with the most magnificent sapphire eyes Nan had ever seen. She smiled kindly.

Where had she come from? Nan wondered, as she caught her breath and replied, "No, I was just looking."

"Oh by all means enjoy. Take your time and if you need any help don't hesitate to ask," the woman beamed. However, she didn't return to the register, but instead hovered and eyed Nan amiably. "Are you interested in healing crystals? I see you already have quite a lovely piece of onyx to help guide you, on your hand," she asked and gestured to an array of stones on display.

A bit taken aback, Nan looked down at the snake-entwined ring from the trunk, still on her finger, unsure; she hadn't realized the black jewel was of particular importance. Nan struggled for a response. "Oh um, no not really. This was…um a family heirloom,"—not knowing how else to explain it—"I didn't know it was onyx."

"Oh yes. And very nice quality by the looks of it. May I?" asked the woman, as she reached out for Nan's hand to better inspect the ring. Amazed by the woman's words, without protest Nan held up her hand.

"Hmm, yes very nice. Definitely an old stone of the purest quality, very powerful I'd say. Do you know the purpose of onyx?" When Nan shook her head 'no', the woman's smile broaden as a teacher about to educate an eager student and explained, "It is not a stone commonly picked. Onyx promotes strength, stamina, durability, and self-confidence. It is said, the stone helps one banish grief and that it brings happiness and prosperity, aids in decision-making, and is used for protection. It also helps in the recovery of past lives."

Baffled, Nan looked at the woman's gentle face. She never imagined a rock to be anything but pretty. Speechless, Nan stared back at her hand, which the woman had let go of.

"And the snake encircling it empowers the stone even more. The snake being a symbol of transformation, the cycle of life, guardianship, and death and rebirth, of course," continued the woman.

Dumbstruck, Nan wondered if she should inquire further or just turn and leave, before she bought into what a lot of people would say was hogwash. *What if it's not hogwash*? Nan pondered, still a bit sceptical.

The woman could sense Nan's insecurity, gave her a benevolent look and asked in a quieter tone, "New to the craft dear? It's okay if it all seems a bit unbelievable still. It takes time to fully understand the workings of the powers nature's energy grants us."

Nan didn't want to offend the woman by admitting she wasn't all that convinced magic or witchcraft or whatever people call it, truly existed, being a firm academic who believed nothing without logical proof, and instead replied, "Oh no I'm not a wi...I mean I don't....I've never...Oh I don't know. I don't honestly know what I'm doing here. I've just had so many unanswerable questions lately and a friend suggested I might find some answers here."

"It's okay dear, you don't have to be a believer to come into my store," the woman smiled, almost like she could read Nan's thoughts. "Perhaps your friend is right and I can help you, but if not there's no harm in just being curious. Why don't you tell me what's troubling you?"

Relieved, Nan instantly perked up and took a deep breath. "You see I've been having some really strange dreams lately and my friend thinks they are trying to tell me something."

"Ah," the woman nodded. "Come, I have a place for my readings in the back. Why don't we have a seat in there and you can tell me about these dreams you've been having."

Nan formed no objection and like a lamb following a shepherd, she went with the complete stranger into the building's back room, which was draped with colourful curtains and spring patterned settees, and an altar with candles and other items in the room's centre against the wall.

Nan couldn't explain what had come over her, rather a secretive private person by nature, but here she felt serene and safe. She began to recite all that had happened to her since her father's death, as if she chatted with an old friend.

When Nan fell silent, the woman gave her a sympathetic look and said, "Dreams can be a powerful thing. Clairvoyants, telepaths, and people practicing divination believe greatly in their messages. Some say they are a way for the dead to communicate with us or a way for us to learn things not yet known about ourselves, our lives, or the lives of others. Even people without any psychic abilities say things come to them in their dreams." The woman paused for a moment as if deliberation, then asked, "Do you believe in reincarnation?"

Nan started, unsure, having never been asked a question of the sort. "Well I have never really given it much thought."

"It's fine if you don't. Many don't, but some believe that a person's soul never truly dies, but is continuously reborn until they have fully learnt all the great lessons of life and that people can see glimpses of their former lives through dreams and other avenues," the woman explained. "Some enlist the help of meditation or herbs or gems, such as the one you wear, to see these lives."

"Really?" Nan said incredulously. She debated in her head whether the woman was nuts or if what she said could be plausible. *I did have that strange dream the night after finding the ring,* mused Nan. *No, that's ridiculous; I was having weird dreams way before I put the ring on!*

The woman quietly laughed as she saw Nan eye the ring dubiously and said, "It's alright, you don't have to believe it, I just thought perhaps it may be another path to consider on your search for answers."

Nan decided it was time to go. She had heard more than enough new age spiritual babble then she could take, which had caused her brain to ache in its fight between logic and irrationality. Nan exited the woman's reading room and made for the door.

As the mystic woman escorted Nan out to the shop's public area, Nan thought of what she had said about the snake on her ring and pictured its match on the mysterious book, which sat on her desk. "Who would use a snake for a symbol? I mean, besides my ring, I found this old book the other day and it has a snake in a pentagram on its cover."

"Well," the woman began, eyeing Nan intently, "I haven't run into it much myself, but the serpent is an ancient totem, both revered and feared by many cultures. Even used in modern fields such as medicine, as you've no doubt seen with the caduceus or the Rod of Asclepius. Its duality has made it a powerful symbol. So much so, there are even snake worshipping cults, a practice known as Ophiolatry. Snake charmers and healers have studied these creatures the world over due to their assigned wisdom and connection to medicine, both as a giver of health and rebirth, as well as death. The serpent has even found a place in Christianity, though less glorified."

"Wow," exclaimed Nan in awe, surprised at the wealth of information the woman knew on the subject. "I never realised snakes were such a big deal. I thought people hated them, thinking they were creepy and vicious."

"Unfortunately most do. Snakes are just one of the many animals misunderstood and prosecuted by humans. You say you found a snake pentagram totem on a book?" the woman frowned, the wheels of thought obvious in her stare, which caused Nan to wonder at her inner thoughts.

"Yes," Nan assured. Suspicion rose at the woman's intensity.

"Hmm, it sounds like a book of shadows or grimoire, to me."

"A book of shadows?" repeated Nan, unsure what she meant.

"Yes, it's a personal spell book each witch or coven of the old religion, use to write down their wisdom," she explained, "It's quite common in the practice and is often adorned with the person's totem."

The woman hesitated as she eyed Nan again in search of what Nan could not say, and then said, "I'm rather new to the practice myself, I was raised Christian but converted a couple of years back. Anyways, there are whisperings about a very old coven, now extinct, who used a snake entwined in a pentagram as their totem. Perhaps the book you found has something to do with them. Very little is known about them, but be warned, they are shrouded in tales of dark magic."

"Dark magic?" Nan's eyes widened to the size of saucers at this. She had heard the phrase uttered in movies and knew it was not good.

"Yes, you don't want to get mixed up in that," the woman cautioned.

"Okay, thank you," replied Nan, not knowing what else to say. As she turned to leave, she paused and asked, "Where was this...um coven from?"

"Sorry, I don't know. As I said not much is known about them."

"Oh okay, well thank you for all your help anyways. You've given me a lot to think about," Nan smiled in appreciation.

"Any time dear," the woman beamed and turning to the counter she grabbed a small business card and handed it to Nan. "Here, in case you find yourself with any more unanswerable questions or just need to talk. My name is Casey and I'm glad to help you in any way I can."

Nan thanked Casey again and placed the card in her jacket pocket before she left the store and headed for her truck, parked on the street outside. Nan barely remembered the drive home, her mind overflowed with Casey's words.

Her father had been a sensible man and Nan couldn't imagine him getting entangled with a woman associated with snake worshipping cults, witchcraft, spell books and all that nonsense. Would he? With everything that had happen since his death, Nan didn't know anymore.

But what if what Casey said had really nothing to do with all this, then why did my mom steal a book on witchcraft? She shook her head as logic flooded back in. Nan reprimanded herself for buying into any of the irrational concepts she had heard that night and reminded her brain that she still had no idea what was in the book. *Only D. Greenwick does.*

****

At home, Nan sat at her desk, laptop screen aglow, and stared once again at the undecipherable inexplicable book. Her last thoughts from the drive home suddenly returned. Nan sucked her lips in, in concentration and repeated out loud to the silent room, "Only D. Greenwick does."

"I wonder?" She glanced at the letters on her nightstand, turned to her computer, put fingers to keys, and began typing furiously. It wasn't long before she had found an English directory, in which she typed the last name and initial, along with the return address on the back of the envelopes. A single listing popped up.

There on the screen in black and white, listed under the same address as on the letters, was the name, Abiageal D. Greenwick.

Hmm I wonder. Nan stared at the computer screen. *There is no 'A' or Abiageal written on the letters, but I wonder if it could be the same person.*

Could it really be possible after so many years since the letters were written that she had actually found their author? Could this mysterious

A New Forest Witch

Aunt D. still be alive? It was the only name in the directory associated with New Forest, England. *It has to be her.*

Chapter 12
"To travel is to live." Hans Christian Anderson

Rory opened the house's door, tired and achy, the cruel evening air biting at her neck and ears. It had proven to be a long day. She had stayed late at the restaurant to win brownie points after the reprimand Pierre had given her for being idle with Nan instead of doing her job. Now she craved a hot soak in the tub and her soft bed.

Instead, she was greeted at the door by ecstatic shrieks from Nan as she rushed down the stairs. Panic stricken by her friend's excited bellows, Rory gazed around in wide-eyed alarm. "What? What's wrong?"

Nan landed in the foyer breathless from her mad dash downstairs and overly elated, announced, "I'm going to England."

Rory's expression changed from concern to utter bewilderment in the span of two seconds flat. She tried in vain to get her tired brain to comprehend what she had just heard, but finally placed her hands to her throbbing temples and replied, "Wow, wow, wow, back up the train. You're doing what?"

"I'm going to England," repeated Nan, still bursting at the seams with pleasure, her mind full of thoughts of adventure.

A little less discombobulated and even more concerned, Rory inquired, "When? Why?"

"The day after tomorrow."

Rory's jaw nearly hit the floor. Getting a slight grip, she erupted in complete horror. "What, but why? And how can you…" Rory stopped in mid-sentence, closed her eyes, and shook her head to absorb the multitude of thoughts, which rattled in their cage. More composed, she tried again, and asked a single question, "Why?"

"I'm going to find my mother," replied Nan, in a proud matter-of-fact tone.

"How?" Rory inquired, only being able to ejaculate one-word responses.

"I found the Aunt D. who wrote the letters. Well at least I think I found her."

"What letters?" questioned Rory, painfully confused.

Nan rolled her eyes at Rory's new bout of short-term memory loss. "The letters to my mother, the ones I was telling you about this morning."

Recognition rolled in and Rory exclaimed, "Oh, yeah ok. But why do you have to go all the way to England to see her? Why can't you just write her or better yet call her?"

"There was no phone number listed in the directory for starters and to be honest I'm not sure if it's even the same person. And I don't want to wait for a reply through snail mail, I need answers," moaned Nan in impatience.

Rory racked her brain for any excuse to make Nan stay and listen to reason. "How do you even know that this woman is still alive?"

"I don't," stated Nan honestly. "But it's the best lead I have and if she is still alive I don't want to wait around and lose my chance."

Finally, she realized there was no chance of talking Nan out of her rashness, once her mind was set on something that was the end of it; Rory smiled and said, "Yeah I guess. So do you want me to help you pack?"

"Absolutely," beamed Nan in return; relieved they were on the same side now.

Rory headed to the kitchen, stating she needed some water to wash down the bomb she had just swallowed, and Nan followed to acquaint her with all the details of her upcoming trip, as well as the visit to Casey's shop. Pretty soon they had determined Rory would obviously watch over the house and animals, while Nan was away and that Nan would leave a stash for her share of the bills in the kitchen drawer, in case she wasn't back by their due dates.

"I won't be gone long. Two weeks at the most," assured Nan.

"Don't worry I'll take good care of everything," replied Rory.

"I have faith in you," smiled Nan.

"Have you told Parker yet?" This question caused Nan's confidence to falter. In her excitement, she hadn't thought of Parker or how her leaving so soon after the start of their business venture may affect things.

"No, not yet," she sighed.

"Well you're gonna have to tell him sooner or later. Especially since you're business partners now," Rory needlessly pointed out.

"Yeah I know, today was his first day out in the truck too." Deep down, she wished she could avoid telling him all together. To regain her confident mask, Nan pretended it was no big deal and said, "He's a big boy. He'll do fine without me."

Their time together now limited, Rory decided to give Nan a proper send off. They stopped their mindless chit chatting and turned the rest of the evening into a girls' night. Complete with bowls of chips, candy, and bottles of pop. They ordered Chinese food and went through Nan's immense DVD collection, until they had picked out an array of horror and fantasy epics to suit their ever-clashing styles.

****

The period gown and long flowing raven hair was back. *Oh no, not again,* Nan's subconscious wailed.

Everything was blurred, as if when woken from a deep sleep. *That's it wakeup,* she urged her unconscious mind. To Nan's horror, it was not her world, which came into focus through her eyes.

Nan knew she was once again an inanimate passenger in another woman's body and watched as her avatar sat up from the pallet she had been laying upon and looked down at her gown. What had once been a rich emerald green tunic garment was now ragged and dirty around the edges. Nan could see from the corner of the woman's eyes that her beautiful satin smooth ebony hair hung limp and matted, all the life taken out of it.

What's happened to her or me or whoever we are? Nan wondered. Her anxiety built as her host stood and staggered across a short stretch to a wall, where she peered out an iron barred glassless window, which towered over a night-darkened view of the forest far below.

A faint stream of moonlight entered through it and as the foreign body turned back to the room, Nan saw that they were in a shoebox sized, circular cell. A dense iron studded wooden door barred their freedom and a foul, putrid odour polluted the air, making simple breathing a chore.

I'm a prisoner. A chill crept up Nan's host's spine, like the laugh of the kookaburra bird results in. Her borrowed eyes panned the cold limestone circumference of the room. It was void of all life and human touch. They swept over the imposing door to the floor and Nan shrieked inaudibly in terror.

A large lump of a shadow lay on the floor. Nan could feel her host's body stiffen with bitter agony at the sight of it. There on the cold, hard stone floor was the strewn spiritless, bloody corpse of a man. His detached head thrown to his side; its glazed over dead eyes staring straight up at them.

****

Nan was glad to awaken to the glowing lemon light of daybreak. Dazed from her nightmare excursion and the lingering sugar rush from the muffled events of the night before, she slowly lifted herself out of bed and headed for the bathroom. The dream man's severed head still prominent in her mind's eye.

She turned on the cold water and ran her hands through the chilled liquid. She splashed her face in the hopes of washing away the effects of the vivid horror plagued thoughts. Nan wiped her face with a towel, then gazed at her reflection in the medicine cabinet mirror above the sink and jumped with fright.

The reflection of her ravenous nightmare doppelganger stared back at her. *Oh no. I'm still dreaming*, worried Nan, as she ran a hand over her drawn, pale complexion. Then, Nan looked down at her hands and wiggled her fingers. She could move them. Nan sighed in relief. *I'm not dreaming I'm awake.*

Nan gazed back in the mirror at the sporadically layered black locks, which covered her head, confused. She closed her eyes as tight as she possibly could; little stars bounced off her irises, and then opened them again only to find the same unrecognizable reflection.

As she ran the blue-black hair through her hands recollection began to seep back into her muddled brain and the whole scene of the spontaneous late night makeovers arranged by Rory, flashed before her eyes. Nan couldn't help but laugh at her stupidity and then began to admire her new look. *I have to admit I kind of like it. But why did I choose black?*

She heard the padding of paws enter the bathroom and gasped when she turned to see Blue. Then giggling, she dropped to her kneels and gave the patient canine a remorseful pet. "Oh you poor thing. You were a victim of Rory's makeover to, eh?"

The poor dog was covered in sparkling purple eye shadow, blush and what once had been plum lipstick, now smeared into a clown smile over her furry muzzle. Nan stood up to retrieve a wetted cloth and washed the makeup off the old dog's spoiled face. "What we don't put you through," she laughed.

When both were refreshed and cleaned up, Nan and Blue headed downstairs to assess the rest of the night's damage. The living room was littered with empty chip bowls, candy wrappers, pop cans, takeout containers, and a multitude of strewn pillows and blankets. Nan shook her head at the mess and continued on to the kitchen hoping it wasn't as bad.

Instead, she found a party hung-over Rory pouring herself a huge mug of coffee, still wearing her fluorescent pink sparkle flecked pyjamas and trademark Oscar the Grouch slippers. Her once sleek chestnut hair now a cropped blonde pixie cut with purple and pink highlights.

"Morning Chickipoo, are you as tired as I am?" asked Rory, as she gazed at Nan over her shoulder.

"Yes. I feel like I've been hit by a train," replied Nan weary. She slumped down in a kitchen chair.

"I totally relate, but last night was a blast and your hair looks great," Rory grinned and took the seat opposite Nan.

"Yeah about that, why did we choose black again?" asked Nan, holding a strand of her hair out to examine.

"It was your choice. You said it was your favourite hair colour," replied Rory.

"I did? Wow, I don't remember that."

"Well I don't know, but it looks good. Anyways, I was thinking that I have a few hours before work so we should go shopping," continued Rory.

"Shopping," exclaimed Nan horror-stricken. She hated the tiresome chore at the best of times.

"Yes, we both know that you haven't really travelled anywhere before, so I doubt you're prepared," stated Rory.

"Well yeah, I guess," acknowledged Nan reluctantly. Rory had a point, apart from the odd truck run to the States with her father, Nan had never gone anywhere, making luggage unnecessary, until now.

Rory smiled at her easy victory. "Okay then, well get dressed and let's head out."

Nan left the kitchen to find more suitable attire, then secured the animals and spent the rest of the morning and most of the afternoon dragged by Rory from store to store on Oshawa's downtown strip.

Just before dinner, the worn-out buyers returned with a truckload of bags, the majority of which belonged to Rory, the shopaholic. Nan only obtained a nice simple, inexpensive set of classic grey suitcases. The girls had grabbed takeout for dinner, quickly ate, and then Rory rushed upstairs to don her uniform and leave for her evening shift at the restaurant.

"Are you sure your boss is going to be okay with your new punk rocker look?" asked Nan sceptically, while Rory put on her coat.

Rory shrugged her shoulders. "Yeah, sure, why wouldn't he? Besides who cares if he doesn't like it. It's not like he can fire me for it, it's a free country after all."

"I guess," said Nan unconvinced.

****

Nan carried her luggage upstairs in preparation to pack, her early morning flight from Pearson International airport would soon arrive. She placed the suitcases, open, on the bed and began going through the checklist in her head.

It was fall in England as well, which meant the season's customary pants and long sleeved shirts would suffice. Thanks to Google, Nan had learned her desired destination of Hampshire was in Southeast England, where the weather was said to be windy and have a lot of rain, classed as an oceanic region.

With that in mind, Nan headed to her closet and soon pulled out an ample supply of jeans, sleeved shirts, and a polyester skirt just in case. She carried the neatly folded stack of clothes back to the bed and placed them in the larger of the two suitcases, then closed the lid. *Good, that's done, now what?*

Her personal feminine necessities already packed and left in a small purse size bag in the bathroom for morning use, Nan went through her mental list again to see if she had overlooked anything. Satisfied, she threw a couple of pairs of extra socks and underwear in just in case and then turned to the still empty, smaller case. *Now what should I put in there?*

All requirements accounted for; Nan gazed around her bedroom for inspiration. Her sight landed on the little handcrafted bookcase her father had made her—being a devoted bibliophile—Nan decided she should take a couple books for light reading. However, upon looking at the shelves contents, which she had all read a hundred times, Nan turned away disappointed.

Suddenly she remembered the three hardcovers from her mother's trunk and walked over to the desk to retrieve them. Having given them little attention before, Nan surveyed the old editions and read their strange titles, *The Mabinogion*, *Book of Taliesin*, and *Black Book of Carmarthen*, found they were unknown to her. *Well it couldn't hurt to give them a chance*, she smiled and walked back to the bed where she placed them in the small suitcase.

Nan's mind remained on the topic of books and she stared back at the secretary desk to the unusual leather bound book and wondered, *should I take it to?* Decided, she strode back over to the desk and took the book in her hands. *If this really is the book from the letters, then I should take it to show this D. Greenwick and see if I can get some answers*. Nan rushed back to the bed before she changed her mind and placed the book in the small suitcase with the rest and closed the lid.

Nan decided to call it a night and went to change into her pyjamas. Just as she was about to do so, she saw a pair of headlights through the window as a truck made its way up the night-darkened driveway. She knew by the sound of the engine it was Parker and peered out of her window, which overlooked the yard and watched as he effortlessly parked the truck and closed the pushbutton garage door behind him.

Well it's now or never, Nan sighed, the dreaded moment now at hand. *You can't just leave without talking to him. What are you so afraid of?* Her mind prodded while she watched him shut the shop's lights off, lock the main door, and head up the laneway to the barn. As she turned for the door, she looked down at Blue and said, "Want to come give me a hand girl?"

****

Nan sucked in a deep breath as she knocked on the loft's French doors at the top of the fire escape-Nan's father's method of outside access-and hoped to find Parker in the shower or otherwise indisposed. She waited only seconds before she was about to chicken out and leave, but then her face fell in disappointment as she caught sight of Parker's happy expression coming towards her to let her in.

"Hey you," he beamed, when he opened a door for her to enter. "This is a surprise."

"You know me, just full of surprises," Nan joked, trying to keep the mood light and hide her unease.

Nan took in her surroundings and realized it was the first time she had been in the loft since her and Rory had moved out. The large open concept room was humbly decorated with shelves of modal cars and the odd poster, which hung on the sanitary white walls. Their old purple couch, television, coffee table, and Nan's old bed, the only furniture in the space, which made it look sparse.

"It looks nice," Nan chimed politely, perched on the arm of the sofa, which had seen better days. "Very homey."

Parker smirked at her generosity and flopped himself down on the couch's other end. "You don't have to lie."

"I'm not," she smirked, "The model cars give it that extra bit of flare."

"You like them eh?" he laughed in return.

"Oh yes, they're every woman's dream."

Nan almost forgot her secret preservations about her purpose in coming to see Parker, as they bantered back and forth like normal. "So how are things going with the towing?"

"So far so good. Not too busy, but things will pick up once the business's name gets around. Not too much for you to do yet in the bookkeeping department," he answered. "How goes it with you? Aren't you heading back to work soon?"

"No, I had a meeting with my boss yesterday and he extended my leave."

"Oh, I thought you were doing better now," Parker frowned. He wondered what he had missed.

"I am, it's just with all the stuff going on with my mother, I'm not ready to deal with work yet," answered Nan. She could feel her anxiety grow inside her as the moment to reveal her trip loomed closer.

"Oh, I see," replied Parker. He turned a scrutinizing eye on Nan's looks and cocked his head to the side in thought. "Did you do something to your hair?"

Nan couldn't help but giggle at just how unobservant men really could be. *It seriously took him this long to notice.* She smiled and replied, "Yes. Rory and me kind of got bored last night and dyed our hair."

"Cool, I like it," Parker smiled genuinely.

Nan decided there was no point in prolonging it any further; she took a deep breath and said, "Hey, you know how you found those letters?"

"Yeah."

"Well they have been really helpful and the person who wrote them may still be alive and have some answers about what happened to my mom," Nan related.

"That's great," beamed Parker, honestly happy for her.

"Yeah it is," Nan smiled back. Perhaps it wouldn't go as badly as she thought it would. "So anyways, I've decided to go to England to find her and hopefully my mother."

Parker stared at Nan stone-faced for a moment, before he burst forth, "You can't go to England. Are you nuts?"

Though Nan hadn't expected him to be happy, she was taken aback by Parker's outraged expression. "What?" she exclaimed bewildered, but then anger crept into the mix. "What do you mean I can't go?"

With dark eyes and a furrowed brow, Parker launched to his feet. "You can't just go running off to England by yourself, to find some deadbeat who abandoned you!"

"My mother is not a deadbeat," roared Nan.

"Oh please, what kind of a person abandons their family?" sneered Parker.

"Who the hell do you think you are?" shouted Nan, now on her feet in a blind rage. "You have no right talking about my family like that and you can't tell me what to do."

"I'm your friend, that's who. Someone needs to knock some sense into that stubborn head of yours," yelled Parker.

"Well some friend," Nan cried out in anger. She scrambled to think of a more dignified comeback. "I don't need your permission, thank you. I just thought you'd like to know that I won't be here for a while."

"How nice of you," he exclaimed through clenched teeth, still seething with rage. "It's not like you're much help with the business anyways."

"Aw," Nan sucked in her breath. She felt as if she had just been slapped in the face.

"Drop dead," she hissed, turned for the door, reefed it open and stormed out of the room. Nan yelled back over her shoulder to the almost forgotten dog, "Blue come on." The poor discombobulated animal scurried out from her hiding place under the coffee table and bolted through the door before Nan slammed it shut, rattling the glass in its panes.

Nan stocked across the yard to the house, foaming at the mouth, while Blue jogged behind her. "Of all the nerve. Who does he think he is?" she raged. Her mind whirled with infuriating thoughts.

Not noticing Rory's car parked in the driveway, Nan charged into the house, slammed the door, and stocked up the stairs like a soldier on patrol. She was met on the landing by a groggy Rory, who peered out of her bedroom door. Rory rubbed sleep from her eyes and asked, "What's the matter? What's going on?"

Nan glared at her from the threshold of her own room and yelled in response, "He's impossible!" before she slammed her door, nearly cracking the doorframe in the process.

Rory yawned, shook her head and rolled her eyes, then retreated to her room and her warm cozy bed.

Chapter 13
"I know not all that may be coming, but be it what it will, I'll go to it laughing." Herman Melville

Nan yawned, awakened by the pilot's voice over the plane's loudspeaker as he announced their upcoming descend into Bournemouth International airport of Hurn, Dorset, in the district of Christchurch.

A first time flyer and not one fond of heights, Nan thought she had done quite well on the ten and a half hour flight. The mysterious tranquilizer Rory had given her at the boarding gate before the flight had of course helped.

As Nan fastened her seat belt, she watched as the evening darkened vision of a faraway land appeared through the plane's small window. Parker's face flashed before her eyes as her mind wandered back home. Still cross over the unexpected altercation they had had the night before, Nan had left to meet her eight thirty am flight, without saying goodbye. A fact she now regretted.

His words still burned in her ears, "Deadbeat who abandoned you." However, she couldn't deny Parker was right about one thing, her mother had abandoned her. *Is this all a mistake? Is trying to find her just crazy?*

Nan shook off this newfound apprehension and collected herself, distracting her mind by reaching inside her purse to retrieve the letters she had grabbed before leaving, along with a framed picture of her father.

She took out the third and final letter, dated the year she was born, from the bunch, relaxed in her seat and read.

Dearest Rhiannon,

I have failed to protect our family once again I'm saddened to report. After your mother's death, I brought our dear fragile Gwynedd home to New Forest. However, neither the house nor I could protect her from your grotesque uncle.

Using his sway in society, he convinced officials that after your mother's passing and your abduction poor Gwynedd had become unhinged. Then caught her unexpected out on the grounds and spirited her off to an asylum. Where I cannot say. Though, I have made many failed attempts at finding her. She seems to have vanished.

I fear for the innocent child's safety. I'm afraid I have failed all of you, my dear sister, as well as her girls.

My only hope of redemption and that of our family is that you and your beautiful little girl remain safe in the new world.

Blessed Be,

Aunt D.

My mother has a sister? Nan refolded the letter, placed it in its envelope and back in her purse. *Could that be the reason she left, to come home and help find her sister?* So many questions flittered through her head.

Glad to be back on solid ground, Nan wasted no time. She retrieved her luggage, bought a map of Southwest England, and then headed out into the quiet country streets of Hurn—population four hundred and sixty eight. Nan hailed an airport taxi and asked the driver to take her to the nearest hotel.

As the man put the car into gear and pulled away from the curb, Nan panicked as the car drove down the wrong side of the road. *They drive on the reverse side here you idiot,* she grumbled in her head, as she caught her breath.

Nan settled back in her seat and attempted to relax, while she gazed out the window at the picturesque little village (not much different from the hamlet she called home), but within minutes the driver pulled up to her assumed destination. After some hold up with payment, Nan not yet a master of the currency change, she got out of the car. In front of her was an old thatched roofed, Tudor style, corner building, with a sign above the door, which read The Bull & Boar.

When Nan entered, her heart sank at the driver's obvious mistake. He hadn't brought her to a hotel, but to a local pub. Its patrons laughed and conversed gaily, enjoying an evening pint, while they watched English football on the telly. Nan felt out of place as she stood at the threshold bags in hand. Sheepishly she turned to exit.

"Can I help ya luv?" a voice called above the crowd's jovial rumble. Nan looked back and saw the barmaid staring at her.

Nan paled with embarrassment at the many eyes, which now looked in her direction. She replied, "No it's okay. I think I've come to the wrong place."

"I can't hear ya luv, ya'll hav to come a bit closer," the girl, about Nan's age, said pleasantly in her thick accent.

Head down, Nan proceeded to the bar, trying not to knock any of the locals in the head with her suitcases. Once there she repeated her earlier statement. The bartender laughed and said with a smile, "Ah no luv, ya've come to the right place. Tis rooms above."

"Oh wonderful," exclaimed Nan in relief.

Still smiling the girl pulled out a roster from under the counter and flipped through it to find the evening's date. "How long will ya be stayin than luv?"

Nan placed her luggage on the floor to give her aching arms a break and answered, "Just for the night. I'm heading to Hampshire in the morning."

At this, the girl gave her a curious look, but kept her smile in place. "Tis a rather bad time of year ta be sight seein. Goin ta visit family are ya?"

Uncertain how to respond, Nan lied, "I'm going to see the fall colours."

The girl nodded and looked back at the book. She smiled, "Tis luv'ly this season. Now then, ya'll be in num'er four at the top of the stairs to the right." She handed Nan a key after she got her signature, then added, "The loo is beside the stairs on the right and the phone boxis on the left."

Nan mentally scrambled to commute all the girl said to memory, then asked, puzzled, "What's a loo?"

"The toilet luv," replied the girl, as she poured another pint for a man at the bar.

"Oh right." Nan felt like such a fool.

She lifted her suitcases off the floor and headed for the stairs, following the barmaid's simple directions until she came to a door with a brass number four on it. The room was plain, with unadorned white walls, small window, double bed, nightstands, dresser, and a single chair in the corner. It reminded Nan of one of the rooms you saw in a horror movie where the serial killer lived. *Thank goodness, I'm only staying one night*; she thought, as she entered the room and closed the door.

Nan draped her coat over the back of the chair and set her suitcases on the seat, then sat down on the edge of the bed and wondered what to do next. It was going on seven pm, but still being on Ontario time (it only being one thirty in the afternoon at home) Nan knew she couldn't go to bed.

I could go out, she considered, *or go downstairs*. Not being much of a drinker she decided against it, figuring there was little else to do in the already evening abandoned village. *When in doubt read.*

Nan jumped back to her feet and reached for the small suitcase to retrieve one of the books she had brought. She picked the first one her hand touched, entitled *Book of Taliesin*, then returned to the bed. After she pulled back the blankets and fluffed the pillows, Nan was soon curled up and absorbed in the written word.

****

Parker pulled the truck into the shop after the last tow job of the evening. It had been a busy day of hauling cars out of ditches and towing broken down jalopies back to their houses or to a mechanics, giving him little time to think. Yet no matter how much work there was, he couldn't get Nan out of his mind.

Why didn't I say goodbye to her? He mentally moaned. Nan's pickup parked in its usual place didn't help; giving the illusion she hadn't gone and was still there.

Parker kicked himself for letting his hot temper get the best of him that night. *If only I could take it back and handle things better, I would have done things different*, he thought, but deep down he knew that wasn't true, his temper still would have gotten in the way. Even now, the thought of Nan so far away, all alone and unprotected, made his blood boil.

What if something happens to her? What if she never comes back? I should have stopped her, tried harder to change her mind, gone with her, done something, he agonised. *I should have said goodbye.*

Chapter 14
"This is my letter to the world. That never wrote to me."
Emily Dickinson

The next morning Nan was in a conundrum over what to wear to meet the mysterious Aunt D. Never in her life had she felt so self-conscious about her appearance, intent on making a good impression. She tried on every article of clothing she had packed in search of the right combination, before finally deciding on a black shirt with grey dress pants and black square-heeled boots.

Nan stuffed the rest of her clothes back in her suitcase haphazardly, then headed down to the bar to pay her bill. Once done, she hailed another taxi and arranged for the driver to take her the seventeen miles into New Forest. The location documented on the letters and hopefully the home of D. Greenwick.

The twenty-five minute drive felt like mere seconds as Nan sat back and enjoyed the many faces of the Hampshire countryside. Caught up in the view, she was astonished when they actually arrived in the parish hamlet of Burley, New Forest. The village itself looked like something right out of a Jane Austen novel, with quaint whitewashed brick and mortar country shops with timber roofs. Streets where the odd pony or cow was seen roaming. Instead of concrete there were trees and shrubs surrounded by seas of green. Its inhabitants walked the streets, greeting each other joyfully and instead of mass vehicles and smog, there was fresh air and bicycles. It was like stepping back in time.

Nan soaked up every inch of it, as she walked down the main street. She came across the local inn, a charming little building with ivy-covered bricks; Nan entered and was immediately greeted by the sweet smell of fresh baking.

A pleasant, plump elderly woman in a chicken patterned apron turned from a shelf of china dolls she dusted in a corner at Nan's entrance, smiled and said, "Hullo dear, how may I help you?"

Nan returned her smile, the woman's pleasantry being contagious, and replied, "I'd like to rent a room."

"Certainly dear, I have just the room for you." The woman squeezed her short robust figure in behind a cherry wood desk and began flipping through the register.

Nan couldn't get over how welcoming and personable British people were. Back home people, even neighbours, went to great lengths to avoid one another. Whereas here Nan was greeted with smiles and good manners, not distaste and rudeness, it was refreshing.

The woman found the day's date in the register and got Nan to sign. "What brings you to our little neck of the woods dear? We don't get many visitors this time of year."

"I don't know why, it's beautiful here," Nan grinned, already attached to the town's charming atmosphere. "I'm actually here to visit family," she admitted.

"How lovely, and who might that be my dear?" the woman asked nonchalantly. She grabbed Nan's room key and emerged from behind the desk.

On any other occasion Nan would have been bothered by the woman's nosy nature, but here in this oasis away from the modern world, Nan took no notice and answered, "Mrs. Greenwick."

Unnoticeable to the unobservant eye, the woman's expression stiffened and became almost grim. "Ah, you mean Lady Greenwick, my dear. Old Birdie, we call her. You'll be heading on to Magewebb Manor then?"

Nan being a master at silent observation caught her hostess's alteration. "Yes, that's correct." Even though in truth, she wasn't sure of anything, let alone the name of 'Lady Greenwick's house.

Maids, sway in society, London houses, rightful places, and now the title of lady and a manor house. What type of family does my mother belong to? Nan pondered. She thought back to the contents of the letters and what the amiable innkeeper had just said. *Perhaps, this Lady Greenwick is not the Aunt D. I'm looking for. But what are the chances of two people with the same name living in New Forest?*

The woman scrutinized Nan's facial features before she turned in the direction of a small-enclosed staircase, motioning for Nan to follow. "A distant relation are you?" the woman pried further.

Nan felt like she was being interrogated for some unknown misdemeanour. "Yes, I'm her great niece," answered Nan. She had grown suspicious at the woman's cool tone.

"I wasn't aware Old Birdie had any relations. Living that is."

Curious at her last statement, Nan frowned, as she followed the woman down a hallway full of closed doors. "Do you know Old Birdie, I mean Lady Greenwick, well?"

With a slight snort, the woman replied, "No one knows Old Birdie well, she keeps to herself."

"Oh, you mean she doesn't live here in town?" Nan felt anxious at the woman's vague, unpleasant replies. Maybe she had come all this way in search of the wrong person after all or even worse a freaky outcast.

"Oh no, thank heavens. Old Birdie comes to town every now and then, but that's all." The innkeeper stopped in front of a door at the end of the hall and opened it, then turned to Nan and said, "Here we are, dear. It isn't much, but it's cozy."

"It's perfect, thank you," Nan smiled courteously, as she looked in at the small floral wallpapered room.

The woman nodded, handed Nan the key, and then turned to head back down the hall. "If you need anything else dear, just ring. The bell is on the desk. When you're ready, Henry will take you where you want to go."

"Oh okay, thank you," answered Nan in surprise.

Nan left her bags in the room to go wander around the village and get some lunch—being just after twelve—at a homely little café across the street from the inn. Full and satisfied, she arrived back at the inn and saw a communal phone. With her international phone card she tried calling home—having left her cell phone at home, not wanting to pay the extra expense of putting international calling on it.

There was no answer. Nan left Rory a message with the inn's name and number in case of emergencies. Then, figuring there was no need for delay, she rang the bell on the desk and when the innkeeper appeared, told her she was ready to leave for Magewebb Manor.

****

As the car drove down the dusty dirt country road out of town into the heart of the serene New Forest countryside, Nan was stilled in awe. *It's a nature's wonderland,* she thought, as she looked out the passenger window at the rolling green hills, patchwork of stonewalled pastures, the golden orange/red autumn splendour of the native trees, and flowing crystal blue water of one of the three New Forest rivers that brought nourishment and hydration to everything they touched.

Dad would have loved it here, she sighed.

A voice from the driver's seat broke through Nan's utopic thoughts, its owner looking at her through the rear-view mirror. "Off to Magewebb Manor then, are ya?"

"Yes," replied Nan to Henry's wrinkled genial face in the mirror. "I take it not many people go there?"

"No, folks steer clear of it. The young folk call it Witchwebb Manor," Henry chuckled. He seemed a lot more laid back on the topic then the innkeeper had been, who Nan assumed was his wife.

Nan found the town people's views on Lady Greenwick and her house more peculiar all the time. *Why is she such an outcast?*

"Why is that?" asked Nan.

"Tis due to all the strange stories about the family over the years, a bunch of superstitious fiddle fuddle," explained Henry, still laughing to himself. "They say the place is cursed."

"Cursed?" yelped Nan. *Oh great, maybe Casey was right. Maybe I'm walking into an occult den?*

Despite the unnerving information she had collected, Nan was absorbed in the growing mystery. "Why do they call her Old Birdie?"

"She's an odd way about her, Old Birdie. It causes folks to think she ain't all there and then there's that raven which follows her around everywhere. Some even say they've seen her talking to it."

Oh no, the woman's lost her mind. She's gone crazy, just like Parker said my mom was. This disheartening thought in mind, Nan looked back at Henry's smile in the mirror. "Why do people think the house is cursed?"

"Some say you'll drop dead if ya so much as lay eyes on the place. Others just tell of strange happenings there. It all stems from the families misfortunes."

What misfortunes? Nan was about to ask, but just then the car pulled to a stop at the side of the road and Henry exclaimed, "Here you go, Miss."

Nan looked out her passenger-side window, first to the left and then right, and saw nothing. No house, no grand structure, no signs of humanity, nothing but miles upon miles of green fields and forest.

"Where's the house?" asked Nan, bewildered.

"Oh tis down the way a bit, about a mile or so. But you see this is as far as I go," answered Henry.

"What? What do you mean this is as far as you go?" Nan half shrieked, confused and anxious.

"The rest of the way is down that there path." Her sight followed Henry's arm as he pointed out the right window and Nan saw a small pony cart width of a laneway.

"No car will fit down there, ya'll have to go on foot," he continued.

The long narrow, overgrown cart trail was speckled with bushes and rocks and was shielded by a thick canopy of fall leafed trees. A broken fence ran down either side of it and at first glance, one would never have known man had once travelled on it.

"You mean I'm supposed to go down there, alone?" exclaimed Nan in wide-eyed disbelief.

"I'm afraid so, Miss" replied Henry.

"But what if I get lost?"

"Just follow the path down to the end, you can't miss it," he encouraged.

Still unsure, Nan got out of the car as Henry put it into gear and pulled away from the side of the road in order to make a U-turn to head back to town. "Good luck, Miss," he said and drove away.

****

Dumbfounded, Nan turned to the untamed trail. Once she might have considered it enchanting with its avenue of hugging trees, but after hearing the local's unsettling opinions of the house, which awaited her at its end, she couldn't help but swallow a lump growing in her throat.

Resolved to push on, having come this far, with no real choice in the matter as she was stranded in the middle of nowhere in a foreign country. Nan zipped up her fall jacket and began walking, glad she was an expert in walking in her typical thick-heeled boots.

Though raised on a farm and a lover of nature's splendour, Nan had no real talent when it came to being outdoors. Which she discovered now as she clumsily laboured down the path, tripping over rocks, twigs, roots, and the long weeds. Her feet began to ache with every step, which caused her to hope her unpleasant hike would soon end.

Thirty minutes later Nan halted in her tracks. There on a large rock dead centre of the laneway was a hostile three-foot ebony scaled snake, ready to strike. Nan's rustling movements had disturbed it, while trying to sun itself during the afternoon's peak heat on the cool autumn day. The snake coiled itself up, threatened; it moved its head in mimicry with every step Nan took to escape.

Nan froze, her pulse thundered. She breathed as little as possible in case it provoked the menacing serpent. *Now what do I do?* She pondered, trying to come up with a solution to her predicament.

Then, as if in answer to her silent prayers, an immense wolfish canine sprang out of the bordering sun shaded trees to her rescue, teeth barred and growling at the slithering assailant. With the dog's arrival, the snake retreated into the opposite thicket. The mighty dog barrelled off after it in hot pursuit.

Elated at her fortune, Nan watched the bushes where both dog and snake had disappeared and wondered if she should go after her gunmetal grey knight. A willowy aged woman materialized on Nan's left at that moment and called out in summons, "Beowulf, come now."

"I'm sorry, I didn't know if I should go after him or not," Nan apologized to the dog's obvious owner.

"He'll come back when he's through," the woman replied, uncommitted. "Once he gets on the trail of a common adder, he's unstoppable."

"An adder, aren't they poisonous?" asked Nan in surprise. She pulled up a *National Geographic* article she had read once in her mind.

"Extremely," the simply dressed yet imposing woman answered.

Nan swallowed at the thought of her close shave with death, then scanned the bushes, haunted by the aspect of the deadly reptile's reappearance. Instead, the large blue-brown grey dog stormed out and went over to his master's side.

Nan eyed the mutt suspiciously. "What kind of dog is that?"

"He's not a dog, he's a wolf," the woman replied.

"But I thought wolves have been extinct in Britain since around the late seventeenth century?"

"They have," was the only answer the woman provided. She stroked the animal's mighty head and eyed Nan in a cool manner. "What brings you here?"

"I was told this is the way to Magewebb Manor," answered Nan, a self-conscious chill ran through her at the woman's stare.

"This is Magewebb. All this property belongs to Magewebb Manor," the woman assured.

"Really?" Nan exclaimed, stunned. She looked around her at the vast countryside with not a house in sight. *All this belongs to my mother's family.*

With almost an indiscernible nod, the woman turned away, commanding, "Come Beowulf," and proceeded on down the trail without another word.

How rude, Nan scowled as she watched the stranger leave. But then, the woman yelled back over her shoulder to Nan, "Follow me."

No more instruction needed, Nan rushed after her. Who was this silent stately newcomer? At first glimpse, one might assume the woman was a farmer's wife or rural hermit due to her Wellington boots, course grey wool sweater, jeans, and straw hat. However, there was a sylphlike elegance about the woman and the rich soft sheen of her long salt and pepper braid said she was use to a finer life.

Perhaps she is a neighbour of Lady Greenwick's. Though, there is no houses in sight. Whoever she is, I'm sure glad she came along, Nan smiled to herself.

The trio continued in silence for what seemed like hours. Nan racked her brain for an icebreaker to initiate some conversation. Instead, she once again tripped over something on the path. "Beowulf eh, are you a lover of epic poetry?" she inquired.

"I've read it," the woman's clipped answered came.

Okay, so much for small talk, Nan reflected.

"Do you know someone at Magewebb?" the woman inquired after a long pause.

Nan stumbled behind. She dusted herself off and answered, "Um, well not really. I'm hoping Lady Greenwick can help me with something."

"I doubt you'll find what you are looking for there," the woman stated tersely, as she strode on with her wolf—even larger than an Arctic wolf Nan speculated—which protectively trotted at her side. Nan frowned at the woman's last statement as she continued to follow her and wondered at her odd negative manner.

Nan's feet felt as if they were going to fall off, so she was relieved when the woman's cold tone announced, "There it is."

She stared up from the path and saw a pair of giant stone ravens standing guard on either side of an opening in a large stone parameter wall. Cast-iron, spike tipped gates, which dangled vicariously on their broken hinges, stood open. The name, Magewebb Manor was etched into a weathered bronze plaque on the base of the right guardian.

The wolf bounded through the entrance, as his master walked behind him in a solemn fashion. She paid no heed to the 'No Trespassing' sign posted on a wooden stake at the entrance. Apprehensive, Nan watched her escort disappear around a bend in the property's driveway, and eyed the stone ravens one last time before following her.

Inside the walls was a gardener's nightmare, with shrubs of all types, hedges, flowers, grand willows and elms, ponds and fountains. Left to grow wild and free, untouched by human hands, they laid claim to where ever and whatever they pleased. It was Frances Hodgson Burnett's *Secret Garden* come to life right before Nan's awestruck eyes.

Nan travelled down the pea stone path and watched as a monstrous stone masterpiece rose before her. Not a mere home, but a private complex. It towered three storeys high and expanded as far as the eye could see.

"This is Magewebb Manor?" Nan gaped. She stopped dead in her tracks.

The woman turned at the foot of the manor's stone stairway at Nan's beguiled utterance and raised her brow. "Oh come along, it's only a house," she said in an uppity fashion.

Nan was bejewelled by the innate Gothic, English country manor house's hammer bean roof, mullioned windows, flying buttresses, ogival and many arches and peaks. It was like nothing she had ever seen before. A child's dream castle, though the years of neglect visible on the aged

A New Forest Witch

stones, gave it a formidable feel. She stared up at the structure's vast arched oak doors.

Nan watched her guide brazenly stroll up the limestone steps to the doors in anticipation to enter. "Shouldn't we wait and announce ourselves first?" she protested.

As the woman opened one of the mighty doors, letting the wolf bound in unsupervised, she turned and stared. "You didn't come all the way from Canada to stand out in the cold did you?"

Flabbergasted, Nan's mouth fell open. "How did you know I was from Canada?"

"I'm old girl, but not senile and I can tell my own flesh and blood when I see it," the woman snapped.

"You're Lady Greenwick?"

Chapter 15
"I do not want people to be very agreeable, as it saves me the trouble of liking them a great deal." Jane Austen

"Abiageal Druantia Greenwick, to be exact, but you may call me, Druantia," Nan's great aunt stated. "Now don't just stand there gawking girl, I'm not getting any younger." She walked into the house and left a stunned Nan frozen to the spot.

I found her, I actually found her, Nan mentally stammered, walking up the grand manor's stone steps. *I found her and she knows who I am.*

The manor's interior blew away the remaining sense Nan had after the shock. Her eyes sparkled as she looked over the foyer's magnificent marble floor, vaulted ribbed ceiling, towering ivory pillars, and great three person wide stone staircase, in the room's centre.

"Wow," Nan exclaimed.

Druantia paid no attention to Nan as she removed her hat and boots and donned a soft pair of loafers, before she reached for a sash in the corner and gave it a sharp tug. Finally, she glanced in Nan's direction and when she saw her star struck appearance, Druantia barked, "Good gracious girl, is that all you do is gape?"

However, before Nan had the chance to reply, a plump white haired woman in a dull green dress and white apron entered the entry hall from some unseen location.

"Ah, Cora," said Druantia upon noticing her. "There will be one more to dine tonight. This is my great niece..." She paused and turned to Nan to inquire, "What is your name girl?"

"Anabel. Anabel Weststar, but everyone calls me Nan."

"Yes of course," Druantia nodded, as if she had known the answer all along. Then, she turned back to the cook/maid and continued, "This is my great niece, Anabel. She will be staying with us for a while. See that the rose room is ready for her."

The wordless Cora nodded her head and was about to turn and take her leave, but stopped when Nan quickly objected. "Oh no that's alright; I've already got a room at the inn in town."

"Nonsense," uttered Druantia with an authoritative stare, "Family stays in the house." She turned back to Cora and added, "Have Shamus fetch her things from the inn and pay whatever bills she has acquired."

"Yes, my lady." Cora nodded again and then disappeared to whence she came.

"Come with me," commanded Druantia and she turned to head up the stairs. Nan jumped into action and hurried after her.

At the second floor landing, Nan followed the stoic figure in front of her down the windowless west corridor, a gallery of oil portraits of people long deceased between imposing doors.

Nan tried to keep pace and not get distracted, but almost ran into Druantia's back when she suddenly stopped to open a door on their left. "This will be your room during your stay. Cora will freshen things up for you. Now I'll leave you to refresh yourself." She didn't wait for a reply, just turned on her heels and left.

Well, it's nice to meet you too; Nan frowned at her great aunt's back. Nan ran her hands over her face in exhaustion and tried to absorb it all. *My mother is a part of the English nobility.*

Nothing had ended up like she had imagined, not the house, the grounds, and certainly not Lady Greenwick. The unexpected facts about her mother's family shocked Nan, but to find the frail gentle old woman she had pictured in her head to be in reality a sharp-witted cruel tongued, cold mannered aristocrat, boggled Nan's mind.

Nan entered the room assigned to her. Her eyes marvelled at the burgundy and wood paneled walls, stone hearth, damask curtains, ancient tapestries, and arched lead diamond patterned windowpanes. Even the rich furnishings were spectacular, but nothing could top the centuries old walnut canopied, four postured bed with its deep crimson draperies.

Immediately, Nan straightened her appearance and within twenty minutes returned to the entrance hall. She noticed another pair of large oak doors left of the entrance, which stood open and Nan stepped inside and found it to be an elegant drawing room, in which Druantia was patiently awaiting.

Nan smiled shyly at Druantia, then took a seat in one of the high back chairs opposite her and stared down at her feet feeling nervous. Her elder's penetrating cold stare fixed upon her. *Say something,* Nan urged herself.

"I trust everything was to your satisfaction and you had no trouble navigating your way back to the foyer," stated Druantia rather than asked.

"Oh yes, the room is lovely and I had no trouble," Nan assured. She wondered how much longer she could sit still without fidgeting under the woman's glare.

Druantia nodded her head, pleased, and gestured with a nonchalant wave of the hand to a side table laden with a silver tea set and petite cakes and pastries on a china platter. "It's late, but would you care for afternoon tea?"

"Oh yes, thank you," replied Nan. She forced herself to smile as she got to her feet and poured herself a cup of tea. Nan avoided the tempting treats as she wasn't yet sure her shocked system could hold anything down.

She returned to her seat and placed the dainty china cup and saucer on her lap. As Nan crossed her ankles politely, she mused, *Rory would be busting a gut if she saw me now.*

"You mentioned the room I'm in is called the rose room," Nan commented. It seemed Druantia's intent was to do nothing but stare at her.

Druantia deemed the statement to not to require an answer and simply inclined her head and waited for Nan to continue.

Not getting the conversational reaction she had hoped for, Nan took a deep breath and continued, "No doubt due to its unique rose window above the balcony's glass doors. If I'm not mistaken they are uncommon in England, aren't they?"

"Well, well, there is a brain in that gawking head of yours after all. I'm impressed," responded Druantia with a hint of a grin. "Yes, a distant ancestor of ours was a patron of the arts and loved Gothic European architecture."

"I can tell," Nan uttered, pleased to be making some progress. "But I noticed that not everything is from that era."

"No, the house has been in the family throughout its entire existence and has been enlarged and remodelled with each century. One can only find remnants of the original structure in the east wing," explained Druantia, tutor like.

"How interesting," said Nan enthralled, her passion for history lusting out of her.

Then, as if shaking off the hint of normal humanity she had let slip, Druantia resumed her cold inhuman demeanour and remarked in a dry tone, "But you're not here for an architectural history lesson, are you?"

"Well no, I guess not," uttered Nan meekly.

Nan didn't know where to begin. She suddenly remembered her arrival and turned a curious eye on Druantia. "How did you know who I was?"

Druantia rose to pour herself another cup of tea and to avoid any chance of eye contact. "I've been expecting you."

Nan's jaw hit the floor like a sack of flour. Druantia didn't let on that she had caught Nan's stunned expression and continued, "It was only a matter of time before you would show up at my door. Though I had hoped I'd be mistaken."

Druantia's words injured Nan to the quick. *So I'm really not wanted.*

She knew only too well what being the black sheep in a flock felt like, having grown up in solitude. Her peers teased and avoided her mercilessly. Her father being the only person who truly understood her. The aspect of more rejection hit Nan hard.

"Oh, I see," squeaked out Nan, as she tried to push back the tears, which threatened to escape. "I had hoped to find my mother here."

"I know, as did your father. But as I told him, I cannot help you. I have no notion of Rhiannon's whereabouts," replied Druantia in an uncomfortable manner, which Nan couldn't quite understand.

Nan's worse expectation had turned into reality. She temporarily pushed the disappointment aside and looked back at the grand woman and said in amazement, "You knew my father?"

"No," answered Druantia in a matter-of-fact way. "But he wrote me after your mother left and I assured him, as I do you, that I do not know where she is."

Nan's heart plummeted at this, her vision of finding her mother faded into oblivion. With the hot liquid still biting at her tear ducts, in final despair, she asked, "Then, perhaps you could just tell me about her?"

Druantia's brow furrowed. "What does your father think about you being here? Surely he has told you all you need to know about your mother."

"He's dead," stated Nan, a quiver escaping in her voice. "He wouldn't talk about my mother when he was alive and told me she was dead."

Visibly taken aback, Druantia replied in a bit more delicate tone, "Oh, I see. Well that changes things then."

Why, Nan was just about to ask, but peering at the claw footed clock on the fireplace mantle, Druantia got to her feet and announced, "Come along, it's time for high tea. Then you can retire to your chamber, for I'm sure you must be exhausted after your trip."

"Oh, I had hoped we could talk some more," voiced Nan, timid as a mouse, as she followed Druantia out of the room.

"There will be plenty of time for talk tomorrow," replied Druantia, upon entering the dining hall.

They ate in complete silence at a table fit for a king. Cora's cooking was superb, but Nan found that after the day's upsets she had little appetite, even for the delicious roast pheasant on her plate. Once the meal was over, Nan excused herself and went straight up to her chamber.

The room was a lot less welcoming now that night had set in, the dark colours giving it an eerie atmosphere. *How am I ever going to sleep in here*, thought Nan, though sleep was the farthest thing from her mind.

Thankfully, one of the many generations who had inhabited the manor over the decades, had seen fit to install electricity, Nan shed some artificial light on things and sat on the velvet-covered bench at the foot of the bed and sulked. *Maybe Parker had been right*, she sighed, *I shouldn't have come.*

A calculated knock on the door roused her and she rose to discover Druantia on its other side with an armful of linen. "I thought you might be in need of these, since your things have not yet arrived," she stated, as she handed Nan the few towels, washcloths and a long white silk nightdress.

Druantia watched Nan's expression intently and added, "It is a bit out of date, but it was the best I could find under the circumstances."

"No, it's perfect, thank you," Nan smiled in assurance.

"Well then, goodnight," said Druantia, before she hastily turned and walked back down the hall.

Nan smiled to herself as she closed the bedroom door. *Maybe Druantia's not as bad as she seems*, she pondered. She felt as if she had just been given the regal woman's version of an olive branch.

Nan put on the nightgown, pulled back the rich covers, and climbed into the enormous bed. She thought of the countless number of people who had slept in it before her and soon drifted off to sleep.

****

It was still as the grave. The only sounds coming from the odd leaf, which rustled in the evening breeze from the trees above.

Nan's host took hesitant steps; her unshod feet crunched twigs as she proceeded through the darkened woods alone. The tattered gown Nan recognized from her earlier dream of the tower cell, hidden beneath a dark hooded cloak, trailed through the leaf-laden ground.

Where is she going? How did she get out of the tower? Nan questioned, as she watched through her host's eyes as they continued to walk amongst the trees. Nan no longer questioned what state she was in or why, she was fully aware she was again in one of her strange dreams.

They looked over their shoulder in terror as if pursued and Nan realized that her host concealed something in a scarf under her cloak. *What is she hiding?* Nan anxiously wondered. She felt like a thief in the night.

Suddenly, an old hag dressed in earth woven rags and adorned with strange blue markings, appeared from within the trees and motioned silently for Nan's host to follow. *I've seen her before,* Nan pondered, as the crone led them to a streambed, which cut through the centre of a forest's clearing.

Nan continued to watch, having no choice in the matter, and gazed nervously out her host's eyes as she moved closer to the crone. Without a word she handed her the scarf wrapped package.

The woman turned to the stream and dropped it into the night-blackened waters, muttering some words Nan could not understand.

They peered into the water and watched the object sink slowly to the bottom. But before it reached it, the package began to unravel. Their eyes adjusted to the darkened state and Nan could see all that lied within the water's depths.

She wanted to flinch away and scream. The stream's bottom was littered with human skulls. The parcel the hag had cast down, was now uncloaked and revealed the most chilling sight of all. The dead man's severed head from the tower prison.

Chapter 16
"Toto, I have a feeling we're not in Kansas anymore."
L. Frank Baum

When Nan awoke from her dream, she was perspiring. "It was only a dream," she repeated to herself.

She turned on the Tiffany lamp on the nightstand to cut the ever-consuming darkness. Then sat up in bed and leaned against the headboard, trying to steady her breathing and palpating heart.

What is going on with me? Am I losing my mind? Why do I keep having these dreams, dreams of someone else's life? Nan pondered. She shook her head to ward off the horrible images of the nightmarish world she had been delivered from.

After some deep breaths, Nan tried to divert her mind. She shut off the lamp and curled back under the bed's covers, hoping this time she wouldn't be plagued by bodiless heads.

As she closed her eyes and let her head sink comfortably into the pillow, she was moments away from sleep when she heard a woman's whisper. *Anabel*, the voice called.

Nan sprung back up in the massive bed and surveyed the dark room, but saw nothing. She must be hearing things, Nan thought as she laid back down and settled in for more sleep. It was an old house after all with no doubt an abundance of creaks and noises.

Anabel, the imageless voice called again.

There was no mistaking it this time. Nan sat bolt upright and reached for the lamp. She was sure she would find the culprit standing in the shadows. No one was there.

"Druantia?" she called out, in hopes her great aunt was hidden somewhere in the shadows and was the owner of the eerie voice. Though Nan couldn't understand why she would be. No reply came.

Just when Nan thought she truly was losing her mind, the bedroom door swung open, unattended. Her heart pumped a hundred beats per minute as Nan scrambled to her feet and rushed to the door, positive she would find someone standing in the hall. She walked out and peered in both directions, but the hallway was deserted, not a soul was a foot.

Anabel, it echoed again.

Nan whipped her head to the right in the direction of the sound and squinted down the dimly lit hall in hopes of seeing something, a person, a ghost, anything that would explain the voice. She saw nothing.

Relax, someone is probably just playing a trick on you, she told herself. *Who though, the maid? She doesn't seem the type and I doubt Druantia is into pranks. Maybe it's a ghost like at home.* However, even that thought didn't provide any relief, for the ghosts at home Nan knew, these she didn't, and none of them had ever talked to her before.

She gulped in a breath of air and cautiously paced down the hall. *What am I doing*? She questioned. The odd wall mounted lamp provided her with little light and casted shadows on the walls.

Nan slowed when she reached the landing and looked down at the unlit foyer below. "Hello," she called, the sound amplified in the great space. "Is anyone there?" No reply came.

Anabel, the chilling voice said. It came from the depths of the manor's uninhabited east wing.

Nan felt an apprehensive terror twist her stomach as she inched closer and stared down the dust filled vacant corridor. The hall was ebony black, only the window at its end visible. She ran her hands over the walls of the corridor's mouth in search of a light switch, but found there was none.

You are such a chicken, she chided herself. Nevertheless, she turned on her heels and jogged back to her room, where she closed and locked the door behind her.

****

The light of day streamed through the balcony doors, as Nan's eyes cracked open to the sound of nature's symphony humming from the grounds outside. Still tired thanks to the little rest she got after the night's unnerving occurrences, Nan yawned and reluctantly got up, hoping she hadn't over slept. The time was unknown, having no clock in the room and her wristwatch forgotten at home.

Still devoid of her luggage, Nan dressed in her clothes from the day before and headed off in search of Druantia on the main floor. She walked down the corridor and thought of the night's unexplainable excursions. Had she really heard someone or was it just the moaning of the house's old plumbing or some other trick of the mind.

No, I definitely heard someone calling my name, she concluded, as she proceeded through the unusually quiet house, even the wind outside inaudible.

Nan was thrilled as she descended the stairs to find her luggage neatly stacked at the bottom by the banister. She flew down to it and was tempted to rush back up to her room and change, but decided to first make an appearance in fear of seeming tardy.

Nan could find no sign of her great aunt in any of the rooms she came across and continued on to the dining room. The whole time she felt as if she was being watched by a concealed pair of eyes. *There's something strange about this place.*

To Nan's astonishment, the banquet size table had a single place set upon it and the sideboard had serving trays still warm on a hot plate. As Nan approached the table, she looked up at the mantle clock, which read ten o'clock. *Oh my, I really did sleep late.*

As if materializing by magic, Cora appeared in the room. "Good morning, Miss Anabel. Would you like your breakfast now?" she asked in a pleasant manner.

"Oh, yes thank you," replied Nan with a start. She sat down at the table, then suddenly realized her delay had put the poor woman out. "I'm so sorry for any inconvenience I've caused you," she apologized.

Cora smiled as she served Nan some eggs and sausage, one of Nan's least favourite meats though she was not going to tell the kind woman that. "Oh it is no bother, Miss Anabel."

"Please call me Nan," Nan pleaded, as she placed the handcrafted, embroidered napkin on her lap.

"Oh no Miss, it would not be fitting. My lady would not approve," assured Cora. She poured Nan a glass of fresh squeezed orange juice.

Wow, it is going to take me a while to get use to how they do things around here, Nan smiled to herself. She was amazed at how proper things were done in this household and decided she really needed to brush up on her etiquette.

"Has Druantia eaten yet?" she asked, after she swallowed a mouthful of eggs.

"Oh yes, Miss. My lady eats sharply at six thirty every morning," answered Cora. Nan made a mental note to be more prompt at rising in the days to come.

Cora caught the concern in Nan's eyes, grinned and added, "Don't worry, Miss. She doesn't expect the same from you. You are a guest of the house."

Oh great not only am I in all honesty, unwanted, but am given special treatment, which puts everyone else out. Nan gave a half-hearted smile and asked, "Where is Druantia now?"

"My lady is in the conservatory," replied Cora. Nan had finished, therefore Cora began to clear the table and trays from the sideboard.

Nan got directions from Cora before she disappeared back into the kitchens below, then hurried off in search of her great aunt.

The conservatory was a large oval shaped room with a domed, glass ceiling and large windows, which extended from floor to ceiling the full length of the room. Nan stepped down a pair of stone steps into the room and marvelled at the jungle of green, which spanned before her eyes. Any plant one could have imagined was before her, radiant with life. She breathed in the fresh scent of nature, dazzled by the abundance of colour, as she walked further into the room.

Nan shrieked and shrank to the flagstones, thinking she was under attack, as a large black mass dove for her head. "Stranger," it squawked in a discontented tone.

Her arms encircled her head, shielding it, as she tried to distinguish what had assaulted her. She peeked out from between her arms and looked around cautiously, but her attacker was gone. Instead, the familiar grey face of her former rescuer, Beowulf, stared back at her with almost human eyes.

"Mercy girl, there is no need to shout. You disturbed Hexia." Druantia's reproach came from the far corner of the room.

Nan straightened and smoothed out her already wrinkled clothes, then headed in the direction of her great aunt's voice. She found her, misting bottle in hand, interrupted from tending to her beloved plants, with a large menacing raven perched on her shoulder.

"There, there, old girl. You'll have to get use to her, she's family," cooed Druantia to the bird, which glowered at Nan from her shoulder.

She really does have a raven, Nan gawked in disbelief, *and she talks to it.*

"Aren't you worried it will hurt you?" asked Nan, trying not to look the corvid in the eyes.

"Oh nonsense girl," said Druantia indignantly, as she turned back to her plants. "She's not too fond of strangers, but she is harmless. And she is much older and wiser than you'll ever be." She added and gave the raven's black feathers an affectionate stroke. "Animals will not hurt you as long as you give them the respect they deserve."

However, Nan doubted that included the bird, as she ruffled her ebony plumage and croaked "Stranger" once more in Nan's direction.

"She's still looking at me as if I was lunch," Nan winced.

"Oh don't be ridiculous girl. She may be an omnivore, but she doesn't eat people."

Nan made a distasteful face and turned her gaze away from the raven's ominous stare, back to the plants and envied Druantia's natural herbocultural abilities. A lover of beautiful gardens, after several failed attempts, it became clear to Nan she lacked a green thumb.

"Your gardens are lovely."

"They care mostly for themselves. I do very little, though Shamus is always insisting we prune the shrubs and hedges. Every now and then, I catch him knee deep in one of the beds, pulling out the helpless wildflowers. He calls it weeding," replied Druantia absently. The first time she had spoken in detail since Nan's arrival.

Nan smiled to herself. Perhaps she would reach the summit of the almost limitless mountain after all. She continued to look at the flowers, but out of the corner of her eye glimpsed a quick movement on the floor.

She looked down and screamed so loud it could have been heard by the ships on the English Channel. Beowulf jumped into action and flew to her defence, while Nan leapt onto a nearby turned up milk crate. An equally frightened little green water snake slithered between the flowerpots for safety.

"What's wrong?" inquired Druantia. She turned in alarm, causing Hexia to flutter in the air above her.

"There's a snake," shrieked Nan. Still safe on her milk crate perch she pointed at the ground where the serpent had disappeared.

"Is that all?" Druantia sighed in relief. With a roll of her eyes and stared at Nan with irritation."I thought you had poked your eye out or something. Jake won't hurt you either, now do stop overreacting, you're giving me a frightful headache."

Nan frowned at Druantia's odd array of pets, as she scrutinized the ground for the scaly spook before she stepped down off the crate. After some thought she decided against questioning her great aunt on her reasons on the subject and turned once more to the plants.

A lovely blue bell shaped flower caught Nan's attention and she reached out to touch it. "By the way did you happen to hear someone in the halls last night?"

"Don't touch that!" Druantia snapped, having turned at Nan's question and caught her before she touched the plant's soft petals. Nan looked up at her in shock, scared half to death, surprised Druantia was so possessive of her plants.

Druantia took a calming breath as a parent would with an insufferable child and explained, "Some of my plants are far more dangerous than my pets, as you call them. And no, no one was a foot in the halls last night, except you."

Before Nan could ask how on earth she had known that, thinking she had been quiet, Druantia added in exhausted exasperation, "Why don't you go out and see the grounds. The fresh air will do you good."

Nan looked injured at this and began to object, "But I had hoped we could…" However, Druantia cut her off. "There will be plenty of time for talk after tea. Now run along and leave me to my gardening."

"Oh okay," sulked Nan.

****

Frustrated with herself for annoying Druantia to the point of being dismissed and ceasing all chance of conversation, Nan walked out one of the double sets of French doors outside the conservatory onto the back terrace. She wondered all the while how a plant could be dangerous.

Druantia was correct, which Nan hated to admit, the crisp fresh air instantly rejuvenated her lungs and the beauty of the grounds cleared her troubled mind.

Not vibrant and colourful as in the spring, the rear gardens were still just as full of wild life and untamed splendour, as Nan watched the late

113

autumn sun touch their leaves. Nan walked down the terrace's steps to the cobblestone path and sauntered through the maze of nature. She breathed in the intoxicating air and almost wished she never had to leave. So fresh, so full of life, it was as enchanting as a Siren's call.

As she rounded a bend in the path, Nan came upon an elderly man kneeling in one of the unruly flowerbeds. He struggled with a reluctant weed, while a fat lazy calico cat lounged by his side. A rusty old wheelbarrow and rack stood at attention behind him.

This must be Shamus; Nan smirked. She had found him in the exact same criminal act—in her great aunt's opinion—which Druantia had moments earlier accused him of.

Her unexpected appearance scared the poor man pale, for which Nan quickly apologized. "Oh pardon me, I didn't mean to startle you."

The old gardener got to his feet and tried to wipe the dirt from his scrawny knees, before he took off his cap, which exposed his balding scalp and replied courteously in his thick British, Gaelic laced accent, "Tis well lass. Pay no mind"

"You must be Shamus," Nan smiled.

"Aye, Lassie," he nodded in assurance.

"Thank you so much for getting my things from the inn," Nan went on.

"Tis no bother Lassie," replied Shamus, still standing at attention, like a man in the presence of a queen.

Uncomfortable with his formal mannerism, Nan gestured towards the garden and said, "Please, don't let me interrupt your work." Then, knelt down and stroked the unmoved cat. "And what's your name?"

Shamus relaxed his rigid stature, replaced his cap and resumed his place in the garden. "Tis Tuppets, a right ruly beggar, but seems ta hav taken to ye Lassie."

"There seems to be an abundance of animals around here," Nan grinned and wondered what type she would come across next.

"Tis so, the daft beggars," answered Shamus, trying to coax a weed from the ground. "The mistress has a way with the beasts."

"It's a wonder," Nan went on as she watched the green pile of ripped weeds grow at Shamus's side and giggled. "You know my aunt would be some cross if she saw what you were doing now."

"Oh aye, she would at that," he smirked, "How about it be our little secret?"

Nan's laughter rang through the trees as she gave the amicable man her oath of eternal silence. There was an instant comradery between the two. Nan eyed the overgrown wilderness as she continued to pat the cat, who loved the attention, and pondered the property's odd animal inhabitants.

All she had learned and observed since her arrival twined together and with a coy gleam to her eyes, Nan asked, "Is that why the people in the village call her Old Birdie and this place Witchwebb, because of all the animals and how engulfing the grounds look?"

"Aye it tis," answered Shamus. "Folk think the mistress tis a cailleach."

"A cailleach?" Nan questioned, puzzled.

"Aye, a mage or a witch tis what ye callin it now."

"Seriously," Nan laughed, but it was a hollow sound as the fingers of unease crept up her spine. *Why does everyone I meet keep talking about curses and witchcraft?* She hoped there was no truth in it and wasn't sure if she would believe it if there was.

Eager for more answers since Shamus proved to be an obliging source, Nan continued, "What is with the raven?" Before Shamus could reply, a shrill cry came from the distant trees and Nan perked up in alarm. "What was that?"

"Tis not but old Beauty. A storm's a brewing, daft old beggar," answered Shamus. He looked in the direction of the continued call and then up to the sky, which had begun to cloud over.

"Beauty?" Nan repeated. She got to her feet in an attempt to see over the foliage for the distressed creature.

"Aye, the mistress's carriage horse," Shamus groaned, as he rose and collected his utensils. "She coddles the beast. Let's it hav it's way, when it should be actin it's nature."

Nan's smile broadened at the old gardener's gruff exterior. He reminded her of Matthew Cuthbert from *Anne of Green Gables*, quiet and a little grumbly, but kind and humorous on the inside.

Drops of hard rain began to fall and taking his wheelbarrow in hand, Shamus headed down the path. "Best be gettin in Lassie. There be hell ta pay if ye get soaked on my watch," he said over his shoulder.

Nan bid him farewell and then ducked her head against the flooding rain and ran back up the path to the house, with Tuppets leading the way. Cora stood in wait at the terrace doors, holding one open and peered out over the soggy grounds in search of Nan.

Tuppets entered through the open door first, with Nan at her heels. Cora closed the door. "My lady sent me after you once the storm was upon us, Miss. For fear you'd get drenched."

Nan thought of Shamus's parting words and smiled. She rung out her wet hair and said, "Sorry, I got caught up in the gardens with Shamus and lost track of time."

"Oh dear me, you're soaked through, Miss," Cora scowled. She handed Nan a towel she had on the ready, draped over her arm. "Any longer and you would have caught your death out there."

Nan's smile widened at the old maid's concern. "No fear Cora, I'm fine. I'll dry in no time."

Cora didn't look at all satisfied as she surveyed Nan's wet clothes once more. She shook her head, retrieved the towel when Nan was through with it, and turned to leave. "My lady is waiting for you in the ballroom."

Chapter 17
"You can discover more about a person in an hour of play then in a year of conversation." Plato

The ballroom, Nan mused. After Cora disappeared into the shadows, Nan wandered around the manor's main floor in search of Druantia's whereabouts. She opened every closed door she came across in the vain hope Druantia might be behind one of them.

As Nan toured around, she realized the majority of the manor's rooms were unused, shown by the obvious signs of neglect. Most had their furnishings draped in white cloths and the curtains drawn, but others left idle as if whoever had occupied them last laid their task aside in a hurry. Books open to a marked place left upside down on tables; cups and saucers waiting for their contents to be consumed. Now all stood coated in a thick layer of dust.

It's kind of creepy, thought Nan, with a shiver after she closed a door to another abandoned room. *Like a preserved haunting memory of another's life, paused; frozen in time. Waiting for the day, their occupant will come back and claim it.*

This glum meditation coursed through her mind as Nan continued to saunter through the halls. She came to a large elaborately carved set of doors in an alcove, right off the entrance hall. Nan opened one to peek inside and saw a massive room, expanding nearly twenty feet, with vaulted ceilings, grand chandeliers and a mosaic designed marble floor.

Nan stepped inside, concluding she must be in the right place, and walked deeper into the room. The history of the room seeped from its walls and Nan envisioned grand debonair lords and ladies in beautiful flowing gowns, dancing through the great expanse of the room. *Oh how wonderful it would have been,* she sighed.

However, it didn't take long for reality to set back in and Nan noticed that where crowds of guests and musicians once stood now supported an array of crates, cages, and aquariums. Odd and probably illegal animals occupied them. There was a fox, a polecat, toads, newts, a robin, a couple turtles, and even a Roe fawn.

Suspicious, Nan eyed the cages until finally she spotted Druantia in the distance, doing who knows what with the malignant raven still perched on her shoulder. Beowulf laid sentry not far away, with a wolverine sitting squarely by his side—*another animal that is extinct in England,* Nan frowned.

"Stranger," the tiresome bird cawed upon Nan's approach. *Well there's definitely no sneaking up on Druantia.* Nan huffed and glared back at the bird.

"Ah there you are girl. I was beginning to think you had gone off with the gypsy's or something."

"I lost track of time," replied Nan. She scrutinized a birdcage, which housed a bat with a bandaged wing.

"No matter, no matter," Druantia fluffed her off. Then turned to face Nan and added disapprovingly, "Gracious girl, you are soaked through."

Nan stifled a giggle. She found the overwhelming British concern for wet things hilarious considering the climate. "I'm fine. Just a bit damp that's all."

"Nonsense girl, you must go up and change before you catch your death," Druantia scowled.

Annoyed at being treated like an idiot child, Nan retorted rather crisply, "Will you please stop calling me girl, I have a name you know."

"Very well," Druantia stiffened. She turned back to the turtle she had been caring for.

Instantly, Nan regretted her forcefulness and tried to think of a way to clear the air and relieve the tension in the room. "What is with all the animals anyways?" she asked.

Druantia ignored Nan's presence and moved on to the next cage. However, after a moment she replied, "My home is their sanctuary. Most of them come to me for help when they are in need. Others, I merely provide a home for until their new caretaker has been discovered."

She always talks in riddles, cryptic-like. What does "until their new caretaker has been discovered," mean anyways? Nan subconsciously huffed. She scowled around the makeshift shelter, thinking it such a historical travesty.

Druantia sensed Nan's disapproval. "It's not as if there is much use for the room these days." Nan couldn't argue. Her great aunt had a point; lavish balls had become a thing of the past.

"What about him?" asked Nan and she gestured to the watchful small-eyed wolverine that flanked Beowulf.

"Gambit is an old friend. He's been with me, as Beowulf has, for many years. He's a shy, secretive creature though, who likes his privacy," answered Druantia, as if she talked about a person rather than an animal.

Nan filled with horror as she watched Druantia move to her next refugee. "Is that a..." but the word wouldn't come out as Nan glared at the four-foot glass terrarium with a long glistening black scaled snake housed inside. Identical, to the untrained eye, to the one she had encountered the day before on the path.

"An adder," Druantia finished for her. "No. It is a harmless black king snake, not native to this country. He is not venomous. His name is Onyx. I'm simply watching over him until his true master reappears."

Thankful, Nan took a relieved breath, but continued to stare apprehensively at the reptilian beast as Druantia slid the screen lid off the tank and dangled the lifeless white furred body of a mouse by the tail above the serpent's head. Quick as lightning, it struck, and grabbed the mouse in its dislocating jaws and soon devoured it whole.

A sickened ripple twisted Nan's throat as she looked away from the nauseating scene and saw Druantia replace the snake's lid. She locked it and put the key into her sweater pocket.

"If he's not dangerous, why do you lock the cage?" questioned Nan.

"To keep people on their toes," Druantia smirked. An odd sight Nan had not yet seen and one which made the cross woman look ten years younger.

Nan lifted her brow at this impish statement and was about to ask what she meant, when Druantia abruptly turned and said, "Now off with you. Go get out of those wet clothes before we dine."

Though her clothes were almost dry, Nan knew there was no point in arguing and complied by heading for the doors. She turned back at the threshold to observe Druantia tenderly caring for her assortment of creatures one last time. *Maybe there really is more to her then I thought,* she smiled.

****

Her luggage already in her room and unpacked in the closet, no doubt thanks to Cora, Nan quickly changed, ran a brush through her tangled hair, and headed back downstairs to join Druantia in the dining room for high tea.

Anabel, Nan heard as she was about to descend to the main floor. It had come from the east wing. The remembrance of the strange events of the night before sprang to Nan's mind.

The corridor was not quite as dark and formidable with the faint light of day shining through the end window as Nan stepped forward to investigate it closer.

Anabel, the summons rang again.

Unsure she really wanted to meet the voice's owner, Nan took some cautious steps down the dust laden, rust coloured rugged corridor, heavy with cobwebs and decay. The décor was beyond archaic. Unlike its sister corridor, there was only one door on the right near the mouth of the hall, while the rest was covered with paintings.

Cora obviously doesn't clean down here. Nan eyed the dust and grime collected on the rich frames. Not a great knowledge on art, She was able to distinguish some pieces (though uncommon), such as *The Witch of Endor* by Nikolai Ge, *The Magic Circle* by J.W. Waterhouse, and *Boudicca* by John Opie. The art selection was captivating yet odd.

Nan inched her way further down the hall until she reached the end. She stared up at the hall's large chapel style window and listened, waiting for the voice to call again and give her direction. All was quiet as a corpse.

Nan's neck tingled with the feel of unseen eyes upon her. She whipped her head around and stared back down to the hall's mouth. She watched, waiting to see movement from someone lurking in the shadows. She saw no one. *I would have sworn someone was watching me.* Nan scowled and turned back to the hall's end.

Sunken in from the walls, on either side of her, were two doors. Both closed, concealing their contents. Nan furrowed her brow as she debated which to investigate first. She pivoted to approach the door on her right.

"Miss Anabel, is that you?" a voice inquired from the landing.

Nan spun away from the door in surprise and squinted down the hall. Cora stared back at her with a questioning gaze. "Yes Cora, it is me."

How long has she been there? Was she the one I felt watching me?

"My lady has been waiting for you to dine for nearly fifteen minutes," she reproached. Cora eyed Nan suspiciously, as she walked back up the hall towards her. "What were you doing down there?"

"I was just touring the rest of the house," Nan fibbed.

The old maid looked unconvinced, but gave a curt nod and followed Nan down the stairs to the dining hall, where Druantia was waiting at the head of the table. Neither an impatient nor pleasant expression on her face. Druantia wordlessly retrieved her utensils and began to eat the duck meal, as Nan seated herself to her right.

"You must be careful where you wander," she commented after what seemed a lifetime of silence. "The east wing is in some state of disrepair and could be hazardous."

How on earth did she know? Nan wondered in astonishment. She knew Cora had not been able to rat her out, as she had followed Nan the whole way.

"Yes, I noticed that it has not been setup with electricity like the rest of the house and that it seems neglected," replied Nan, in an attempt to weed out the reason why.

"The east wing is the only original part left of the initial manor, though it too has been slightly altered since its construction. It is the truest part of the house and instead of renovating it or replenishing it, over the years the family has added and expanded elsewhere," explained Druantia.

"That's rather sad."

For the first time throughout the meal, Druantia lifted her eyes from her plate and studied Nan curiously. "How so?"

"It just seems sad to neglect something that is such an important part of the house's history, and yours," answered Nan, surprised to have gained her great aunt's attention.

"Hmm." A slight grin appeared on Druantia's otherwise stone face, as she turned back to her meal.

****

Supper was finished in silence and once concluded the two adjourned for a glass of sherry in a less formal parlour. After they settled back onto the plush high back duel couches, which faced a blazing fire in an old hearth, they began idle conversation.

"Tell me about yourself. Do you have a house in Ontario?" questioned Druantia.

"Yes, I inherited my father's farm in Myrtle," answered Nan, happy for some communication at last.

"Oh yes, I believe your mother mentioned a farm once in one of her correspondence. Do you raise livestock?"

Nan shook her head vigorously and tried to swallow a mouthful of the dry, mildly sweetened amber wine. "No, I rent the land out to one of the local cattle farmers. My father drove transports for a living, so we never kept animals."

"I see. Much the same as my operation here," continued Druantia. "The neighbouring farmer leases my property in return for beef and milk."

Nan was almost giddy at the fact Druantia was actually opening up to her, but tried her hardest not to show it in case it might discourage the woman and make her relapse into distant coldness.

"If not farming, what is your occupation?" Druantia inquired, honestly interested.

"I am an ancient history graduate and am currently employed with the L.M. Montgomery Heritage Society."

"Interesting," exclaimed Druantia, impressed."That is not a profession commonly sought after these days." Nan smiled from ear to ear at the implied complement and felt less uneasy around her newfound relation every minute.

However, the wise woman's next question made Nan's heart flutter and her complexion pale. "And do you have a suitor or perhaps a husband?" inquired Druantia.

"No, not really," answered Nan shyly. Parker's face instantly flashed before her eyes, causing her heart to race with desire and a sudden longing to swell up inside her. *Get a grip,* she grumbled to herself.

Druantia caught the alteration in Nan's appearance and demeanour, and gave her a coy smile. "Ah, I see." Embarrassed, Nan let the conversation die and remained quiet for some time.

"You said you had come here to find your mother. Why?" asked Druantia.

This caught Nan off guard. "I discovered after my father died that she hadn't died like he told me, but had left us instead. I assumed, back home to England."

Then, as if devoured by her own thoughts, Nan voiced aloud, "It must have hurt my father tremendously, because he made up that story and would never discuss her, no matter how hard I pried."

"Understandable," exclaimed Druantia softly, deep in her own thoughts.

"It wasn't until I found your letters in an old steamer trunk, that I decided to come to New Forest, in the hopes you could help me find my mother or at least tell me what happened," continued Nan.

"I see," Druantia sighed. She turned her gaze from Nan to the lapping flames of the fire.

"She contacted me by mail not long after she left your father and told me she was returning home, but that was the last I heard from her," Druantia finally remarked in a strained tone after a deliberating silence.

"You never saw her?" uttered Nan, confused and deflated.

"No," Druantia stated. "I made inquiries, contacted airlines, and ship yards, but to no avail. No one had news of her and she never contacted me again."

"I don't understand. She couldn't have just vanished," Nan bleated in desperation.

If she didn't come here, where did she go? Nan tried to stretch her analytical mind to the brink to make sense of it all, but came up dry. Her theory of her mother's abandonment to return home in search of her sister cracked into oblivion. *Maybe the simple fact is that she just didn't want a family? The bare truth is she abandoned us, because she didn't want us.*

The reminder that she honestly knew nothing about the woman whom she had strived to find, suddenly hit her full force and she looked back at Druantia with solemn, pleading eyes. "Tell me about her, please. Tell me what she was like?"

"Rhiannon was the apple of my dear sister, Elaine's eye. She pampered and fussed over her, which caused Rhiannon to grow into a vain, self-absorbed creature, who believed life revolved around her every wish, instead of fitting into the world around her. She would do things for others to serve herself, for her glory, to make them feel indebted to her and if something failed she loved to play the martyr," related Druantia with a mournful sigh. "But Elaine allowed it with her misguided favour for your mother, sometimes forgetting all about her other daughter, Gwynedd all together."

"She sounds horrible," Nan whimpered, sadden to think her absentee parent had been such a monster, but finally saw the unexplainable pieces fall into place.

"It wasn't her fault really," continued Druantia, after she saw the disappointment in Nan's eyes. "My sister had made Rhiannon what she was, but Rhiannon changed. Before leaving England, she had come to realize her flaws and I truly believe she loved you and your father."

At this Nan fell silent for a while, not sure what to think or feel. She thought on all Druantia had said, then remarked, "Gwynedd, I remember you mentioning her in one of the letters. She disappeared too didn't she?"

"Yes, the poor sweet child. She was your mother's twin, but they were two entirely different people, Gwynedd so sweet, shy, and loving. She disappeared the year after Elaine's death, the year you were born," Druantia answered. "Beowulf was hers," she added sadly and reached down to pet the wolf's strong head as he sat by her side, listening, almost like he could understand what they had said.

"The year my mother left," whispered Nan in wonder.

"Yes, it was a sad year indeed."

Frustration crept up on Nan as she thought about the ghost of a woman she had been chasing, the person who probably never gave her a second thought. "But if she loved us so much, why did she leave? Why did she abandon us?"

"To protect you," answered Druantia simply.

"Protect me from what?" Nan huffed, the growing irritation of the unknown clawed its way to the surface.

With a serious expression, Druantia rose from her seat and replied, "To answer that I must relay a very sad and sinister tale. Come with me," and she left the room.

"Come," the raven echoed as it flew out of the room above Druantia's head.

Chapter 18
"To be ignorant of what occurred before you were born is to remain always a child. For what is the worth of human life, unless it is woven into the life of our ancestors by the records of history?"
Cicero

The storm raged outside the stonewalls as Nan followed her great aunt's deaf form up the soundless grand staircase. The whips of thunder and fists of the water raged its war against the old country manor and caused her to shutter and wonder what she was in for next.

They climbed to the second floor landing, then Druantia turned left; bird perched on her shoulder witchingly, and headed down the darkened east wing. *Where is she taking me,* wondered Nan. Her heart pounded as they progressed down the tomb-like corridor.

They walked all the way to the end of the spider-infested hall. Druantia turned to the door on the left and opened it. It creaked on its hinges, which sent chills up Nan's spine in the ominous atmosphere.

Nan followed Druantia inside, unable to see a thing in the room's pitch darkness, and was relieved when the unexpected familiar glow of electricity suddenly illuminated things.

She turned back to the door in wonder, having thought this wing to be void of hydro, and saw Druantia step out of the shadows behind the door. At the sight of Nan's puzzled look, she explained, "I had electricity installed in this room myself."

Nan smiled and turned back to investigate the mysterious room Druantia obviously deemed worth the expense. Her mouth fell agape as she stared at the largest, most glorious wonder she had ever seen. They stood in the house's own private library.

Completely forgetting her earlier tribulations, Nan crept forward, beguiled by all she could see. Floor to ceiling gold leafed mahogany bookshelves ran the entire expanse of the football field sized room. Spiralling staircases led up to the many balconies and levels of the upper shelves. An immense limestone fireplace, with ivory busks and armless statues, rich high back leather chairs and window seats, grand reading desks, gorgeous crystal chandeliers, and a freestanding world globe adorned the space.

However, it was the books, which captivated Nan, a never-ending paradise of books. Books of every colour, texture, height and size, surrounded her, calling her to crack their spines and read their pages. Books which looked as if they had withstood the test of time and others as if they had never had a hand upon them.

Many times Nan had envied Belle when the Beast had told her to open her eyes and revealed the most spectacular library one had ever seen in Disney's *Beauty and the Beast*. Now as she stood and eyed the treasures around her, Nan felt like she had been plucked from real life and placed in Belle's shoes. She had died and gone to bookworm heaven.

"It is magnificent, isn't it?" smiled Druantia, as she came up to stand by Nan's side, enjoying her obvious pleasure. "It is one of the largest private collections in all of England."

"It is glorious," Nan sighed.

"Yes, it has always been one of my favourite rooms," admitted Druantia. "Your mother's as well."

"Really?" exclaimed Nan, surprised.

"Oh yes. She visited me often, practically grew up in this house, as we all did. This house has been passed down the lines of our entire family throughout the ages," Druantia related, a proud smile spread across her face.

"It is rare, but rarer still is that it has been passed down on the matriarchal side rather than through the sire," she continued. This surprised Nan; the fact a female lineage could have so much power in the male dominated English nobility.

"She actually used to stay in the room you're staying in now."

"Really?" exclaimed Nan, with a tingle of pleasure.

"Oh yes. But anyways, this is not the reason I brought you up here. Follow me," and Druantia led Nan deeper into the library.

Nan gazed around the written paradise as she walked and pictured her mother wasting away hours of a day comfortably reading. *Maybe we would have had something in common after all, if she had only stayed,* she sighed.

In a little alcove at the far end of the library, Druantia came to a stop in front of a large glass door cabinet, which contained what to Nan seemed to be scrolls. Hexia fluttered onto a table, when Druantia opened the door to retrieve one of the ancient rolls of parchment and laid it out on a nearby desk.

Nan gazed at the archaic text in wonder. "This is our family tree. It spans all the way back to the Bronze Age," Druantia announced.

Stunned, Nan took a seat in the desk's chair and stared at the document like it was the Holy Grail itself. Mute, she read down the calligraphic names in wonder until she came to the end and beheld her own.

Pleased by Nan's obvious respect, Druantia smiled down at her, and pointed to a name near the top of the page. "The story you seek, began with Blodwen."

****

"During the time of the Roman decline and the Viking rise to power, there remained a small Insular Celtic settlement from the days of old; hidden away in the shadows of Somerset, England, existing virtually untouched. In this community of farmers and peacekeepers there was a maiden named, Blodwen, who it was whispered to be a descent of Creirwy herself, the daughter of the legendary enchantress, Cerridwen.

Blodwen was a lovely creature, with skin of white porcelain and hair blacker then the raven's feathers. Orphaned young, she had grown independent, fended for herself, and never found the need for male companionship. However, most of the men in the settlement found themselves bewitched by her beauty, which caused their wives to call her a sorceress, enchantress, or a witch.

As a result, Blodwen lived a rather solitary life, in her tiny straw thatched, circular cottage on the outskirts of the village, near the forest. There she tended to the sick and needy, as she had great insight and was skilled in the ways of nature. Some said she was a druidess.

Then, one night a band of drunken Vikings happened upon the serene village and sacked it, killing most of the men and raping all the women they could find, including Blodwen.

Shamed and destitute by the inhumane act of brutality, Blodwen travelled with the few scattered survivors of the attack to their cousin settlement on the far shores of the Isle of Man. They sought shelter and provisions where they could find them. Blodwen grew heavier each day with her assailant's unwanted child, a curse from the gods for her weakness.

Once in their new home they were welcomed graciously by their fellow clansmen. A newly widowed smithy, a prosperous man and pillar of the community, admired Blodwen's beauty and noted her urgent situation. He offered to marry her and adopt her unborn child in return for the care of his three motherless children and wifely duties. Blodwen accepted and lodged with the smith, where she soon gave birth to a set of daughters.

One was a silk-skinned jewel, adorned with her mother's ebony black locks, whom she named Anwen, while the other was a green-eyed temptress, enflamed with the blood red mane of their Viking sire. Her name was Boudicca."

"Wait a minute," interrupted Nan, much to Druantia's irritation. "Wasn't Boudicca a Celtic queen or something; the one in the painting in the hallway? And Cerridwen is just a myth, isn't she?"

Perturbed, Druantia rolled her eyes and answered, "Yes there was a queen named Boudicca, whom is the subject of the painting, but that was an entirely different time and different person. Or is it a crime for more than one person to bear the same name? And yes, some say Cerridwen is a myth. Now do you want to hear the rest of the story or not?"

"Yes, sorry." Nan allowed Druantia to continue.

"Anwen was the light of her mother's life, much like Rhiannon was for Elaine, and had inherited her mother's talents for herbs and healing. However, the tides soon turned on the happy duo. Boudicca grew jealous of her mother's affections and laid fault with her to her stepfather, claiming Blodwen intentionally prevented herself from bearing the man more sons, which he desired.

The man felt cheated and enraged by Blodwen's revealed deceit and distain for her marriage vows. He sought to punish her and sold Anwen in marriage to a black hearted travelling Saxon-Norman lord, Ucrane Wraithgart.

Despondent by her eternal separation from her beloved parent and false marriage promises, for in truth her heart belonged to another, Anwen was spirited away by her deplorable new husband to his cliff side fortress in Gloucestershire.

Grief stricken and wretched with unhappiness, Anwen became desperately ill. Having little love for her apart from her beauty and the whispers he had heard of her talents, Ucrane thought Anwen's state some cruel trick to avoid his bed, as he knew of her former lover, and forced himself upon her.

When the dastardly deed was done and Anwen lay trembling and deflowered, Ucrane remained still unsatisfied and sought revenge by throwing her into the highest tower cell.

As if his injustices had not been treacherous enough, still angry Ucrane ordered Anwen's lover brought to him, then had him beheaded and his lifeless body strewn into the tower chamber Anwen then occupied.

Within a week Anwen was nearly without her wits and mortally ill. Not only from grief, but the putrid stench filled circular room where her true love's headless corpse decomposed.

Not able to bare the tyranny any longer, Anwen's handmaiden besieged Ucrane to release her mistress before it was too late and implied she believed Anwen to be with child.

Intrigued at the prospect of an heir, Ucrane immediately ordered Anwen's removal from the tower. However, still unforgiven, he sent Anwen and the handmaiden to the secluded country manor he had presented to her as a wedding present, in the remote forest of New Forest. Anwen remained there, imprisoned, away from the world, until the time came for her to deliver."

"Wait, so you mean Anwen was imprisoned here? In this very house?" interrupted Nan.

Druantia scowled, "Yes, now do stop interrupting."

"Word from Ucrane's many spies came that Anwen was about to give birth and he rushed to the hidden manor to see the long awaited event. He arrived in the dead of night and discovered his wife had borne twin girls, as her mother before her.

However, upon beholding them Ucrane instantly claimed Anwen to be an adulterous, as one of the babes was not dark like him, but tangerine. Anwen bitterly denied his ludicrous accusations and assured him she had been with no other man but him. Anwen watched in horror as Ucrane thrust the child at the handmaiden and ordered its destruction.

Anwen screamed and implored him from her bed, too weak to stand. The maid looked at her lord, terror struck, gripping the child in her arms. Scared she gave him a brief nod and rushed from the room, leaving Ucrane to bereave Anwen some more for her so-called unlawful act. When Ucrane finished his rave, he picked up the remaining child and departed. Anwen was left, childless and mournful.

Shut up from the world as if in a tomb, Anwen remained a prisoner in the manor for many years, only her grief for the child lost and longing for the survivor as company. Little did she know that against Ucrane's demonic wishes, the handmaiden, unable to be so treacherous, had stashed the infant in a basket in the kitchen. Later that night she secretly whisked it out of the house and gave it to an old crone who lived deep in the woods, for safekeeping, where the child grew and prospered.

After some years had passed Ucrane softened and restored Anwen to the castle and life at court. Methodically Anwen resumed the flow of society after such a great absence and attended to her noble duties, her husband titled baron in her leave. However, she stayed withdrawn and solemn. Her daughter still kept out of her sight, under the tutelage of nuns at an unnamed convent.

Within a fortnight, Ucrane made his presence in Anwen's chambers once more, as he did so many years prior and her heart sank. However, this time it was not her womanhood he sought, but her powers. She soon learned her reinstatement was not an act of mercy or forgiveness, but a means to an end.

Ucrane thirsted for power and though a baron, he was not satisfied. He proposed that in penance for her earlier crimes against him and for the return of their daughter, Anwen would use her extra ordinary abilities to help him rise even higher in his quest for succession.

Horrified at his designs, Anwen blatantly refused. Even though it meant the loss of her child forever. Instead, she looked him straight in the eyes and vowed as long as she had breath and her descendants thereafter her, he would never achieve his frightful plans.

Ucrane smiled like a hangman at a public execution. He threatened the life of his own daughter to win Anwen's compliance, but she remained strong. She shrank back from him in terror as he approached to forcibly bend her will. Anwen side stepped him and raced from the room in search of freedom.

She ran through the stone halls of the formidable fortress, but found no solace, only locked doors. Out of options, she whirled on and finally came to the top of the highest battlement with nowhere else to go. She looked out over the forested cliff side floor, with its scattered rocks below and knew her life was at an end."

"Nevermore," the all but forgotten raven shrieked at that moment. Nan jumped out of her skin with fright and Druantia frowned at the bird, then continued.

"As if he stepped out of the night itself, Ucrane appeared behind Anwen, with his devilish gleam and menacing Cheshire cat grin. Once more, he requested her compliance, but Anwen held fast, hatred seeping out of her very pores.

Venom spewed from Ucrane's eyes as he lunged forward and seized Anwen's shoulders. He hurled her fragile form over the stone parapet and watched as she plummeted down the cliff side to the rocks and trees below.

A surge of power electrified the night sky as Anwen's body disappeared into the dark. At that moment, Ucrane realized Anwen's curse was real and as long as Anwen's blood still walked the earth, he would never prosper. Desperate to thwart her powers, he sent riders to the nunnery to extinguish the life of his own daughter. However, she was gone.

The guards hid their failure for fear of repercussions. Ucrane played the martyr and cried over the loss of both his beloved wife and daughter, though he relished in his victory of his wife's curse.

In his ignorance, Ucrane lived happily. He found himself another witch to do his bidding and proceeded with his plans for succession. However, after multiple failed attempts Ucrane realized not all was right. He tortured the unfortunate guards, along with Anwen's old handmaiden, and soon the truth came out that not one but both of Anwen's daughters lived.

Now feeling the effects of his age, but desperate to get his revenge on Anwen's bloodline, Ucrane went back to his witch and bid her enable him to hunt those who escaped him, without fear of death, until all those who carried Anwen's blood were destroyed.

The ill-advised witch did so and Ucrane vowed he would rid himself of Anwen's illustrious children no matter how long it took. He began his bloodhound search for his own daughters and made it a personal vendetta along the way, to burn, torture, hang or just extinguish the life of every witch, soothsayer, sorceress, fortune-teller and so on, he came upon. He became more feared than the Witchfinder General himself.

And so, never dying, Ucrane has transformed himself into someone new with every century. Anwen's curse has prevailed, but our family's deathblow in the name of revenge does too. For you see this is no fairy tale, Ucrane is real and has brought generations of our bloodline to tragic ends, including my poor sister, Elaine."

****

"What a horrible story," said Nan solemnly. She could not explain it, but it was almost as if she had heard it somewhere before. However much she wanted to dismiss its bizarre allusions of sorcery.

Nan looked down the list of names on the scroll, saddened to think of how all those people had suffered. "What happened to Anwen's daughters, did they live?"

"Coventia and Druantia, lived long enough to see their children born and grow, before meeting their father's wrath. They lived in this very manor," explained Druantia.

"Druantia, that's your name," stated Nan, as she let it all settle in her mind.

"Yes, I am her namesake," answered Druantia.

"But wait, how did they live in this house unharmed, when Ucrane knew of its whereabouts?"

"The manor is protected, charmed. Seeing Ucrane's evil heart right from the start, Anwen put a protection spell over the house to prevent him from harming her or their children within its walls. No dark magic can withstand the house's ancient purity. For you see, Anwen had planned to retrieve her daughter from Ucrane's clutches and escape back to Magewebb, where they could live away from his harm. But she didn't succeed."

"Okay, wait a minute, let's see if I've got this straight," Nan interrupted. "You're telling me I'm supposed to be descended from a long line of witches, who are being murdered by a crazed immortal baron, who just happens to be our sire?"

"Precisely," replied Druantia, stone faced.

"Ha," Nan laughed, mockingly. "Next you're going to tell me that I'm a witch."

"You are."

"You're crazy!" exclaimed Nan outraged. She got to her feet and paced like a caged tiger. "I'm not a witch. I don't even look like a witch."

"Oh and pray tell me what a witch is supposed to look like?" scowled Druantia indignantly.

"I don't know," Nan admitted, flustered. "But not like me. And what about my mother, was she supposed to be a witch too?"

"Rhiannon rejected her faith and the traditions of old, in order to live what she perceived as a normal life," replied Druantia, "Which is probably why you have no knowledge of any of this."

"It all sounds like some ridiculous tale from a German fairy tale, to me," grumbled Nan. "Where's your proof? And if we are all so powerful witches, why is this baron guy still hunting us down and killing us?"

"We are only safe when we are within these stonewalls. Outside we are fair game and without the words of the original witch we cannot finish Anwen's curse and vanquish Ucrane forever," retorted Druantia, annoyed at Nan's prejudice attitude.

"As for the proof it is all around you," and she gestured to the many books and newspapers, which filled the little alcove. "Stop being a narrow minded ostrich with your head in the sand and read it for yourself." Druantia turned on her heels and stormed across the library for the door, leaving a stunned, confused Nan alone with her doubts.

Nan yelled across the great expanse of the room as Druantia opened the door to leave. "What does all this have to do with my mother?"

Druantia halted, turned and stared back at Nan with vexation in her eyes. "Your mother fled England because of Ucrane, though he now goes by the name of Lord Vespir Meldun. In this century, he has disguised himself as the half-brother of the late, Lord Percy St. Clair, your grandfather. Elaine was unaware of this when they wed.

However, once aware, Elaine and I waited for Meldun to strike and protected your mother and Gwynedd as best we could. However, Percy insisted on moving his family to his London house and out of Magewebb's safe haven, which allowed Meldun to use this disadvantage against us.

Your mother, being the senseless thing she was, soon fell in love with Meldun's ward. A kind and handsome boy who Meldun took in after he found him abandoned in his stables. No doubt, he planned to use the poor unsuspecting youth to his advantage later and Rhiannon brought that plan to light.

They were wed against Elaine's protests and as a wedding gift, Meldun gave them the west wing of his castle, the same fortress where Anwen fell to her death.

Meldun seized his opportunity and advanced on your mother one night in the privacy of the belvedere and tried to kill her, but was stopped by his ward. In his rage Meldun struck the boy dead and your mother fled with only the clothes on her back. She ran barefoot over miles of countryside, until she found her way home where she retrieved some personal items and left the island to seek a new life in Canada. And that is how you came into it."

Druantia said no more, just turned and walked out the door. Nan stared, transfixed, at the spot where Druantia had stood moments before and replayed her words over and over in her head. Nan had never imagined her search for answers would lead to such a sorrowful, dastardly story.

It must have been horrible to watch the man you love murdered right before your eyes, mused Nan. *And then to flee for your life, leaving everything you've ever known and loved behind. I can't even imagine what that would be like.*

Nan's mind and emotions whirled inconsistently. She sat back down in the desk chair and stared again at the scroll of names. *So many innocent people murdered.*

Was everything Druantia said true? Am I really a witch? Or is it just some old fish tale passed down throughout the ages? Nan tried to decide. She gazed up at the books, newspapers, and folders Druantia had gestured to and concluded that the only way she would discover the truth was to look for herself.

Chapter 19
"Books let us into their souls and lay open to us the secrets of our own." William Hazlitt

Words, letters, and pictures, all swam before Nan's eyes as she flipped the pages of yet another archived edition of a United Kingdom newspaper. There was no more doubt, having found sufficient evidence of the truth in the library's centuries' worth of family records. Nan couldn't help but feel she still missed something though.

Her search was a disheartening process. The hundreds of newspaper clippings, police reports, court records, and historian's notes, all described tragic deaths. One by one, her family members had been poisoned, drowned, bludgeoned, accidentally killed, committed suicide, or simply vanished without a trace.

There was also evidence of the occult, black marks, curses, and strange happenings, which supported Druantia's assurances of witchcraft. It was obvious that over the years the public had begun to believe the family's misfortunes were penance for their sacrilege.

That explains the town folk's odd opinions of Druantia and Magewebb Manor.

Nan had concluded her examination of the contents of the little alcove and was about to search the rest of the library when she heard Druantia's soft soled shoes approach from behind.

"My goodness, Anabel, you have been cooped up in this stuffy library for days now. It is high time you put aside this obsession of yours and abandon these walls of books for the land of the living," protested Druantia, as she gazed deep into Nan's blood shot eyes.

At least she has stopped calling me girl, Nan smirked. "I know, but I feel like I'm so close to finally understanding it all," she answered.

"I understand, but you can't remain like this. It is unhealthy," Druantia cautioned. "Now come along, we'll start by getting some breakfast into you."

"Okay, but there are a few things I want to do first."

"Now, Anabel," commanded Druantia, not taking no for an answer.

"But there's still so much I don't understand," complained Nan, as she followed her great aunt to the library door.

"Such as?" inquired Druantia. She waited for Nan to exit the room and then closed the door behind her to prevent Nan from re-entering.

"Well, all the records describe how the women of our family perished, but what happened to the men? Why did Ucrane or Meldun or whoever he is, only kill the girls and not the boys?"

"Because there were none," answered Druantia simply.

"What do you mean?" Nan frowned.

"Sons, there were no sons. The gods' punishment for Blodwen's weakness and inability to protect her people caused a chain reaction and our bloodline, Anwen's bloodline, only produces daughters, twin daughters, one light and one dark," informed Druantia. "As for the husbands, well they moved on, probably remarried, but usually left unscathed."

Shocked at this, Nan fumbled to understand. "You mean there are never any boys? How is that possible...you don't honestly believe that nonsense about gods and punishment, do you?"

"Yes, I do," declared Druantia.

Wow, she is out to lunch, Nan scowled. "But wait a minute, I'm not a twin," she verbalized in realization.

"No, you're not," replied Druantia, but instead of elaborating any further she simply added, "Now forget all that and let's get some food into you. I've had to fend Cora off from disturbing you for almost a week now."

Resolved to drop the issue for the time being, though the question of her singlehood hung heavily over her, Nan followed her great aunt to the dining room where Nan polished off her porridge and poached eggs. Only looking up from her plate to take a sip of juice or grab another honey-glazed croissant.

"My, my, you would think you hadn't eaten in months," Druantia smiled, as she watched Nan devour everything in sight.

"I guess I was hungry after all," replied Nan, between mouthfuls.

"I would say so," agreed Druantia and then added, "I need to get a few supplies in town this afternoon if you care to join me. It would do you good to get out of the house for a bit and get some fresh air."

"I'd love to," beamed Nan at the unexpected invitation. "I assumed you always sent Shamus on errands."

"Not always. There are a few things I need for my wards and Shamus is hopeless at getting it right," Druantia huffed in exasperation.

Nan smiled, pleased. She knew full well that most of the animals' needs could be provided for with items found on the property, which made the trip unnecessary and entirely for her benefit.

When breakfast was finished, Nan and Druantia walked out the manor's front doors to where Shamus waited for them with Beauty hitched to a trap. The horse itself was small in stature, but stocky with long flowing mane and tail, much like the ponies one saw pulling the gypsy's caravans.

Shamus removed his hat and bowed at the sight of Nan and his mistress, then offered his hand to assist them into the cart. "Mornin Mistress and Lassie."

"Good morning Shamus, how are you today?" smiled Nan, as she took her seat beside Druantia. It felt quaint and exciting not to be travelling by motorized vehicle.

"Just fine Lassie," answered Shamus good-naturedly, and then looked at his mistress and added, "Ye be needin me ta drive ye than mistress?"

"No, that won't be necessary today Shamus, thank you," replied Druantia with regal authority, yet kindness. "I'm sure Cora could use your help in the kitchens today."

"Aye mistress," Shamus smiled, like a boy given permission to eat sweets before dinner and without further ado, he headed off around the side of the house to the servants' entrance.

As they trotted off down the lane, past the stone ravens, Hexia flying close by, Nan turned to Druantia with a curious expression and giggled. "Well I wonder what got into him? If I didn't know better I would say Shamus has a crush on Cora."

"I should hope so," replied Druantia with a coy smile. "They are married."

Completely flabbergasted, Nan stared at her with bug eyes and exclaimed, "Really? I had no idea."

"They don't make a public affair of it. Though we live in the modern world, it is still held in some circles that the help normally are unwed. However, I'm known for going against tradition to some extent and gave them my blessing."

At that moment, Nan felt she and Druantia were kindred spirits after all. The graceful noble woman proved to be kinder and more generous than Nan had given her credit for. She smiled at Druantia's romanticism. "That's so lovely. Where do they live though?"

"In the servants quarters of course, on the third floor," answered Druantia as if only natural. "Being that they're the only ones up there, they have converted it into a nice suite for themselves."

"No doubt."

****

The rest of the glorious wildlife filled ride was spent in idle chitchat. Once in town, all pleasantries evaporated as Nan could feel the villagers' eyes on them, full of misgivings, burning holes into their skulls. *Wow, they really do dislike Druantia, and now me by association,* thought Nan. She had never felt so conspicuous and queer in all her life.

Druantia reined in Beauty out front of the grocers and dismounted from the trap. As she tethered the mare to a lamppost, she said, "I just have to get a few items if you want to go shop around while you wait."

"Oh okay," answered Nan, unsure, intimidated by the gawkers. "I think I might try to phone home and check in." She dismounted as well and headed for the nearest pay phone.

Impatient for an answer, Nan sighed irritably as the phone continued to ring. *Oh come on, answer already.*

"Hello," Rory's jovial voice said on the other end. Ecstatic when she realized the caller was Nan, Rory exclaimed, "Heavens Chickipoo, where have you been? I've missed you so much. I called the hotel, but the woman said you had left."

"I'm sorry it's been so long since I called," Nan apologized. Rory's familiar frenzy brought a smile to her face. "I'm still in England, but there is no phone at the house."

"What house? Did you find who wrote the letters? Oh and what about your mother?" Rory's roller coaster of questions zipped out.

"Yes, I found Druantia. That is where I'm staying," answered Nan. For the first time she acknowledged just how much she missed Rory.

"And your mom?" Rory inquired again.

"No, Druantia doesn't know where she is," replied Nan, with a regretful tone in her voice. "I don't think I'm going to find her."

"Oh, I'm sorry Chickipoo."

"Yeah well. How are things there?" inquired Nan.

"Oh the same," replied Rory nonchalantly. "My hours are still all over the place at work. Poe pretends Blue and I don't exist, until feeding time that is, and Blue hogs my bed at night."

"Sounds like you're spoiling her," Nan laughed. Then, in a shier tone, inquired, "And Parker?"

"I try to avoid him as much as I can, but the truck is rarely here, so I guess that is a good thing," answered Rory, her voice crisp with dislike.

"Oh okay. Well that's good I guess. Say hi to him for me, okay?"

"Yeah sure," agreed Rory reluctantly.

After a slight pause, with a hesitant note, Rory said, "By the way, your boss called."

"Oh yeah, I should call him," Nan commented, unconcerned.

"He fired you sweetie," Rory reluctantly revealed. "I got your record of employment and last pay in the mail last week."

"Oh," exclaimed Nan, shocked. She didn't know how to react.

"Maybe you can talk your way back in when you get back."

"Yeah maybe," answered Nan, unenthused.

"Anyways, when are you coming home? It's pushing the two week mark."

"Soon," answered Nan vaguely. "There's stuff here I have to do first. Besides it's not like I'm needed there, it sounds like you have everything under control."

"Yeah I guess, but..." but before Rory could finish her sentence, Nan spotted Druantia emerging from the store and said quickly, "I have to go now, but I will call again soon alright. Love you guys. Take care, bye."

"Nan, wait!" Rory shrieked, but the line went dead and Nan was gone.

****

"Is everything well at home?" asked Druantia, while she untied the mare, as Nan climbed back into the trap.

"Yes, thank you," smiled Nan falsely.

On the journey back to Magewebb, Nan remained quiet and withdrawn, deep in her own thoughts as she pondered the unexpected news from Rory. *What do I do now? No job, my father's gone, no real*

A New Forest Witch

reason to return to Ontario, I failed to find my mother, and can't stay here...can I?

Druantia eyed Nan's distant expression, while she tended to the mare's reins, then ventured to ask, "I hope you did not receive disappointing news."

How does she always know stuff? Nan wondered, roused out of her stupor. "No, everyone is fine." Then after another bout of silence, she admitted, "I got fired from my job."

"Ah," exclaimed Druantia, everything became clear. "And you don't know how this makes you feel?"

"No, I don't," sighed Nan. "I know I should be more panicked or something, but I'm just not. I'm almost happy in a way."

"Relieved?" suggested the wise woman.

"Yes, but I don't know why. I admit it wasn't my dream job, but it wasn't horrible," continued Nan, as if trying to hash things out, out loud. "I've just been so lost since dad died and so much has happened. It's almost like I simply don't care anymore. I miss him so much and I'm so confused."

"Understandable."

Druantia deliberated as to whether to comment further, reminded of Nan's previous cynicism on the subject, but finally said cautiously, "Our ancestors believed death was a type of rebirth. That the soul never truly dies, for nothing in the universe can be destroyed, only changed, and death is merely a change of place till the soul is ready to be reborn."

"Our ancestors, you mean the Celts, right?" questioned Nan, unsure, but intrigued. She wanted to learn more about her family after her days locked in investigation in the library.

"Yes, that is right," Druantia grinned.

"So you're saying my dad is still alive somewhere?"

"Basically," Druantia affirmed. "You just can't see him. He is in the world parallel to our own, out of our scope of sight."

"Hmm," mused Nan, not sure if she believed what Druantia was saying or not. "Well whether he is alive or not, it still hurts all the same. And now my mother is once again just a lost memory."

"Pain and death are just facts of life Anabel, they are not evil. The only evil in this world is moral weakness," replied Druantia.

"And what my mother did to my father, was that not evil? Abandoning him like that and shattering his heart. Was that just a fact of life?" Nan challenged bitterly.

"Ah, well no, that was not essential to life's plan. However, she had her reasons."

"I know, you told me, to protect us," grumbled Nan.

"After your mother heard of the fates of her mother and sister, and that Meldun still pursued her, she believed leaving you and your father was the only way to protect you," Druantia tried to sooth.

"Even if that was her reasoning, until I find her and hear it from her lips myself, I'm not sure I could forgive her for all the pain she caused my father. But it doesn't look like that is going to happen," said Nan flustered."I need to find her and we need to rid our family of Meldun once and for all."

Druantia gave her a little sombre laugh and replied, "Ah tis a noble aspiration, but many before you have tried and failed, people who didn't look down their noses at magic."

"Okay so maybe I haven't been open minded about the whole witchy thing, but I get it now, I believe you and if it helps find my mother and defeat Meldun, then I'd better learn how to be a witch," Nan stated decidedly.

"Even if I was to instruct you in the ways of old and I'm not saying I'm going to, you would still be ill-equipped to stop Meldun," Druantia frowned.

"I understand that I'm a novice and all, but I'm sure with the two of us we would come up with something," urged Nan.

"Without the words of the original witch I'm afraid it is hopeless," she sighed.

"The original witch?" repeated Nan.

"Anwen, the one who created the curse. It is only by knowing her exact words that fateful night, that one could expand and thwart Meldun's efforts, but they are lost to us."

Nan's eyes gleamed with triumph, as the picture of the great serpent engraved leather spell book flashed before her eyes. "No they're not, I have them. I have the book."

"Ah so you have the family grimoire, do you?" said Druantia coyly. "Yes it is true that it contains writings from Anwen and her mother compiled by Anwen's daughters and granddaughters, but unfortunately it does not house the curse we need. Those words were never written down."

"Oh," moaned Nan. "So I brought the book for nothing."

"I'm afraid so, but it is reassuring to know that it is in good hands," Druantia smiled.

"Okay, but be that as it may, will you still teach me, please?"

"You are incorrigible, aren't you?" snorted Druantia. "Oh very well then, but if I am to teach you, you better leave that condescending attitude of yours at the door and listen to exactly as I say. No back talk."

"Oh thank you," squealed Nan with glee and threw her arms around Druantia's neck in a happy embrace.

Druantia stiffened, her cold British mannerism not use to such displays of affection. As she wiggled free, she exclaimed, "Yes, yes, now enough of that. Oh and another thing, since you will be remaining with us longer than originally expected, you must start pulling your weight around the manor and help with the wards and gardens."

"Of course," answered Nan, happy to do anything she could in exchange for her great aunt's tutelage.

"Good, then we'll start tomorrow."

Excited, Nan continued to pick the elder witch's brain the rest of the way to Magewebb, sponging up everything she knew about the Insular-Celts, before the Romans invaded and Christianity demolished their old ways.

Chapter 20
"Men more frequently require to be reminded than informed."
Samuel Johnson

Parker unlocked the garage to get the truck ready for another busy afternoon, having just finished his lunch break. He saw Rory exit the house and head for her dilapidated old Bug and called out for her to wait a second. He was surprised to see her actually halt and turn in his direction, though her facial expression revealed her irritation.

"Hey, thanks for waiting," he said as he approached.

"Yeah well, I'm going to be late so what do you want?" Rory growled. It was obvious she hated the fact she had to share the same air as him, let alone talk to him.

"I was just wondering if you had heard from Nan?" inquired Parker, unaffected by her typical hostility.

"Actually yes," replied Rory, astonished at Parker's timing, as she had just hung up from Nan moments earlier. "I just got off the phone with her and she said to say hi."

"Cool," Parker grinned, happy Nan had remembered him or cared enough to include him, especially after their parting argument. "Did she say how things were going over there?"

"She said she had hooked up with some Druantia and was staying with her, but that there was no phone and she hadn't found her mother yet," Rory conveyed to try to end the conversation and quit Parker's company as soon as possible.

"Oh okay," he frowned, unsettled at the aspect of Nan in a stranger's house with no means of calling for help.

He took a chance and pressed for information one last time, just as Rory was about to turn and leave. "Did Nan say when she was coming home?"

Rory's contemptuous look fell away at this and a worrisome gaze took its place. "No. I told her about her boss calling to say she was fired and then she made some sarcastic remark about not really being needed here and that she still had stuff to do there and was staying longer."

"Oh I see," Parker muttered. He could sense the unsure tone to Rory's voice and decided something was just not right.

143

"I don't think she took the news about her job well, but I'm not sure because she was really evasive," Rory continued. "Anyways I really have to get going or I'll be late."

"Yeah of course." Parker broke out of his daze. "Thanks for telling me," and he turned back down the lane, while Rory headed for her car.

Rory's uncertain answers caused a pit to open up at the bottom of Parker's stomach. *I knew I shouldn't have let her go there alone. But what can I do about it now with a whole ocean between us?*

He entered the shop, headed to the office instead of the truck, and flipped through the directory Nan had organized for him on the desk. Within minutes, he found the number for a friend who was also in the towing industry and Parker called him to ask if he could cover the rest of his jobs for the day, to which the man eagerly agreed. Parker then switched the phone to go directly to automated message and headed to his loft.

Inside Parker grabbed an empty duffle bag from under the bed, threw it on the unmade mess, and stuffed it full of random clothes. "I'll just have to go get her back myself," he said to the empty room.

****

By the time Nan and Druantia got back from the village, supper was ready, which left them only minutes to freshen up and meet back in the dining room to be served.

They dug into the scrumptious shepherd's pie Cora had presented them with, but then were interrupted when Shamus appeared at the door, cleared his throat, and apologetically said, "Pardon mistress, tis a message for ye."

"Oh?" exclaimed Druantia, she arched her eyebrow and held out her hand for the note. Nan perched on the edge of her seat eagerly awaiting her great aunt to disclose the contents of the mysterious note.

Druantia read in silence, which kept Nan in heated suspense, but then smiled slyly and exclaimed, "Well, well, my dear, it appears your desired audience with Lord Meldun will commence sooner than you had anticipated. He has learned of your arrival and requests our presence for high tea tomorrow evening."

"So soon?" Nan stammered, baffled. "But what will I say to him? I'm not prepared."

"Well, 'Hello' would be a customary start," Druantia teased and turned back to Shamus, "Tell the courier my answer is yes, we will be there tomorrow evening."

"Aye, mistress," Shamus bowed and exited the room.

"But what will I wear?" Nan continued to fumble.

"I'm sure we can dig something up for you that would be appropriate," replied Druantia unconcerned, as she placed the note to the side of her plate and resumed her meal.

Nan sat transfixed. She stared down at her plate and wondered what tomorrow night would bring. *Should I act like I don't know who Meldun really is, our family's arch nemesis Ucrane? Just exchange common pleasantries with him or should I confront him head on about the disappearance of my mother and the centuries' worth of torment he has bestowed on our family?*

Cora entered the room then and began clearing the trays. Druantia wiped her mouth delicately with a napkin and said, "Ah Cora, we will be in need of an evening gown for Anabel tomorrow night for a private gather with Lord Meldun at Falconhurst. Can you see what you can find in the robe room? Nothing too flashy. Simple yet elegant."

"Yes my lady," replied Cora. Then turned to Nan, eyed her critically and added, "I would say you're about a size 6, is that correct Miss?"

"Um yes, I believe so," Nan mumbled, never putting much thought into her dress size and surprised how accurate Cora's eye was.

"Grand, I'll take care of it then, Miss," Cora smiled and guessing Nan had finished, though there was a fair amount of food still on her plate, she lifted the china and said, "Now you best get off to bed, you have a big day tomorrow."

"What? So early?" Nan whined and looked to her great aunt for help.

"Your wits must be sharp if you expect to cram years of knowledge into that head of yours tomorrow, so best do as Cora says," Druantia ejected, with an amused grin.

"Very well," Nan huffed and reluctantly rose from her chair. She said her goodnights and headed upstairs. Much to Nan's surprise once changed and in bed, it wasn't long before she was fast asleep.

****

Nan's eyes flew open. Something or someone had just shaken her awake, calling out her name in the cool stillness of the room. She reached over, turned on the lamp and gazed expectantly around the shadow-filled chamber. No one was there.

"Who's there?" Nan whispered into the night, as she searched every crook and cranny with panicked eyes. She rubbed her arms for all the hairs stood on end. "What do you want?"

Anabel, the haunting voice called out. *Let her out Anabel.*

The echo came from behind the door. Nan sprung to her feet, grabbed a pocket flashlight from the nightstand she had stowed there after her last midnight adventure, opened the door, and entered the hallway.

She turned right and then left. Again, no one was a foot. Nan wasted no time and made straight for the mouth of the east wing. "Where are you?" she called into the dark. She knew in her gut the voice she searched for was down there.

Let her out Anabel, it cryptically repeated from the darken depths of the corridor.

Nan turned on her flashlight and cautiously crept down the hall, starting every now and then as the light illuminated one of the painted faces on the walls. When she reached the end, she found herself at an impasse. *What door do I pick?*

"Where are you?" she asked again, but received no answer. The contents behind the door on the left already known, Nan slowly turned to the right, grabbed hold of the knob, and entered the room.

She was in an eerie bedchamber. An unkempt room that was obviously part of the original twelfth century manor, with bare stonewalls, low beamed vaulted ceiling, an iron candelabra, stone hearth, and heavy green brocade drapery. The only furniture was a high wooden box top canopy bed, an archaic crowned chair, a coffer, a petite vanity with a pitcher and washbasin, and a handcrafted cradle, which stood at the ready at the foot of the bed. It was like walking into Castle Udolpho.

However, much to Nan's surprise, what the room lacked in décor it made up for in charm, giving off a serene almost welcoming feel. *It's like I've been here before*, thought Nan, as she shone the flashlight around to investigate the long forgotten room.

As the light moved over the small dark ashen fireplace (once used to warm to the quaint room on many of cold nights), Nan saw a portrait of a beautiful enchanting young woman, hung regally above its mantle.

Nan's retinas consumed every inch of detail captured by the artist's hand and committed it to memory. The woman was breathtaking in a deep crimson tunic with sweeping sleeves and a woven gold rope belt. Her hair was as black as the new moon and waved down her back freely, unmoved. Her skin was as fair as porcelain, with eyes the pale grey of the sea after a storm, just like Nan's. She stood in the midst of a lush green field, bordered with dancing trees. It was unlike any portrait Nan had ever seen.

Nan stared deep into the mysterious woman's eyes, captivated by their depth and truth. *I know her*, she thought. *I've seen her before. She's the woman from my mother's drawing. Those eyes, they are the same ones, but who is she?*

Nan forgot about the summoning voice and edged deeper into the room, away from the portrait's burrowing stare, to ponder this new discovery. Her mind churned as she approached the bay windows and gazed out of their diamond leaded panes at the festering storm outside.

Dry lightning filled the night sky. Out of the corner of her eye, Nan saw a white female figure looking up at her from the garden path. Nan blinked in disbelief and stared at the spot where the ominous form had stood. It was gone.

No, someone was just there. Nan panned the grounds below from the window, but saw no one.

She raced from the room and sped down the daunting corridor to the stairs. Nan flew down them two at a time and soon exited the terrace door and ran down the cobblestone path in search of the ghostly figure. She cared little for the treacherous sky overhead or the cries from the distraught mare in the stables as she ran on. But to no avail, the woman's apparition was gone.

Nan sighed in frustration. Just as she was about to head back to the house, the cold night air biting at her bare arms, she saw peculiar shapes in front of the distant tree line at the gardens end. Nan walked forward, flashlight still firmly in hand, and discovered them to be headstones in a private graveyard.

Like a Dalmatian's spots, an array of tombstones from every age, in every size, shape, and colour, littered the ground. Decades' worth of people, her family, beneath her feet.

Nan proceeded through the stones in silent repose, feeling as if she was personally crushing the bones of her ancestors. She shone her light to read their names, yet never knew she was being watched. Then out of the night, she saw the raven sat upon the ground before her.

"Hexia?" Nan hissed in surprise. She cautiously moved towards the bird. Before she was able to get much closer, the raven took flight and revealed a headstone, which she had been sitting on.

The stone's cracked, pitted surface was almost completely disguised by the overgrown weeds, which adorned its flush ground level top. Nan knelt down and wiped away its veil to expose its occupant's name. When cleared a single solitary name blazed back at her, Anwen.

All at once, it became clear to her. Her mother's sketch, the story of the original witch, the portrait in the abandoned room, it all was Anwen. The woman who had started it all, the one clouded in secret, the person Nan had never known yet felt connected to. She was the one who linked it all together.

Hexia was giving me the answer, realized Nan, as she placed a hand on the cold, immortalized tombstone. *Hexia was showing me the nameless woman who I've been searching for all along.*

"Anabel," a crisp voice called from behind her. Nan jumped to her feet in fright. Druantia stood at the end of the path, her woollen sweater coat pulled tight around her body. Hexia was perched on her shoulder. "Anabel, goodness sakes girl, what are you doing out here? You are going to catch your death dressed like that in this storm."

Nan felt the first drops of rain hit her already numb skin and rushed to Druantia's side. Without further delay they headed back to the house. Druantia lead Nan down a set of steps to a side door, which opened into the cellar. Nan was flummoxed to find it to be a cozy wide-range kitchen.

She smiled to herself as she walked into the room. "Ah so this is where Cora hides out."

"Yes, she is very particular about her kitchen and does not like it when people mess about unsupervised," replied Druantia. She retrieved a cotton sheet from a nearby closet and wrapped it around Nan's blue tinged shoulders. Swaddled like an infant, Druantia vigorously rubbed Nan's arms to regain circulation and scowled. "What a fool hearted thing to do, going out this late at night and in this weather. Whatever enticed you?"

"You'd never believe me if I told you," chattered Nan, not sure whether she believed herself.

"Try me," Druantia stated. She turned towards one of the great gas range stoves and grabbed a copper kettle from a burner to fill with water.

"I thought I saw someone in the garden and tried to follow them, but they disappeared," explained Nan, as she perched on a stool by a big butcher-block table in the room's centre.

"And where do you think they went?" Druantia took two china teacups out of a cupboard and placed them in preparation on the counter next to the stove.

"I'm not sure," groaned Nan, confused. "I don't honestly know if there was anyone there to start with."

"You can't see that part of the gardens from your chamber," commented Druantia, mixing some dried leaves together for the tea.

"Oh, well no," Nan stammered, not prepared to explain why she had been creeping around the manor like a thief in the night. "I wasn't in my room. I was in a room in the east wing."

"I see," nodded Druantia, almost knowingly.

Then, Nan took a deep breath, feeling as if she was about to burst at the seams if she harboured the burden much longer and said. "I keep having all these strange dreams. Like I'm watching someone else's life, as if we're one. And now on top of it all I'm seeing things and hearing voices in the night."

"Why have you never mentioned this before?"

"I figured you would think I was crazy," Nan admitted.

"You may be many things Anabel, but crazy is not one of them," Druantia reassured. "Tell me more about these dreams and happenings."

"They're more like nightmares and none of them make sense. It is as if I am a prisoner in another woman's body and am forced to watch all these horrible things happen to her. And I think she's crazy, because in one dream she gave this old woman a severed head to drop in a river. Then when I'm not dreaming I keep getting woken up by someone calling my name and tonight they told me to "Let her out", but who?"

Frustrated, Nan collapsed her head onto the table and said no more.

"The Celts believed that the soul dwells in the head and to show honour to a person, often times the head was removed and taken to a sacred place. Rivers, lakes, and stream beds were quite often used and it was not uncommon to find a river full of skulls," enlightened Druantia. She poured the steaming hot water into the cups.

"Really?" Nan perked up, curious, but grimaced at the thought. "So you think the woman I'm dreaming about is Celtic?"

"Perhaps, maybe the head belonged to someone the woman loved." This sparked a sudden inkling in Nan's mind and all at once, Anwen's story came back to her, about how Ucrane had beheaded her lover. *Could that be what my dreams are about?*

Druantia approached the table, placed one of the hot beverages in front of Nan, and then took a seat on one of the other stools. "Someone is trying to tell you something, Anabel and that person is you."

"Me?" Nan all but screeched, shocked.

"Yes, you," replied Druantia calmly. "Do you remember how I told you the soul never dies, but keeps getting reborn? Well your dreams are just your soul's way of reminding you of the past, of your former life."

Nan's jaw probably rang out through the entire house as it hit the floor at this proclamation. Speechless, she stared at Druantia's composure and waited for her brain to revive.

"I believe in the Western world they call it reincarnation," continued Druantia.

"So you are saying that this woman I keep dreaming about is me in a different life? That all I'm seeing actually happened to me back in medieval times?" Nan asked, her vocal cords having relaxed.

"Precisely," Druantia grinned.

"This is insane, it's nuts!" Nan bellowed out in horror.

"Just think about it, Anabel," Druantia urged. "Think of all you've seen and how strange things seem familiar to you."

"I don't know," faltered Nan, too overwhelmed to grasp it all. "Say it's true and I am dreaming about myself, who was I then?" she challenged.

"Anwen, of course" answered Druantia simply.

The room fell deadly still, not even the storm could be heard outside. The drawing, the dreams, the woman's eyes, the painting, the familiar story, and the grave, all danced around in Nan's mind. The raven had shown her the answer she was looking for, but Nan hadn't realized then that it was the answer to everything.

I'm the girl in the drawing, from my dreams, in the painting. I am Anwen, the one who doomed our family. Nan mentally scrambled, unsure if she believed it.

"I've had my suspicions from the moment you walked through my door," continued Druantia, when she realized Nan was to dumbstruck to speak. "The way you were continuously drawn to the east wing, to Anwen's chamber, and how your eyes hold that same sultry knowing look as hers did. Then tonight when Hexia showed you her grave, I knew I was right."

"But it can't be. There's no way," Nan baulked. "And how did she know?" she continued to fumble, as she stared at the ever watchful raven, now perched high in one of the kitchen windows.

"Here, drink this. It will help calm you," smiled Druantia sympathetically. She pushed the teacup closer to Nan. She understood it was a lot to take in.

Nan raised the cup to her lips, still frothing over the bomb Druantia expected her to digest. As the unusual liquid swam down her throat, she scowled and asked, "Argh, what is this?"

"It is an old recipe of mine. Just some valerian, catnip, mugwort, and a pinch of mistletoe, mixed with honey for sweetening. It will soothe you and help you relax and sleep."

"Catnip? Seriously? I better not start purring or something. And isn't mistletoe a Christmas decoration?" Nan frowned.

"It has many medicinal purposes and was highly revered by the Druids," explained Druantia.

Nan suffered down another mouthful of the bitter tasting concoction, the honey not doing much to cloud the fluid's vile bite, and tried to relax and think logically. *None of this is logical though. How am I supposed to just buy into it?*

"I just don't know if I believe it," Nan sighed, doubtful. "How is it possible to know things that never even happened to me and how did a bird know about it?"

"Don't force it, Anabel," cautioned Druantia sweetly. "It will all come to you in time. The gates of your mind are open now. Just relax and all will be revealed, but don't fight it. You can't fight who you are, who you were, your past. It is all a part of who you are." She smiled and decided to avoid the question of the raven, leaving it for another time, as it would be information overload for her already overwhelmed niece.

"But how can I be two people at once?" whimpered Nan, tormented.

"You're not," Druantia assured. "You're still the same insightful adventurous girl who came walking up my path; you've just opened a new chapter of your development. You are Anwen and Anwen is you, you're connected, you're one."

Druantia looked at the weariness on Nan's face and added, "How about you sleep on it? All will be better in the morning."

Nan blinked with tired indecision. She heaved a strained sigh and agreed. Then got to her feet, clutching the sheet around her now shock-numbed body, and headed for the stairs, which led to the main floor.

"Aren't you coming," she frowned, after she looked back and found Druantia lingering in the kitchen.

"Yes, but first I'm going to erase all evidence of our trespass in Cora's kitchen," Druantia winked coyly.

Chapter 21
"Of course there must be lots of Magic in the world, but people don't know what it is like or how to make it."
Frances Hodgson Burnett

Groggy thanks to the sleep inducing tea she had drank the night before, Nan awoke to a knock on her bedroom door. The glare of the morning's blazing light made her blink, as she propped herself up in bed and said, "Come in."

Cora entered the room with a garment bag draped over her arm and a smile on her face. "Good morning, Miss. Here is your dress for this evening. I'll just drape it over this chair for you."

Nan tiredly watched Cora move across the bedchamber to a red velvet armchair in the corner and gently set the bag along its length. "Thank you, Cora. What time is it?" she mumbled.

"It is nearing eight o'clock, Miss. My lady instructed us to let you sleep late, for you had an eventful evening," answered Cora.

And eight o'clock is late? Nan felt like she had been hit by a locomotive.

Lighting on the 'us' reference Cora had almost slipped by her, Nan swivelled her head back to the open door and caught sight of Shamus's tall arthritic riddled frame, skulking in the corner behind the door. He was in the process of easing a large rectangular object onto the top of a small chest of drawers.

Nan watched him, briefly puzzled, until the item became clear. She recognized it and leapt from the bed (not caring she was only clad in her skimpy nightclothes) and rushed to Shamus's side.

"What is that doing here?" Nan shrieked. Her eyes glued to the familiar glass snake terrarium.

Shamus removed his cap as usual and fumbled with it nervously, then uttered uncomfortably, "I was told ta bring the beast up ta ye, Lassie."

"What?" she bellowed, causing the poor groundskeeper to jump with fright.

Goosebumps ran up Nan's arms as she stared at the ominous terrarium and its ebony scaled occupant, who at that same moment observed her with his glossy hematite orbs. The thought of sleeping in the same room with the loathsome reptile made Nan's skin crawl. *A deal is a deal remember*. She reminded herself.

"Very well, but you kept it locked, right?" questioned Nan.

Shamus jumped into attention as if zapped by a cattle prod and with shaky fingers reached into his vest pocket and produced a small bronze key. He handed it to her and said, "Aye here ye are Lassie."

"Thank you," she mumbled. Nan took the key and fingered it uneasily, as if its mere presence near the tank might cause the lid to spring open and release its slithering prisoner.

At this point, the all but forgotten Cora reappeared from the closet holding out an already assembled outfit for Nan to wear. "Here you are Miss, you're all set. Now we'll leave you to change. My lady is waiting for you in the library," and she ushered Shamus out the door.

Alone with her new reptilian roommate, Nan stood in shocked silence for a moment. The night's revelations seeped back into her consciousness, along with the knowledge of her lessons ahead. After another steadying breath, Nan donned her clothes and sighed. "I'm really going to do this, I'm going to become a witch."

But you've always been one, a little voice in her head echoed.

****

"Ah, Anabel," exclaimed Druantia, as Nan walked through the library door. "Good morning, I trust you slept well."

"Excellent," assured Nan. "That tea of yours is a lethal weapon."

"Yes, well my plants have many uses," Druantia smirked and gave Nan a playful wink.

"You'll have to teach me," Nan grinned in return.

"All in good time."

As Nan neared the large reading table Druantia sat at, she noticed that not only Hexia—roosted near one of the towering windows on a large tree root mounted to the floor—was there, but Beowulf and Gambit lurked in the room as well.

Trays of fresh fruits, biscuits, and a chilled pitcher of ice tea was spread out on the table, compliments of Cora. As Nan took a seat opposite her great aunt, she eyed Druantia glumly and said, "Did it have to be the snake? That's as bad as giving me her," she added, gesturing to the minatory raven.

"Stranger," the disagreeable bird cawed in return.

"Oh come now you two, it's time to put this grudge you seem to have for one another behind you," suggested Druantia diplomatic-like. "And you agreed you would help with the wards for the remainder of your stay, Anabel," she added.

"I know, but a snake, really?" Nan groaned.

"Just give Onyx a chance; I think you'll be surprised. Besides he belongs to you."

"What do you mean? You're giving him to me?" Nan frowned.

"He was never mine to give," stated Druantia. "He has always been yours, I've only been watching over him."

"Huh?" Nan felt more confused than ever.

"I didn't want to explain it last night for fear of giving you a meltdown, which is why I avoided your questions about Hexia, but tell me Anabel what have you heard in your Western world about witches?" probed Druantia.

"Well, the usual stuff. That they are old crones who fly on broomsticks, have warts, wear pointed hats, dress in black, cast spells and curses, dance with the devil around bonfires, cook in cauldrons, and keep black cats as familiars," recited Nan.

"Ah ha, I see," Druantia scowled, "Old crones indeed! All misguided propaganda the church has infused into the innocent naive minds of society."

"So you're saying all of it is made up?" questioned Nan.

Druantia composed herself and answered, "Well no, not entirely, which brings me back to my point. Witches, as we're so commonly labelled, do not consort with the devil; fly on broomsticks, and all the rest of that mumble jumble. However, our ancestors did cook stews and that in cauldrons, used bonfires for warmth and for celebration, and we did and still do cast spells, and have familiars."

"Ha-ha really? So where's your black cat," laughed Nan.

"She's right there," Druantia smiled and pointed to the watching raven.

"You're shitting me?" baulked Nan, eyes as wide as saucers.

"No I am most certainly not 'shitting you'," retorted Druantia. "How do you think she knew who you were and showed you? Familiars are not what you've heard them to be."

"What do you mean?"

"Familiars are the ancestral protectors of the next generation," explained Druantia. "They are ancient members of a coven's family. Once a witch's soul has been reborn to its fullest, learning all they need to know, they are reborn one final time in the form of a familiar to help guide other members of their family and are continuously passed down the lines."

"So you're saying that that bird is a dead member of our family?" queried Nan, unconvinced.

"Yes."

"Then why does it keep calling me a stranger," she countered, in the hopes of tripping Druantia up to reveal the whole theory to be a sham.

"Because she's a disagreeable old goat," answered Druantia, as she scowled at the raven.

Nan was quiet for a couple of minutes. She tried to absorb it all. Was she truly open minded enough to believe it? *Hexia did show me the gravestone, as if she was trying to tell me something,* she mused.

She looked around the library as if to find the decision making answer. Her gaze fell on the mighty wolf, which laid beside Druantia's chair and said, "You said Beowulf belonged to Gwynedd, does that mean he's a familiar too?"

"Yes, he's Gwynedd's familiar. He wasn't walking with her when Meldun swiped her from the grounds and so he remains with me." The wolf looked up then, sadly, as if he understood the conversation.

"But he's a boy. I thought you said our family members were only girls?"

"As humans we are, but when we come back as familiars our sex can change," replied Druantia.

Hmm, she has an answer for everything, doesn't she? Nan frowned, deep in thought. *There's no way she could be making this up.*

"Gambit," continued Druantia, "Was my sister, Elaine's familiar. He remains in the sanctity of the house until the day comes when his next companion is revealed. He has been with the family the longest, his first charge being Blodwen."

"Wow," exclaimed Nan. She stared at the aloof small bear shaped wolverine in awe. "And you say Onyx is mine?"

"Yes, that's right. He's been waiting for you for a long time," she smiled. "You two go back a long ways, for he was your familiar in your past life, when you were Anwen."

Nan was dumbstruck at this. She pictured the snake's black eyes staring at her every time she was near him as if he waited for her to recognize him, though she didn't realize that at the time. *Could he really be a link to my past,* Nan wondered. The snake suddenly took on a new light.

"Do they have magic to?" inquired Nan once her voice came back to her.

"Not so much in the way of casting spells, no, but they communicate with us and guide us," answered Druantia.

"That's why people have seen you talking to the raven...I mean Hexia."

"Well yes, though I try to avoid doing so in public," admitted Druantia sheepishly.

"So she can talk to you as we are doing now?" Nan became eager to learn more of the new secret world she had stepped into.

"No, they can understand our speech, but can only communicate telepathically. They can communicate with us over great distances."

"Wow, I would never have believed any of this was real if you had told me a month ago," exclaimed Nan, still flabbergasted. "Wait, is that how you have known my movements since I arrived?"

Druantia smirked. "Yes, Gambit here is pretty good at being stealthy and watches much of what goes on around the manor, unseen."

"Oh, so it was you sneaking around behind me," smiled Nan, as she eyed the black op wolverine.

"Now, let's get on with your lessons, shall we," announced Druantia, getting down to business. "First off, magic is not about waving wands and casting spells, though we sometimes do. Magic is found in the minds of those who believe in it and manifests itself in everyday life. It is merely a suspension of what is known and a belief and trust in the unknown. A source of respect and befriending of nature, its miraculous elements and energy pools one petitions for help. It is neither evil nor un-divine, but a natural connection to one's self, with nature and the universe surrounding us."

"Okay, but if it is so pure and innocent then why did my mom denounce it?" Nan frowned.

"It wasn't that your mother didn't believe, Anabel," Druantia assured. "She was tired of living under the cloak of bias and suspicion our family has suffered from the outside world. Rhiannon desperately wanted to fit in and live what she perceived was a normal life, but she still believed. You see my dear, what is called the modern world still rejects and labels those of the old ways as pagans, witches, heathens, and heretics, who continuously feel the strangling condemnation of the Christian revolution."

"But how will I know if I have what it takes to be a witch?"

"All you have to do is believe. Listen to your heart and it will come to you. It is your hereditary right and besides, you have Anwen's power coursing through your veins. If nothing else her ring which you're wearing will empower you."

"This was Anwen's ring?" exclaimed Nan and she stared down at her hands in wide eyed bafflement.

"Yes, the ring is a powerful talisman and the soul of Anwen's power, of your power. Plus it embodies our family's totem, the serpent."

So Casey's suspicions were correct. There really is an ancient secret coven of witches who use a snake totem, and I'm in it!

"So how does it work?" urged Nan.

"All you have to do is respect nature and yourself and remain open to continual growth and learning. It's very simple, Anabel. Our ways are all about being at peace and staying connected with yourself and the world around you and the possibility of new things. But keep in mind that with every action there will be an equal reaction."

"You mean like karma?" questioned Nan.

"Precisely," Druantia assured.

"Karma is not a sure thing though. People don't always get what they deserve," Nan countered.

"Perhaps not in this life, but the crimes of the past follow us and eventually it all gets resolved in the end," Druantia schooled. "Now enough chatter, let's get down to business. We're working against the clock you know."

"Whatever you do you'll never teach me enough before tonight," Nan moaned, suddenly feeling overwhelmed.

"Of course not, that would just be absurd. But I can awaken your inner strength and help you tap into the hidden knowledge you already possess," confirmed Druantia.

"The gifts of our past are old and pre-date what some say is logical thinking and it all started with her." Druantia pointed to a large copy of Christopher Williams's *Cerridwen*, which hung majestically over the library's stone hearth.

"The goddess Cerridwen, the keeper of the cauldron, represented knowledge, regeneration, inspiration, and magic itself. Her gifts laid in herbs, animals, prophecy, enchantment, death and rebirth, and much more."

Nan gave her a questioning look, but before she could ask Druantia cut her off and exclaimed, "Yes, I know she's a figure of mythology, but there is always a hint of truth to all myths. Our Celtic ancestors did not see their deities as divine untouchable beings, but as ancestors themselves. So who's to say that this mythical goddess was not originally just an ordinary woman?"

"I've read a little about her actually, in one of my mother's books, called *The Book of Taliesin*," Nan added. She tried to sound optimistic.

"Good, that's a start," smiled Druantia. "Each one of our family members has displayed one, if not more, of Cerridwen's bountiful traits. Be it herbology or simple spell work. Your mother was a clairvoyant; unfortunately, her gift didn't let her perceive her own future. Your grandmother's ability was augury, Gwynedd's talent was telekinesis, and mine is communing with nature and its creatures.

However, Anwen was special, you are special. She was not only an oracle, but was talented in spell work and could communicate with animals and the otherworld. Powers, which lie within you. All we have to do is find them," stated Druantia confidently.

"Easier said than done," grumbled Nan.

"Oh don't be so pessimistic, Anabel. Now, pick up one of the apples off the tray beside you and tell me what you feel," instructed Druantia.

Nan reached over and grabbed one of the fresh smelling, green apples off the tray and replied, "It's roundish and hard."

"No, no, Anabel, you have to actually try," Druantia scolded. "Close your eyes and hold the apple in both hands. Good! Explore out with your mind and focus on the apple, nothing else around you and tell me what you feel."

Eyes closed and brow furrowed, Nan sighed. She felt ridiculous. She ventured to feel the illustrious sensation Druantia expected her to, but felt nothing. However, just when she was about to open her eyes a slight tingle began to needle up her fingertips.

Stunned, Nan held her mind tighter on the vibration, which moved up her hands. Her senses burrowed deeper into the energy travelling within her. Then, as if a great dam burst forth under the pressure of a mountainous wave of water, she felt the barrier let go and opened her eyes to find the apple floating over her upturned palms.

Druantia's astonished expression was a mirror of her own. Nan was elated as the age-old witch said, "Well, well, that was unexpected. There's no doubting it now my dear, you are a true born witch."

****

The rest of the afternoon was spent with Druantia setting up a bunch of different exercises to test the limitations of Nan's untouched powers. Before the evening was upon them it had been revealed to both stunned parties, that not only could Nan levitate fruit (an ability Druantia did not expect her to possess), but could reach out with her mind to the world around them and perceive what neither could see.

They had made great progress for such a short time. Druantia leaned back in her chair and proclaimed, "Unbelievable, you have definitely surprised me my dear. I knew Anwen's abilities...your abilities, were unprecedented, but I never imagined you could do so much. Based on what I've seen today, there's no doubt you still possess all of your former powers, which means you can probably commune with the dead."

"Do you really think so?" Nan gave an involuntary shudder at the thought, but had to admit it explained a lot. All she had learned explained a lot about herself, her bizarre sixth sense and knowledge of ghosts. It all made sense to her now.

"Oh yes, which is why the white lady came to you last night," Druantia revealed. "Now that your mind is open there is no stopping the flood of information and power you will begin to discover. The key is to relax and focus. Don't rush it."

"Okay I won't," Nan promised.

"Come, we best be getting ready or we'll be late for our engagement this evening," Druantia announced. She rose, which cued Nan to do the same.

As they made for the door with the string of familiars following behind them, Nan gazed over the two four legged companions and frowned. "What about my mother, didn't she have a familiar?"

"Ah yes, she did," sighed Druantia mournfully, as she held the door open for them all to file out. "The night Meldun attacked her, Rhiannon did not just lose her husband, but her familiar as well. Meldun killed them both."

"What?" Nan gasped in shock. "How horrible. I didn't think familiars could die."

"Oh yes," assured Druantia as they walked down the east wing back to the civilized part of the manor. "They can be killed, but only by another witch or warlock and it is a devastating travesty for a witch to suffer. For you see, when a witch's familiar dies, it kills a part of her soul as well, because they are connected. She never recovers from it."

"My poor mother," moaned Nan. She found she sympathized with the woman more every day as her tragic history unfolded.

"Make sure you guard yours well, so the same doesn't happen to you," Druantia cautioned.

****

Nan's heart was electrified when she returned to her room. Her newfound powers and hidden aspects of herself swirled around inside her just waiting to be explored. Never had she felt so alive, so vibrant, like she could take on the world.

Though she had promised not to overdue it and knew she should be getting ready for the evening ahead of her, Nan spun on the spot. She yearned to test her abilities some more. Then her gaze fell on the glass terrarium, which sat half hidden in the corner behind the door.

A New Forest Witch

With an anticipated breath she took a step forward and lifted the little bronze key from her jean's back pocket. Nan put the key in the lock on the tank's lid, then took another deep breath to quiet her accelerating pulse and opened it.

After the distinct click of the lock was heard, Nan removed the lid and slowly lowered her hand to where the watchful serpent laid expectant on the aspen. *I hope this works*, she thought to herself.

Onyx investigated Nan's smooth skin with his flickering tongue, as she lifted up his bulk gently with both hands. She watched him, enthralled, as his lustrous cool onyx gem coloured scales slithered explorative over her arm. His studious round, unblinking eyes caught the slightest movement or shadow, while his tongue continuously licked the air to orient himself with her scent.

A tingle ran up Nan's skin from the snake's movement as it coiled itself around her limb. Never had she expected letting a snake slither over her body to be so intensely provocative. It felt natural, invigorating, as if his cylindrical body belonged on her.

All she had known slipped away and opened up to a new road, which stretched out endless before her. Nan eyed the reptile, then reached into the depths of her soul and brought him up closer to her face. "Can you understand me?" she asked.

Yeeessss Anabel. Welcome home, came the reptile's reply in her mind.

Chapter 22
"The life of the enemy. Whoever lives for the sake of combating an enemy has an interest in the enemy's staying alive."
Friedrich Nietzsche

With Beauty in harness and Shamus tending to the reins, the little trap made its way down the overgrown tree lined avenue to the awaiting black SUV at its end. The last sun kissed colours of dusk fell beneath the skyline. Nan sat beside her great aunt and clutched a silken shawl around her bare autumn chilled shoulders. She was dressed in a strapless midnight blue evening gown with her hair stylishly knotted on the back of her head thanks to Cora's skilled hands.

"There's something troubling you, Anabel," observed Druantia, seated at her side, clad in a forest green sequenced dress.

"I'm just nervous," replied Nan.

"There's no need to worry, I'll be with you the whole time." Druantia gave her a reassuring smile.

After they said their adieus to Shamus and got into the stationed vehicle, the pair were soon chauffeured off to Gloucestershire, where their greatest enemy awaited them. Nan gazed out the window at the different landscapes, overflowing with nervousness and raked with turmoil over who she was becoming.

Though her new life intrigued her, Nan couldn't help but wonder if these new aspects of her were more of a curse then a blessing. *So much has changed, so many things have happened. Am I still the Ontario farm girl who came here looking for her mother or am I now just some great witch resurrected from the past? Am I Anwen or Anabel?*

"There doesn't have to be a division between the two?" perceived Druantia, as if she knew without being told of the upheaval, which shook Nan's soul. "You can be both. This is only a new chapter in an old life. Embrace it and let your old memories help guide your future."

"But I can feel myself changing and the powers growing inside me. I feel like I'm losing who I was before," Nan whimpered.

"Relax, Anabel. Your heart still knows the true you, it is just making room for the old. Things have been overshadowed by new discovery. Once your past fully reveals itself all will fall into place."

"I hope so," Nan sighed.

Nan fell quiet for a while and thought about the story Druantia had told her about her former life. About Anwen and Ucrane, and grimaced at the thought that she was once more about to walk into the very place which held her doom. The castle she had dreamt of, where she had been held prisoner, where she had been killed.

"What happened to her family? To Blodwen and Boudicca?"asked Nan suddenly.

"Unfortunately not much was recorded about them after Anwen was taken to Falconhurst. It is believed Blodwen lived out her days in the settlement with the smith and that somehow Anwen's daughters found her. But as for Boudicca, no one knows. She just disappeared," answered Druantia.

"How odd," Nan scowled.

"Yes, but enough talk, we have arrived. Anabel, welcome back to Falconhurst," exclaimed Druantia. She made a sweeping gesture towards the windshield where the formidable cliff top castle was visible. Nan stared in stunned terror. *This was my home.*

Lording over the sprinkled timbered cliff face below like an all seeing eye, the bare aged stones of the fortress spoke of its immense years, and the scars from sieges past could be detected on its imposing battlements. The sliver type glassless windows gave little sense of freedom, coincided with the castle's impenetrable perch. A fortress of an era when brutality and war roamed free across the land and fortification was ones only hope of survival.

As the SUV sped through the stone remnants of the once untraversable gatehouse to the devilish castle above, Nan felt like she had been transported to Transylvania and the essence of Vlad the Impaler's vampire abode.

"This is where I...I mean Anwen died?" she sputtered in horror. She waited for a bunch of bats or impaled corpses to spring out at her from the darkness.

"Yes it is my dear, so be on your guard," cautioned Druantia, as she exited the parked vehicle and ascended the giant staircase, which led up to a set of spike armour plated oak doors. Nan mustered her courage and followed her great aunt into the lion's den.

As they reached the landing, they found one of the imprisoning doors held open by a gargoyle faced butler.

"Good evening, Gunther," greeted Druantia stiffly.

"Milady," retorted Gunther with equal disdain, as he gave a slight bow when Nan and Druantia entered.

"Be careful of him," Druantia whispered to Nan when they were out of earshot. "He is a deceitful creature and a loyal minion to his master."

Nan wondered what she had signed up for as she looked around the mausoleum like entrance hall they stood in and awaited their host.

A maid soon came and fetched their wraps. Upon seeing Nan's exposed neck, Druantia hissed in alarm. "Anabel what are you playing at?"

There wrapped around Nan's neck, still as sculpted metal encased with gemstones, was Onyx. He laid perfectly still, his length encircling Nan's neck while his head rested on his midsection as if clasped there and his tail dangled invitingly towards her half-moon exposed bust. To someone who didn't know better the snake looked like an elaborately unique piece of jewellery.

"What? He wanted to come," explained Nan, as she mimicked her great aunt's hushed tone.

"Do you think Meldun is an idiot?" Druantia scowled. "Do you think he will not recognize the snake? He has seen him before."

"Alive, but not as a simple piece of jewellery," countered Nan and she looked over her shoulder at Gunther who was eyeing them curiously. "He'll never expect Onyx is anything more than a necklace. And if Cora had chosen me a dress which didn't leave me half naked then he wouldn't be as noticeable," she grumbled. She felt indecent.

"I'm glad to see you two have bonded and you look lovely, but either way you are playing with fire," but before Nan could tell her great aunt she was needlessly worried and that Nan had everything under control, their family's curse appeared at the top of the castle's elephant staircase.

Meldun descended the stairs towards them, accompanied by an unknown young man. Nan sucked in an astonished breath. The demonic ghoul she had pictured since Druantia had told her their family story was in fact an aged heartthrob, with a salted black as night lush flowing mane, arched studious eyebrows, dark brooding eyes, smooth tanned skin, a straight British nose, David Bowie lips, and a sculpted face.

If Nan had been more girly she might have swooned, but one side-glance at Druantia's unaffected features soon put her in check.

The young man that followed a few paces behind Meldun was no less majestic. Nan felt a heat rise in her as her pulse raced at the sight of his well-defined six-foot figure, chiselled cheekbones, sun kissed skin, diamond blue eyes, and copper blonde tinged hair. He was the human personification of Adonis.

Nan's skin began to feel clammy and her muscles tensed with the desire to have this stranger's hands touch her skin. She couldn't understand what had come over her and embarrassed, Nan diverted her gaze from the model beautiful man to the floor, hoping he hadn't noticed her staring.

"Dearest Druantia, how wonderful it is to be in your company again. Thank you for accepting my invitation, it's been far too long," Meldun chimed in a thick bewitching tone.

"It is a delight to receive such an honour, Vespir," Druantia cooed in return, which caused Nan to gawk at her in disbelief due to her great aunt's sincere and friendly tone.

"This must be Miss Weststar, I presume. A pleasure to finally make your acquaintance my dear. And as lovely as expected," purred Meldun as he turned to Nan and devoured her with his eyes. He lingered momentarily on her bulging bodice before moving to her face.

Under his intense alluring gaze, Nan faltered, not knowing what to say in reply. *Courage, Anabel it's a game of the minds,* hissed Onyx in her mind.

She straightened her shoulders and plastered her most pleasant smile on her face. "Thank you my lord, I am happy to be here. I must say you have a most imposing home."

"Thank you my sweet, I'm glad it still holds its appeal," he grinned and then stepped aside and gestured to the young man who stood behind him. "Please allow me to introduce, Mr. Oron Ravenwood, a visiting associate of mine. I pray you will not be offended if he dines with us?"

"Not at all," assured Druantia and reached out a hand for the handsome young man to take. "A pleasure to see you again, Master Ravenwood."

"The pleasure is all mine, Lady Greenwick," replied Oron, as he kissed the top of her hand.

"May I introduce my great niece, Miss Anabel Weststar," smiled Druantia.

Oron smiled seductively as he moved away from Druantia to face Nan head on. He reached for her hand, bowed, and said, "Charmed, Miss Weststar," before planting a kiss on her hand, which sent sparks shooting through Nan's veins.

Nan's throat all but closed as her mind turned to mush. She practically forgot where she was as she managed to fumble out in response, "Please call me Nan."

"As you wish, Nan," answered Oron. His eyes dancing as he stared into hers.

With the introductions and initial pleasantries aside, the group moved into the great hall where hairy, unwashed chieftains had once gorged themselves on red meat and robustly sang and talked of their conquests.

The four made idle small talk and sipped wine, while waiting for the first course at a table large enough to seat thirty. Nan held strong and allowed nothing to slip about her true purpose or suspicions, as Meldun nonchalantly grilled her about her background. The whole time she sent her feelers out in hopes of picking up some sign or sense of her mother's whereabouts or anything unusual.

She had to admit her task was not at all unpleasant, as their host was by no means hard on the eyes, much like his enchanting associate. However, Nan begun to become discouraged as their meal arrived and she still had not received any insight or clues as to what she desired.

You need to infiltrate deeper, Anabel, Onyx advised.

As dinner proceeded the discussion remained casual, until eyeing Nan with an impish grin, Meldun said, "I must say, Miss Weststar that that is a very unique piece of jewellery you're wearing."

"Why thank you." Nan smiled in return and moved her hand up to touch the unmoved snake around her neck.

To change the subject, Druantia turned to Oron. "Tell me, Master Ravenwood, of what aid does our charming Vespir ask of you this time? The last I heard you were away studying at Oxford."

"Actually, Lord Meldun is too kind for it is I who am imposing on him and seek his approval to enlist this historical castle as one of our commercial attractions," he smiled.

"Oh is that so?" Druantia looked to Meldun for confirmation.

"It seems the Western world covets places as mine for its rich history and young Oron here is begging me to allow it to be a tourist attraction," confirmed Meldun.

"Ah and what a rich history it is," grinned Druantia coyly.

Nan saw her opportunity and jumped on it. "How interesting," she beamed at their host.

"Are you a lover of history, Miss Weststar?" asked Meldun, as he pealed the glare he had set on Druantia and turned his almost black eyes onto Nan.

"Quite, I'm in England on a marketing project for the travel agency I work for back home and it is places like Falconhurst that we look to promote. They draw the most customers," replied Nan, which caused Druantia to eye her in surprise before masking her emotions.

"Fantastic," exclaimed Oron. He stared at Nan with newfound comradery. "That is precisely what I keep telling our lord, but he stubbornly refuses to bend his old ways."

"What can I say," Meldun smirked, "A person's home is a place full of their private secrets."

"Indeed," taunted Druantia.

Now issss your opening, Anabel. Take it, she heard in her mind.

"Still I'd love to see more of your grand home," urged Nan, as she tried to appeal to his vanity.

"I'd love to show you," beamed Oron. He held Nan's gaze in a locked embrace.

"With your leave of course my lord," he added to Meldun, not removing his eyes from Nan's.

"Oh very well," Meldun consented with a laugh. "You two youngsters go off and have fun, while we old souls reminisce about times gone by."

With no more encouragement needed, both Nan and Oron rose from their chairs. As Nan turned from the table, she gave Druantia a sly wink.

****

Oron was a thorough tour guide. He showed Nan the minstrel's gallery, chapel, oratory, scullery, buttery, pantry, storerooms and everything else on the main level. He beguiled her with the amount of knowledge he possessed of the castle's history.

Nan listened to his captivating voice and tried not to get engulfed and lose sight of her goals. *Focusss, Anabel,* chided Onyx, when Nan's inner eye had stopped searching due to Oron's intense retelling of a battle the fortress survived during The Barons War.

Nan refocused and suddenly felt a malevolent unseen force lurking in the shadows. It must be Gunther, she decided, as Druantia had warned and walked on with Oron across the castle's minute bailey. "You said a baron lived here back in the twelfth century, but I don't understand. I thought it wasn't customary for nobles of lesser standing then royalty to own property such as this?"

Excited by Nan's educated inquiry, Oron proclaimed, "You are quite right and it actually makes for an interesting tale. It has been speculated throughout the academic community for some time, that Baron Ucrane Wraithgart, the original owner of the castle and one of Lord Meldun's ancestors, was in fact one of the unaccounted bastards of Robert the Magnificent, Duke of Normandy.

If true, it would mean William the Conqueror was his half-brother and it is suspected William was the one who bestowed this magnificent piece of medieval history on Baron Wraithgart as penance for their father's faults. Did you know that Robert I's lineage can be traced all the way back to Rollo, the Viking who originally founded Normandy?"

"No, how fascinating," exclaimed Nan. *So Blodwen couldn't keep her family safe from Vikings after all*, she thought.

"Yes, it has been suggested that Rollo's kin were responsible for the sacking of a lot of native settlements in the area," Oron went on, glad for Nan's interest.

However, Nan no longer listened. As they climbed the six-person staircase to the private chambers above, her mind began to cloud, as if she had stepped into a dream. The walls around her melted away to reveal their torch lit predecessors from the original twelfth century fortress.

What's going on? Nan's subconscious questioned.

It'sss a memory, go with it, answered Onyx.

Nan watched as her former self appeared on the stairs heading solemnly up to the rooms above, her flowing skirt trailing behind her, along with her trusted handmaiden.

"Thou risk is too great, Milady. Thou's child is not here, we should flee," whispered Anwen's handmaiden. She gazed over her shoulder as she spoke to perceive if she was overheard.

"Courage Eliza, thy quest tis not at an end, but we must make haste," replied Anwen, as she continued to glide up the stairs.

As quickly as it had come, the vision was gone, and Nan was left mystified on the castle's stairs. She blinked and looked around in a haze. "It's all coming back," she muttered barely above a whisper.

Asss I told you it would, assured Onyx.

"Nan?" she heard from above her on the steps and lifted her head to see Oron looking down at her with a concerned expression. Nan regained her composure and hurried after him. "Sorry, I got side tracked by the beautiful artwork on the far wall," she lied with a smile.

"Oh yes, Lord Meldun's personal collection," replied Oron, "He is quite an art lover and added them to the castle's facade when he took over ownership."

The two then continued through the many cabinets, boudoirs, dovecotes, garderobes, and private chambers on the castle's upper levels. Nan's skin tingled with the continual sensation of eyes on them. *Someone is watching us,* she mused, aware Onyx could read her thoughts.

There are many eyessss in thissss cassstle, be cautiousss, the reptile warned.

The dream work of visions plagued Nan even greater the more the pair ascended and descended through the castle's maze of corridors, which caused her to have to mask their affects more skilfully. They were disheartening and sporadic; clips of her past in no particular order. But as their intensity grew, so did Nan's awareness and bond with her past.

As they entered the castle's solar the remembrance of past events hit her like a cold breeze. Soon all Nan could see was Anwen sitting woebegone, gazing out her chamber's arch tipped window at the world she was forbidden to partake in.

"Thine master was watching thou this evening. I fear it tis nay safe for thou anymore. If thou presumes to flee to Magewebb, thou shalt do so forthwith," worried Eliza, as she sat mending one of her mistress's shirts near the hearth.

"Fear tis for the weak, Eliza. I shall not allow thy master's evil to forsake thee. Thou's game is afoot and I plan to see it to thy end," answered Anwen.

Back in the present, Nan stated absent-mindedly, before Oron could even get the words out, "This was her room."

"Yes, but how did you know?" he asked, astonished. "This was Lady Wraithgart's chamber. I'm amazed you knew that though, most don't."

"You can just tell it was the room of a grand lady," fumbled Nan, as she tried to cover up her revealing error.

"Ah yes, but a sad soul I am afraid," he sighed.

Nan didn't need to hear the academic's estimated views on Anwen's personality, for she had better knowledge of her than anyone, and therefore didn't question Oron's statement to avoid the conversation going any further. Instead, the two proceeded on with the tour.

They climbed higher and higher up the castle's vast scale, until they ascended one of the many towers' spiralling stairwells. Bile began to rise at the back of Nan's throat due to the familiar sights, sounds, and smells as they approached the torturous tower prison where she had once been a prisoner.

Breathe, Anabel, urged Onyx. Nan's panic began to grow as she heard her own former stricken cries from days gone bounce off the bare unyielding stonewalls.

Nan was thankful that instead of touring the cell they passed by it and continued onto the tower's battlement, the highest one of the castle. Nan's momentary reprise from the nauseating sensation the tower cell had brought upon her evaporated as soon as her feet touched the battlement's stones.

This is where I died, she mentally hissed. The vision of her helpless medieval clad form flailing over the parapet, while Ucrane, with a murderous gleam, watched as she plummet to the ground, flashed before Nan's eyes.

"And this is where the sad lady's tale comes to ahead, for it is said that Baron Wraithgart's lovely young bride threw herself over this very parapet after losing their first born child," announced Oron, as he stared over the stones at the shear drop below.

He turned and upon seeing Nan's pallor rushed to her side and gave her his shoulder for support. "Oh my, are you alright? Here let's take you back inside."

"Sorry," moaned Nan, "I'm deathly afraid of heights. I should have known better than to come up here."

"No worries," his soothing British accent assured. "You'll be fine once we get you back inside."

Safe (though Nan didn't feel safe in any part of the castle) back inside the stonewalls, they headed down the stairs. Oron continued to grip Nan around the waist, which she made no objection to, even though her weariness had subsided. The feel of his heat radiating body so close to hers caused all her mental anguish to subside, while her instinctual desires raged on.

Anabel, you must ssstop with thisss frivoloussnesss and focusss, grumbled Onyx.

Nan gave her head a slight shake to dissolve the physical responses that rushed through her body and probed conversationally, "How do you know she killed herself and wasn't pushed or something? What happened to her body?"

"Tragically, Lady Wraithgart's remains were never recovered. What are you suggesting that Baron Wraithgart was a murderer?" questioned Oron with a stunned expression.

"Maybe, who's to say he wasn't some male black widow," she suggested.

"Oh no," laughed Oron, "He eventually remarried and his next wife lived prosperously."

"He remarried?" Nan stuttered. She halted in her tracks as if she had hit by a brick wall.

"Yes, he married a girl from the Isle, I believe her name was Boudicca," he answered offhand.

Nan's pulse stopped, her legs gave out, and she almost tumbled down the remaining stairs. Oron promptly caught hold of her elbow.

"My goodness, your equilibrium really must be off from the height. Are you okay?" he asked in horror. He swung Nan's arm over his shoulder and held her firmer about the waist.

"No, I think I'd better return to my aunt," Nan breathed out uneasily.

"But of course," replied Oron and gingerly helped Nan down the rest of the staircase to the main floor.

Anabel you are not finished, we have not found what it is we are searching for, objected Onyx.

I know my friend, but I cannot proceed right now, replied Nan. Her mind raced with the bitter truth that not only had her sister (her own flesh and blood) dispelled Nan/Anwen from their home and those she loved, which hurled her into a torturous existence and caused her death, but that after she had assumed her place, her life, and had prospered. The betrayal ran to deep. How could Boudicca have hated her that much?

****

"There you two are. We were about to send a search party after you," Meldun smirked, as the two adventurers descended the grand staircase to where Druantia and Meldun awaited their return.

Upon seeing Nan's obvious condition, Druantia cut off any reply the young pair could make and rushed forward. "Anabel, you are unwell."

"I'm afraid that is my fault, Lady Greenwick. An ill-advised trip to the battlement," Oron jumped in, as he handed Nan over to her great aunt, who wrapped a protective arm around Nan and guided her away.

"I see," she hissed suspiciously. "Come, Anabel, it is getting late and we'd best be on our way. Thank you, Vespir for your hospitality."

"Yes, thank you my lord and you as well, Oron, for the pleasant tour," added Nan weakly.

"It was my absolute pleasure, Nan," assured Oron. "I hope we can repeat it again very soon," he added with a seductive smile, which Nan couldn't help but return.

"Yes, you are welcome here anytime my dear," grinned Meldun, "For after all, it is your home."

This caused Nan's skin to sprout goose bumps. *He knows,* she exclaimed wordlessly to Onyx.

Yesss he doesss.

173

Back in the chauffeured vehicle as it returned to New Forest, Druantia turned to Nan anxiously and asked, "What happened, did he attack you?"

"What? No," exclaimed Nan, shocked at such a vile suggestion. "No I'm fine really. What would make you think that way?"

"You just looked so pale….like something….and you were with him….I thought," Druantia stammered. "People aren't always what they seem, Anabel. You don't know him after all and he is associated with, Meldun."

"So that makes him guilty by default?" Nan frowned defensively. "Perhaps you're misjudging him, like you did with my mother's first husband."

Taken aback at Nan's words, Druantia gave a defeated sigh and said, "Just be on your guard, okay?"

"Okay," agreed Nan. "Anyways, you were right. During the tour, it all came back to me, my former life. I am no longer disconnected from it. I could smell what I smelt as Anwen, see what I saw as Anwen, hear what I heard as Anwen, and worst of all, I felt everything I had felt back then. Which is why I looked so stricken, the memories were exhilarating, but horrible all at the same time."

"Fascinating," exclaimed Druantia intrigued. "And did the two of you learn anything?" she asked as she eyed the snake, which now slithered down Nan's arm.

"No, I'm afraid the nauseating affliction from the memories caught me off guard and that is when I returned to you," Nan sighed.

"Well perhaps it was for the best."

"Yes, I believe it was. He knows, Meldun knows who I truly am," confirmed Nan and she gave her great aunt a worrisome look.

"So all is lost then," Druantia sighed, "You won't be able to gain access back to the castle and find the words we need and worst of all you have now painted a huge target on your back."

"No, we don't need to gain access again," beamed Nan, which caused Druantia to frown. "I know the words, I remember what Anwen...what I said that night. They are once again a part of me."

"That is fantastic! Now we can rid ourselves of this wretched curse once and for all."

"Yes, but I want to wait a bit longer," revealed Nan.

"For heaven's sake why?"

"To find my mother," answered Nan. "I believe Meldun knows where she is and I want to try and find her before we destroy him."

"Very well," agreed Druantia, willing to wait for the sake of a family member.

"But there is one other thing."

"What?" Druantia queried.

"I know what happened to Boudicca. She became Ucrane's wife and probably the witch he used to create the spell that kept him immortal," replied Nan.

Druantia's eyes widen with indignation. "Well that changes everything," she exhaled.

"It gets worse," Nan added. "I think she's still there. I could feel her watching me."

A brief silence fell over them as they brooded over the night's discoveries. Nan remembered something Oron had said, which she had found odd at the time. "During the tour Oron said that Anwen's body had never been recovered, but what about the grave at Magewebb?"

"It is merely an empty tribute to her. A way our family showed we remembered her...you," answered Druantia.

"How sweet, but sad."

Chapter 23
"If you do not expect the unexpected, you will not find it; for it is hard to be sought out and difficult." Heraclitus

The dream came to Nan much like all the rest, during the first stages of sleep. However, unlike the others, this time she was in complete control of herself, movements, and mind. Accustomed to the *Through the Looking Glass* type scenarios, Nan gave herself over to the vision, eager to see where it would lead her this time.

All was pitch black, as if Nan had been sucked into a black hole. All except for a blue orb, which hovered a few feet in front of her. Hypnotised by its glow, Nan slowly inched towards the blue ball.

"Welcome, Anabel." The voice emanated out of the orbs impenetrable depths.

Nan stopped and eyed her dark surroundings to be sure she hadn't been mistaken and that the voice had indeed come from the light source. Convinced, she stared at it cautiously and once more moved forward.

"Who are you and what do you want?" questioned Nan. She stood inches away from the blue glow and was tempted to reach out and touch it.

"Look to the one who guides and protects you to find the way," the unperceivable voice spoke.

"Who do you mean, Onyx?" Nan frowned, still glued in place by the blue glow.

All at once, a faded image began to appear in the orbs centre. Amazed, Nan watched while the picture came into focus. She sucked in a shocked breath.

There in the orb's centre surrounded by its glowing blue light sat an old hunched over, cloak covered crone, with strange woad markings on her arms. She swaddled an infant in a bundle of earth woven rags. It was the same mysterious woman who had appeared in Nan's other dreams.

I know her. It's the crone, who saved Anwen's...my baby. Nan pushed her mind to the brink to recall her former memories of the secret veiled figure. She strained and forced her subconscious to yield to her will, but something blocked her way, some barrier she hadn't yet traversed.

As if it realized Nan's struggle, the giant blue energy ball spoke once more, as the crone's image faded from view. "Hexia will guide you. She knows the secrets of old."

Then the light vanished and all was consumed by darkness.

****

"I had another dream last night," announced Nan the next morning, as she reached for one of the delicious vapour, warm cinnamon buns in a wicker basket on the dining room table.

"And?" probed Druantia. She fed a piece of ham to the large carnivorous rather than omnivorous raven perched on the back of her chair. Beowulf and Gambit were stationed nearby, politely waiting for their share.

"This time it was strange indeed, nothing like the suppressed memories of my former life. This time I simply stood in front of a talking blue orb," explained Nan.

"And what did you learn?"

"It showed me a picture of the old crone who saved Anwen's baby and then said, "Hexia will guide you," before disappearing."

"Intriguing, but vague," Druantia scowled. "The crone obviously has more to do with the story than we originally suspected, but what do you presume she is going to guide you to?"

"I've been trying to figure that out all morning, but something is still blocking me from recalling everything from my past. Here I thought I was fully connected to my former life after the visit to Falconhurst," Nan huffed in exasperation. "I even asked Onyx, but he was cryptic on the subject, simply saying I needed to let the pieces fall into place on their own."

"In a philosophical mood was he?" chuckled Druantia.

"I guess so," Nan smirked in return, then watched as her great aunt presented the pampered bird with another offering. Nan furrowed her brow and gestured to the raven. "You don't suppose the dream was referring to her, do you?"

"Well now that you mention it, it could very well have been." But before Druantia could say anymore on the subject or question her familiar, the raven ruffled its wings, took flight, and soared out an open window to disappear into the wilderness.

"Hey, where are you going?" yelled Druantia after the corvid.

"Hmmm," Nan uttered, "Well if that wasn't suspicious I don't know what is."

"Yes, quite," agreed Druantia. She glowered at the open window Hexia had made her hasty exit through.

Just then, Shamus entered and announced, "Pardon mistress, but there tis a Mr. Ravenwood here ta see ye."

Druantia arched her brow in interested surprise and turned a questioning gaze onto Nan. "Show him in, Shamus," she replied.

"Well it seems someone made quite an impression last night," commented Druantia coyly to Nan, after Shamus had exited to show their unexpected guest in.

Nan did not reply, only gave Druantia a shy yet delighted smile. However, her great aunt's expression became serious. "Tread lightly my dear, you don't know him well."

Nan nodded, the building butterflies in her stomach at the thought of seeing the male obsession her mind had toyed with since the previous night, froze her tongue and vocal cords. *Could he really be here to see me? Is it possible he felt the connection I did between us last night?* Nan's mind whirled like a crushing schoolgirl's.

Within minutes, Shamus reappeared escorting the young gentleman into their company. "Allow me to apologize, Lady Greenwick for this impromptu intrusion, but I was in the area and had hoped your delightful niece might accompany me to see the sights," said Oron, as he bowed graciously.

Druantia decided to save her reply and looked to Nan instead for her answer. Nan smiled shyly, both flattered and giddy at the thought of being in Oron's company, alone. Though hard to keep her rising excitement at bay but not wanting to seem too eager, Nan smiled and replied, "I'd love too."

"How wonderful," Oron smiled in return. Druantia's unamused expression went unnoticed by both.

Nan rose from her chair and grinned at her great aunt as she went to leave. "I'll be back before supper."

Then she and Oron rapturously exited the room.

Shamus was stationed in the foyer like a sentry and glared at Oron as the two approached. He handed Nan her jacket once they had reached the door. "Tis a brisk one taday Lassie, per'haps I should fetch the cart an escort ye myself," said the fatherly old gardener.

Nan smiled at his sweetness. "Thank you, Shamus, but that won't be necessary."

"Yes, I'm sure we can manage. My car is parked at the end of the path," interjected Oron, which resulted in an even nastier glare from Shamus.

However, Shamus sensed defeat, bowed his head in reluctance, and stepped aside to allow the young couple to leave.

Oron, very debonair, opened the door for Nan to exit, but instead she froze in her tracks. "Parker!" she shrieked in utter horror.

"Surprise," Parker grinned. He enjoyed Nan's stunned expression as he lowered his arm, which had been raised in preparation to knock before the door spontaneously opened.

"What are you doing here?" she exclaimed in mystification.

"I thought you might have forgotten your way home and came to guide you," he teased, "Miss me?"

Oron cleared his throat to regain Nan's attention, resulting in Parker noticing him for the first time. "Not to interfere, but we really should be going, it's a long walk," Oron interrupted.

Parker's face turned grim. Not taking his eyes off his male competitor for a second, he stated dryly, "I see this is a bad time."

"No…well…yes, we were just heading out," Nan stammered. She blinked indecisively between the two men and felt like a caught adulterous.

Get a grip, Nan! She chided herself; *Parker has no claim on me. He's just a good friend.*

Nan reassembled her shocked mind and took a step back into the manor to unblock the entrance. "Please come in." With a triumphant smirk, Parker walked passed his rival, giving him a challengingly stare, and into the house.

Okay, now what? A flustered Nan stumbled. *What is he doing here? And just when I was about to...*but she couldn't finish her train of thought, a red flush crept up her neck and into her cheeks. Just when she was about to what, start a new romance, throw herself at a seductive foreign stranger, Nan could not decide, but Parker's unexpected arrival had definitely thrown a wrench into things.

Nan placed a smile on her face , having concluded she would form a decision about the two men later, and exclaimed, "I'm afraid I'll be out for most of the afternoon, but Shamus can show you to one of the guestrooms upstairs and we can talk when I get back."

For assurance, Nan looked over her shoulder at Shamus who at the mention of his name stepped out of the shadows where he had been skulking. With a bow, he agreed, "Aye Lassie."

"There, see it's all settled," beamed Nan in relief.

"Uh huh," grunted Parker, "And what am I supposed to do while you're gone?"

Nan moved to the door in preparation to leave. She shrugged as she looked back at him over her shoulder. "I'm sure you'll think of something."

Before Parker could say anymore, Oron cupped Nan's elbow and ever so sweetly said, "Shall we go?"

She let him guide her out of the manor, but before the door closed, Nan glanced over her shoulder at Parker's outraged face. "I'll see you tonight," she called back and then she was gone.

Parker snorted in annoyance, his reunion not going as expected, then turned and took in his surroundings. *Maybe this was a mistake*, he thought, as he looked around the grand manor. Then he followed Shamus up the immense staircase to the rooms above. *Why would she leave this....or him?*

****

Nan was almost late for supper that night when she returned to the manor. She entered through the house's huge doors to find Shamus leading a glum Parker down the stairs to the dining hall.

She formed an uneasy smile on her face as she stepped forward and said, "Good evening, Shamus."

"Evenin Lassie," Shamus nodded.

Then she turned to Parker. "I trust you got all settled in."

"I've never been so bored in my life," grumbled Parker.

"Yes, well...," muttered Nan, not sure what to say next.

180

"Did you have a nice time?" he mocked in a sore tone.

Nan straightened with indignation at his tone. "Yes, thank you. It was lovely," she assured.

"How sweet," muttered Parker.

"Yes, well, have you met my great aunt yet?" she asked to change the subject.

"Not yet," he answered unenthused.

"You'll love her, she's great," beamed Nan. "She is cold at first, but once you get to know her it wears off. Oh, but make sure you address her as Lady Greenwick."

"Huh, you really have changed, haven't you?" retorted Parker and he turned and walked away in the direction of the dining room after Shamus.

Nan stood in dumbfounded paralysis. *What does he know anyways,* she grumbled angrily, *he doesn't know all that has happened to me. So what if I have changed, I don't owe him anything. I don't even know why he came.*

"Ah, you must be Mr. Tazman," exclaimed Druantia, already seated at the head of the table, as Parker entered the dining room. "Welcome to Magewebb Manor. I hope you will enjoy your stay."

She doesn't seem cold, thought Parker, as he took a seat in the chair Shamus had pulled out for him.

"Thank you, Lady Greenwick," he smiled politely.

"My pleasure, it is wonderful to meet one of Anabel's friends from home," added Druantia. She gave Nan a coy grin as she took her customary seat beside her great aunt.

"I seem to have arrived at an inconvenient time, though." Parker gave a pointed glance.

Unbelievable, Nan scowled.

"Oh nonsense, I'm sure Anabel is more than thrilled to have such a dear friend here and we have nothing pressing to occupy us otherwise. Do we Anabel?" Druantia smiled at Nan encouragingly.

"No, nothing," mumbled Nan in reply.

The three passed the rest of the meal in cordial conversation, primarily between Druantia and Parker, while Nan said little, consumed by her inner turmoil over the new turn of events. When dinner was through,

Nan and Parker said their goodnights to their hostess and then Nan led him back to his room in case he lost his way.

Nan mutely walked by his side, self-conscious due to Parker's earlier criticism and the awkward situation upon his unexpected arrival. When they reached the door to the room Shamus had given him earlier; Nan casually turned toward him and said, "Well, you must be jet legged. I'll let you get some rest and will see you in the morning."

Parker found Nan's continued standoffish mannerism infuriating. He shook his head in annoyance, opened the room's door, and yelled over his shoulder, "Yeah, whatever!" before slamming it in her face.

Eyes wide as a deer's in the headlights, Nan stared at the closed door in shock. Then stormed off to her own room down the hall and slammed her door in suit.

****

The next couple of days were filled with the same uneasy animosity between the two old friends, as Nan's budding romance with Oron continued. Most of her afternoons being spent in his company as they travelled over the English countryside, while Parker stayed behind, bored, to wander around Magewebb's grounds.

Why am I still here, he continued to ask himself. *It's obvious there is no place for me in Nan's new life.* But still he stayed and held on to the fleeting hope that the girl he loved would return to her senses and to him.

Meanwhile, Nan was no less confused over her heart's desires and the upheaval Parker's presence had created. She couldn't deny that looking into his familiar hazel eyes rekindle the torch she had held for him all these years, but at the same time just thinking of the pleasant afternoons she spent with Oron caused her stomach to knot and her skin to tingle. Was what she felt for Oron just lust or something else? What about Parker, was it-unspoken love or just deep platonic affection?

On the fourth evening after Parker's arrival, Nan returned to the manor after the cessation of another charmed filled afternoon with Oron and found Druantia in the ballroom attending to her wards' nightly needs. Glad Parker was nowhere in sight, the turmoil his presence produced unbearable, Nan sauntered over to her great aunt in the hopes of some diverting conversation.

Upon seeing her niece's approach from the corner of her eye, Druantia exclaimed, "Your friend is beginning to tire of your absence, Anabel."

Oh, here we go again, grumbled Nan in irritation. She sighed, but continued forward. As she reached down to pet Beowulf on the head, she replied, "Yes, I know. But it's not my fault, I didn't ask him to come here."

"Anabel!" Druantia turned with a sharp scowl. "Don't be so ungencrous. The boy obvious cares for you deeply, coming all this way, the least you can do is talk to him."

"Yes, I know," admitted Nan sheepishly.

"Perhaps you are spending too much time abroad with Oron," chided Druantia. "Your lessons and intentions to find your mother are suffering."

"I've been practicing the craft in my spare time," countered Nan in defiance. "And I can feel my powers growing, so don't worry. Besides, I'm remembering more of my old life and abilities every day. Plus I've been using my time with Oron to learn more about Meldun and the castle trying to gain clues. We actually had lunch there today."

At this Druantia arched an inquisitive eyebrow. "And did you discover anything?"

"Unfortunately no, I still can't sense her in the castle anywhere," Nan sighed in defeat. "But I could feel the malevolent presence I told you about before. Something or someone evil, besides Meldun, is in that castle."

"What of Meldun, was he present for this luncheon?" inquired Druantia, concerned.

"No, Gunther said he was otherwise detained," answered Nan. "How about you, have you learned anything from Hexia yet?"

"No, she has been avoiding me, the insufferable fowl," Druantia scowled.

"I'm surer than ever, that she has something to do with the dream I had."

"As am I," confirmed Druantia.

"Either way, there's one more place I want to search for my mother before I confront Meldun. The castle's dungeons and catacombs," announced Nan. "Oron has shown me everything else, but there so far."

"Perhaps there is a reason for that," challenged Druantia.

Nan glowered at Druantia for her continued pessimism towards the male delicacy, but before she could repeat that she was once again wrong, Cora entered the ballroom and announced dinner was served. Nan excused herself, stating she wanted to freshen up, and headed for the door.

"Perhaps Parker would like to freshen up as well. I believe he is in the garden with Shamus, why don't you fetch him. I honestly do believe he's out of sorts with all the attention you've been giving Oron," suggested Druantia before Nan left. Nan nodded and left the room.

"It's downright heartbreaking, watching that boy sulk around the place. He truly loves her, that one," observed Cora, no longer a servant but an old friend, as she walked towards Druantia.

"Yes, I know," agreed Druantia sombrely. "I just hope she realizes her own heart before it is too late."

"Perhaps it is time she learnt the truth," suggested Cora.

"The truth," moaned Druantia. "But what is the truth? No, she's not ready for it yet, my friend. She's had so much thrown at her; so much she needs to digest. It is not yet time to throw another log on the fire."

"She must be told sooner or later. It may prove better for both of them if it was sooner."

"The heart must find its way unhindered," Druantia schooled.

"Ah, but young Oron is…."

But Druantia cut her off, "That's enough, Cora."

Chapter 24
"...There is the heat of Love, the lover's whisper, irresistible-magic to make the sanest man go mad." Homer

Supper that night was another uncomfortable meal, with Parker and Druantia doing most of the talking. Nan excused herself right after the first course, feigning a headache, and headed straight for the sanctuary of her room. Exhausted from the inner battle she had been fighting the past couple of days; it wasn't long before Nan was asleep and entwined in a veil of dreams.

Nan's body involuntarily jerked up in bed, possessed. Her eyes burst open, glued straight ahead into the colourless room. Her mind raced with another's thoughts and vision, her body nothing but a vacant shell.

"Hwar for are I?" whispered Anwen in her strange surroundings. She flailed out from under the bedcovers to free herself and gazed down at her attire, confused to find she was still dressed in a brocade tunic gown and not just a shift for bed.

"Why for are I here? Tis not thy chamber," Anwen panicked and lunged for the bedchamber's door. "Tis one of thy master's tricks," she growled as she searched the hallway from the bedroom's open door for any concealed foes.

She stumbled out of the bedroom into the corridor in confusion. Her eyes darted frantically in their sockets, while she moved towards the east wing. "Hwar for tis Eliza? We must hasten, the time is upon us," she mumbled as her skirt swept the rugged floor behind her.

In his room, Parker laid on the undisturbed bed, restless, unable to sleep, his mind tormented over the disappointments he had suffered since his arrival. As he pondered whether he should stay and fight or call it a day, he heard steps in the hall.

It's three am, who would be walking around at this time of night. He frowned as he got to his feet and headed for the door, in the hopes of finding Nan on the other side. He opened the door and stuck his head into the hall. There Parker caught sight of Nan's rigid form as it slowly moved away from his room and down the dimly lit corridor to the landing.

"Nan," he called quietly, not wanting to wake up the rest of the house. But she did not answer, turn, nor halt. Instead, like a zombie, Nan continued to inch down the hall. Parker exited his room and followed.

Anwen raced down the hall. She felt as if she was being pursued, though she could see no one. "Thou can search all thou wishes, he shall never find thy secrets," she hissed. At the end of the east wing she turned to the right and entered her true bedchamber.

She surveyed the room for foul play, but was somewhat soothed by its customary warm glow from the flaming candelabra and burning hearth, which sent mystical shadows over the stonewalls.

"But hwar for tis Eliza, I cannot waste. Hexia must prepare," she sighed and cast a fretful glance over her shoulder to the open door, before she rushed across the bedchamber.

Parker stood on the threshold and squinted into the blackened dust filled room, where Nan now stood statuesque, as if frozen in time. "Nan," he called again, but got no answer. It was as if she wasn't there, despite her physical appearance.

Anwen reached the head of the plum taffeta draped box top canopy bed and dropped to the stone floor, heedless of her gown. She pressed her slight frame hard against the base of the stonewall, her muscles taut with strain and her breath coming out in pants. She was relieved by a faint whoosh of air as a square section of the wall gave way to reveal a secret passageway.

She gave one last apprehensive look over her shoulder. Then on her hands and knees, Anwen squeezed inside the black hole, before the grey blocks inched back into place, and disappeared.

Parker stood in front of Nan and peered into her cold dead eyes. His brow furrowed with worry. Then he grabbed her shoulders and shook Nan vigorously. "Nan!" he yelled.

With a start, Nan blinked as if coming out of a daze, her body softening under Parker's fingers. "Parker? What's going on, where am I?" she asked.

"You were sleepwalking," replied Parker. His hands dropped from her shoulders.

"I was?" questioned Nan, bewildered as she looked around Anwen's void room. It all came back to her. "But it felt so real," she mumbled, as she moved closer to the old unused bed.

"What did?" Parker frowned, his turn to be confused as he watched her.

"The dream or was it a memory?" she mumbled. She crouched at the bed's side in front of the stonewall. "But it was real; it was one of my memories," and slowly began to push on the wall.

"What?" asked Parker at her mutterings, "What are you talking about and what are you doing?"

"Help me," she yelped, the tension of her strained muscles seeping from her voice.

Immediately, though reluctant, Parker knelt down beside her and used his ample upper strength to move the cube cut-out of the stonewall within seconds. He stared into the crawl space astonished. "How did you know about this?"

"From Anwen's memories," answered Nan, distracted as she crawled through the secret opening.

"What? Who's Anwen?"

"It's a long story," she shrugged, though he could no longer see her inside the darker than night space. "Hey, do you have a light?"

Parker looked down at his bare rippling torso and jeans, and came back with an affirmative, sarcastic "No". "Why don't we do this in the morning, when there's light and you're better prepared?" he suggested to the impenetrable black hole.

"Yeah, alright," Nan's voice said in agreement. She crawled back through the hole and the slab closed into place as soon as Parker released it.

Nan sighed with disappointment as she followed Parker to the door. She gazed over her shoulder longingly at the wall where the now unperceivable secret passage was and yearned to discover its hidden truths and learn what they might have to do with her quest, but realized Parker was correct in that she needed more light to do so.

****

As they returned to the illuminated part of the manor and to her room, Nan didn't object when Parker presumptuously followed her inside in the hopes of having the conversation he so longed for, her mind still lingered on her past life vision.

As Nan closed the door, Parker looked around the impressive room. But when his gaze fell onto the glass terrarium and its inhabitant, he exclaimed, "Wow, you have a snake in your room?"

"Oh yeah, that's Onyx," Nan shrugged.

"But you hate snakes."

"No, I just misunderstood them, that's all," corrected Nan.

"Wow, you really have changed," grumbled Parker, as he turned away from the tank and moved deeper into the room.

"You don't know the half of it," mumbled Nan in return, more to herself then to him.

Parker caught what she said and whipped around to face her, her aloofness finally too much for him to bear. "What is going on with you? Why won't you just talk to me? And what are you still doing here, when are you coming home?"

"This is my home," answered Nan, surprised to hear herself say out loud what she had felt for quite a while. Parker's stunned stare burrowed holes into her soul. "You are right, I have changed."

"Why, because of him?" he fired back, a fury red tinge rose up his bare chest to his face. "Is it this place? Are you suddenly too good for your old lowlife friends?"

His words hurt and shocked Nan. She was horrified he would even think so little of her. "No, that's not it at all. And it has nothing to do with, Oron," she assured him.

"Yeah sure it doesn't, I've seen you drooling when you're around him. Like every other hussy when a pretty boy walks by." The words spewed out of Parker like venom as he pictured Oron's hands all over the body he so long coveted.

"How dare you!" shrieked Nan, her body began to tremble with rage. "You have no right to talk to me like that and you have no idea what I've been through since coming here. You just wouldn't understand."

"Cut the crap, Nan and just tell me the truth," he growled.

Flushed and flustered, Nan frowned, ignored his statement, and then fired back, "Why did you come here?"

"I came to get you," he replied, the passionate conviction thick in his voice.

"Why?" pressed Nan, still assuming her customary oblivion.

Parker decided it was his turn for ignorance and interrogated, "So what, you have a new boyfriend and are just going to forget about where you came from?"

"No, I barely even know, Oron," Nan huffed, annoyed at his continuous referral to a guy who in all honesty she completely forgot about when in Parker's company."I've changed. I'm not the same person. I don't know where I belong anymore."

"You belong at home."

"Do I?" she challenged. "What's back there for me? Dad's gone; I have no career, no family, nothing! So what's left?"

"You have me," he roared.

"What are you talking about?" grumbled Nan, as she turned away from him, growing uncomfortable.

"Oh come on Nan, enough with the games. Stop pretending you don't know," Parker stormed, almost at his breaking point.

"I don't know what you are talking about," she continued in denial. She turned back and stared him in the face with both anger induced hatred and passion and screamed, "Why did you come here?"

"Because I love you," bellowed Parker in return. Nan froze, speechless.

Unable to stand it any longer, Parker dove forward as if to attack. He took Nan about the waist in his arms and kissed her fiercely like his life was about to end.

Shocked at first, Nan's body stood rigid, until the flame of Parker's desperate embrace passed into her and she surrendered, opening herself up to her long smothered desires. She raised her hands to his face and gripped it between them to return his passion.

They broke free, gasped for breath, and clutched each other as the carnal fever penetrated between them. Nan lowered her hands from his face and slowly ran her fingers up and down Parker's muscular biceps. He closed his eyes against his lustful sight to steady his pounding heart.

He could fight off the urge no longer and pulled Nan's slender form hard against him, leaving no space between them. He lowered his lips once more to hers.

In a tight massaging grip, he moved his right hand farther up her back to consume every part of her figure like a blind man discovering unseen territory, while his left travelled south. Nan's body began to tremble with anticipated ecstasy and her rising temperature caused moisture to form under her clothes.

Nan released her lips from their jailer and said between heaving breaths, "I don't know if we should do this. You're my oldest friend; I don't want to lose you."

"That will never happen," reassured Parker before he touched his lips back to hers. With no more protests, Nan bent to her body's will and ever so slowly they moved back towards the awaiting bed.

Their bodies melted together as her fingers gently caressed the nape of his neck and his hands cupped her chest. Nan's breath caught in her throat as the walls around her heart gave way and electricity coursed through her veins.

They stopped at the bed's edge as they continued to explore each other's hidden canvases, peeling off clothes in a fit of frenzied desire. Completely exposed, they again mashed their bodies together and collapsed as one onto the bed's soft coverings.

With their passionate endeavours growing closer to the point of no return, Parker forced himself to break free, gazed into Nan's eyes, then asked, "Are you sure?"

Nan pulled him back down on top of her, wrapped her legs around him, then gave him a lustful nip on the ear and answered, "Yes."

Chapter 25
"As a man, casting off worn out garments taketh new ones, so the dweller in the body, enterth into ones that are new." Epictetus

Nan laid in bed and looked up at the canopy top, while Parker contentedly slept by her side with his arm draped over her naked stomach. Darkness veiled the bedroom as she listened to the rise and fall of his peaceful breaths, uncertain where they went from there.

What have I done? Could they go back to being friends and consider this night an impulsive mistake or would they be something more?

She needed space to think, but didn't want to rouse the man sleeping by her side. Nan gently lifted Parker's arm off her middle, rolled a little to get out of the way, and then placed it back down on the bed. Parker sighed, but did not wake. He flopped onto his back and resumed whatever dream he was having.

Satisfied he was still asleep, Nan inched her way out from under the covers and off the bed. Quietly she grabbed her strewn clothes and put them back on. Dressed, Nan tiptoed to the door and like a thief in the night opened it to flee.

Where are you going, Anabel? A voice in her head questioned. Nan jumped and looked back at the bed in alarm. Parker continued to sleep.

I'll be back, she sighed as realization crept in. She knew Onyx could understand her as she entered the hall and closed the bedroom door. *I just need some air.*

And I can ssssee why. Opened a can of wormsss haven't you? The snake hissed in her mind.

Oh shut up. Nan scowled at his mockery. *I know what I'm doing.* But the truth was, she had no clue.

Very well, but don't do anything esssle rasssh. It might not turn out to your benefit, cautioned Onyx.

All right, all right. Nan huffed, turned, and made her way down the hall to the east wing. The secret passage in Anwen's room was just the distraction she needed from her tormented mind.

Nan entered the dull room, the first hues of dawn colouring the leaded bay windowpanes, and moved across the room to the hidden passage. She dropped to her knees and pressed her weight against the stones to open it.

It took a lot of effort without Parker's brute strength, but soon the stone shifted. Nan cursed herself for forgetting a flashlight in her haste and crawled into the blackened hole. She stuck one of the pillowcases from the bed between the secret door and the wall it slid open against, in order to hold it in place.

Inside, Nan squatted on her knees and waited while her eyes adjusted to the barely visible space. The only source of illumination came from the small square cut entryway from the bedroom on the wall's other side. She tried to focus to the best of their abilities as her eyes panned the chamber and soon it became clear to Nan that she was in a makeshift bedroom.

The ceiling was low, almost too low for her to stand erect, which she found out when she rose to her feet and brushed her head on its smooth stones. The walls of the confined space were unadorned, bare stone. There was a tiny hearth made of rough rock, which had a cauldron attached to a wooden spit suspended over it, a wooden bed covered in straw, and an old rocking chair tucked away in the furthest corner beside a cradle.

"This is where Hexia lived while she cared for my baby, Druantia...Aunt Druantia's namesake," Nan spoke as the once barred memories of her past flowed freely in her mind.

"Okay, but how will this room help me find my mother?" she asked aloud. The sound of her voice helped to ebb off the portentous feel the black engulfed space gave her.

"Hexia will guide you, the dream had said, but how and to what? Think, Nan, think...remember," she urged herself.

Desperation gnawed at her gut. Nan scoured the hidden room for anything to spark her past memories. As she slowly moved around the cramped space, rummaging through the straw and the cradle cloth, glimpses of her former life weaved in and out of her sight.

It was clear to her now. Hexia use to rock in the chair sewing, while the child slept in its cradle and the cauldron bubbled over the warm flames of the hearth's fire. She could hear the familiar sound of her cherished infant crying through her bedchamber's stonewall and then the sweet soothing song the crone would sing to it in her thick Goidelic accent.

Nan took in a deep spell bound breath while the memories washed over her as if it all had happened only yesterday. There was no longer any doubt; Anwen was as much a part of her as Nan was to Anwen's memories. She belonged to both the present and the past, and longed to remain in them both, though she knew it was not possible.

Her memory now as sharp as ever, Nan whirled to face what was the outer wall of the room and knowingly dropped her gaze to the floor. She squinted until she could make out a rectangular hole in the stone floor, which opened up to a descending stairwell.

Even darker than the secret chamber itself, Nan blindly made her way down the walled-in spiralling staircase, never thinking she should have acquainted someone with her expedition before embarking on it alone.

Finally, she reached the bottom after what seemed like an endless winding journey through the manor's bowels. Nan braced her shoulder against a wall, unable to see but inches in front of her face, and explored the impenetrable space she had been delivered into.

I'm sure it's here somewhere, she thought. Her and Anwen's joint memories fresh in her mind as she ran her hands over the wall's cold limestone blocks. Soon her fingers struck a rough, splintered wooden surface.

Ah ha, I knew it was here. She moved her hands over the rudely constructed thick, oval shaped door, and soon alighted on the cast iron slide bolt lock, which secured it into place.

Nan wrestled the unused bolt free and pulled the strange little door open with a grunt. *This is Hexia's secret. This is how she'll guide me,* she triumphed as she knelt on all fours and crawled into the dirt etched man-made tunnel, which ran under the gardens of the manor. However, little did she know she was not alone.

Follow her, Gambit, commanded Onyx to the wolverine who had been tailing Nan unsuspected since she had left her bedchamber.

****

Parker awoke to the peaceful morning light streaming in through the windows of Nan's room. He rose up on his elbows and with a euphoric glow looked over to Nan's side of the bed. His face fell when he found it empty, blankets tossed aside and Nan nowhere in sight.

She snuck out of bed because she regrets sleeping with me, he thought dejectedly. He got out of bed and donned on his jeans to go in search of her. *I knew I shouldn't let it go that far. She wasn't ready.*

He left Nan's room, stopped and grabbed a shirt from his room, and then headed downstairs. On his way, he didn't spy Nan or anyone else in the house. Parker wandered all the way to the terrace doors at the manor's rear. Still no Nan. He exited and meandered down the garden path in hopes of finding some signs of humanity.

He heard the nay of a horse along with muffled voices and took the path leading to the sound. He walked until he came to the barn, where a cross looking Druantia and a disgruntled Shamus stood in a glaring standoff.

The two were paused in what seemed to be a somewhat heated discussion. However, upon seeing Parker's arrival, Druantia fixed a pleasant smile on her face and said, "Good morning, Mr. Tazman. Did you sleep well?"

"Yes, thank you," replied Parker. Beauty was tethered to a hitching post behind Druantia where she happily munched grass, while Shamus stood by broken fence rails that dangled from their posts.

"Splendid," she beamed. Then with a swipe of her hand toward the still sour looking Shamus and the obvious issue, she explained, "I'm afraid you have caught us in rather an unhappy pickle. Shamus and I were just discussing the best remedy to stop our darling Beauty here, from breaking through the fence during storms, which you can see we have failed to do so far."

"Yes, I see that," Parker smirked. He tried not to laugh in what was already a strained atmosphere.

"Daft beggar," grumbled Shamus, as he eyed the mare menacingly. In return he received an equally unimpressed expression from Druantia.

"Now, Shamus," she scolded, "Be kind to the old girl. If she had been in the barn during last night's storm where she ought to have been, then the fence wouldn't need mending, now would it?"

"Aye mistress." Shamus rolled his eyes as she turned her back on him to stroke the content mare, which made it almost impossible for Parker not to burst out laughing.

Parker got himself under control and asked, before the pair could continue their disagreement, "Have you seen, Nan?"

"Anabel?" replied Druantia as if to correct him. "No, as a matter of fact I haven't seen her all morning. Perhaps she has gone out once more with, Mr. Ravenwood," she added with a scowl.

Really, could she honestly be that heartless to spend the night with me and then go off with him? How could last night have meant nothing to her?

However, to Parker's relief, Shamus came to his rescue and after clearing his throat, objected, "Nay mistress, not ta soul has been here nor has the lassie gone out."

Druantia raised her brows in surprise and turned back to Parker. "Then she must be around here somewhere, perhaps she's in the library. I think we are pretty much done here, I'll go check." She nodded to Shamus. As she headed passed Parker, she paused and placed a caring hand on his shoulder. "Don't give up on her yet my boy. She will come to you in due time."

Parker stared at Druantia's retreating form and hoped what she said would prove true. Then he sighed and turned back to Shamus. "Do you want a hand, Shamus?"

****

Nan crawled through the claustrophobics nightmare. Her hands and knees ached from the hard, unevenly compacted earth all around her. It seemed like she had been crawling for hours. Sometimes it became so narrow she had to slither on her belly like a snake. *So this is what it feels like to be Onyx,* she mused.

Every now and then, Nan worried there was no end and she would be entombed in the never-ending tunnel, underground, lost forever. However, her memories would soon arrest her fear and she pressed on knowing there was a fate-finding destination somewhere. *Besides, I can still breath can't I, which means there's air getting in here from somewhere.*

After a while, Nan realized she wasn't as cramped in the deafening earth cylinder and had gained more headroom enabling her to stand. Her more than cramped muscles objected to the change in position at first, which caused her to inch up straighter by slow degrees.

Finally, Nan stood erect and moved from the dirt trodden tunnel end to the rock floor of a natural cavern. Thrilled to be free of the transgressing tunnel, she blinked against the faint sheen of daylight, which

195

her eyes were unaccustomed too after being so long in the dark. She stumbled forward into the cave's heart.

The recesses of the cave opened up to a large chamber burrowed into the rock that was like walking through the pages of the past, long ago inhabited by humans. It was a pagan sanctuary, away from the world and prying eyes, where Anwen and Hexia had been free to embrace their old ways and commune with nature without prosecution.

Nan now remembered it well as she looked around at its heather covered stone ledge bed and tattered remnants of a blanket, fieldstone fire pit in the room's centre with its hanging cauldron, and the collection of earthenware pottery, pestle and mortars, and other instruments strewn on natural rock ledges throughout the cavern. Painted runes adorned the walls like frozen pieces of history, untouched and preserved for generations to come.

This was our safe haven. The one place Ucrane's evil could not find us.

As Nan mournfully remembered, she moved through the conserved memory of her past to the cave's mouth, where she stopped and studied an ancient pictorial on the wall. It was her family's crest, the mark of their coven, the familiar pentagram entwined serpent.

Yes, we are all connected, she thought, as she ran a hand over the painted snake. *For we are all family. Anwen, Druantia, myself, and even Hexia; once my companion, my protector, my child's saviour, my ancestor.*

The door stood fully open in Nan's mind and there were no longer any unanswered questions. She stepped out of the cave into the late afternoon/early evening light (for she had been travelling underground for hours) and gazed around the brilliant autumn coloured, sacred oak nemeton. The place of her salvation and home to her heart, for there dividing its centre gurgled the river where her former lover's soul rested.

Nan remembered it all. Her heart and soul were finally one. She turned to the cave's side and climbed over the forest debris to the greatest mystery of all. Hidden in the rock's shadow, was a long pile of stones. Nan kneeled down before them and placed a hand on her true grave, the unknown place Hexia had laid her broken body after Ucrane had thrown her to her death.

A surge of energy shot up Nan's hand, making its way straight to her heart and all at once, a sense of peace engulfed her.

She looked above the trees at the horizon and took a deep breath. There perched like an unforgiving mythical shrine was Falconhurst castle. "Hexia guided me back to where it all began. Through the secret backdoor to hell," Nan uttered to the towering trees as she rose to her feet, ready to face the music. "My only chance to infiltrating the devil's dome, unannounced."

Chapter 26
"We learn from failure, not from success!" Bram Stoker

Gambit watched from the safety of the shadowed tree line as Nan crept towards the castle. Nan concealed herself by squatting beside one of the parked vehicles along the castle's drive. She surveyed the area for any sign of life. No one was a foot and knowing night would soon be upon her, she raced for the castle's steps.

Nan slipped in through one of the castle's immense doors, undetected, and skulked in the shadows until she was satisfied all was clear, then made her way to the fortress's bowels. She needed no guide, for the way was already imprinted on her memory.

It's too quiet, almost like the place is deserted.

Nan crept along the morbid passages of the castle's underground. However, as she descended deeper into the forgotten depths of the fortress, she had the same distinct feeling there were eyes watching her. *Druantia is right, I'm tempting fate, but I have to know if my mother is here.*

As Nan walked into the medieval corridor, which led to the dungeon, torch holders dotting its walls every few feet, she thought she heard the sound of footsteps behind her. She wheeled around and looked into the gloom to find her stalker, but saw no one. *Weird,* she thought as she turned back and continued down the winding stone-entombed walkway.

A loud resounding 'bang' echoed off the walls, followed by the metallic sliding of a bolt locking into place. Nan ran back up the corridor to its mouth and found the wooden door of the entrance shut. She rushed forward and pushed the door. She looked for its latch, but the door had no handle. It was locked from the outside.

"I'm trapped." Nan panicked in the stale dead space. With no other option, she edged forward down the dome topped narrow walkway, the putrid smell of century's worth of rotting flesh from the dungeon below assaulting her nostrils.

At its end, Nan found herself on a thin ledge, which overlooked a vast expansive torture cavity. Its victims' blood still stained the stone floor a dull red and the deads' foul odours clung to the little air the space contained. The only windows were three slits high on the dungeon's back wall, which had a single iron bar down their centres, barring any chance of escape. There was also no door, though Nan had not expected there to be.

As she moved to take the first step down the steep narrow stone staircase that led to the death chamber below, a prickling warning ran up Nan's spine. Something or someone was behind her.

She spun around, but it was too late. A shapeless black force with blazing hot eyes charged towards her out of the corridor's shadows. Nan screamed as the devilish entity lunged toward her and stepped back. The mass smashed into her and it hurled Nan backwards down the bone shattering steps. She landed at the bottom unconscious, battered, and bloody.

****

The sun made its gradual descend to the west as Parker and Shamus headed back to the manor after the day's labours. Druantia exited the terrace door to meet them and exclaimed in a panic, "There you two are. I haven't been able to come across Anabel anywhere. Have you seen her yet?"

"No." Parker was now concerned.

"This is quite unusual for her and what's even stranger is that Gambit and Hexia are missing as well."

"Maybe she's gone exploring in that secret passage she found," suggested Parker, as the memory of the previous night's odd exploits before they tumbled into bed came back in his head.

"What secret passage?" scowled Druantia.

"The one in that old bedroom at the end of that dusty hall." But Druantia didn't hear Parker's reply for at that moment a voice in her head answered. *She has gone down the trail of old, to Falconhurst, where her doom still lies,* Hexia's inaudible caw came.

Thank you, my friend, she replied before she looked back up at the men sharply.

"I know where she is," stated Druantia. "Shamus hitch Beauty up, there's no time to lose."

****

Anabel. Wakeup Anabel. A sweet siren's call sounded in Nan's mind.

199

Her reluctant lids opened and Nan looked into a world of fog. All except the glowing white form, which stood inches in front of her. *I'm dreaming,* her hazed over mind thought.

No daughter, but you must get up, the ghostly woman instructed.

Mom? The image in front of her resembled the photograph Nan had seen in her father's desk.

Get up, Anabel. You must get up, your purpose is not done, her mother's spectre spoke.

Nan's mind cleared as things began to come into focus. As she went to turn a searing pain shot through her body and jolted her into awareness. She was lying on the hard stones at the foot of the dungeon stairs in an awkward position. Nan tried to rise to her feet as instructed, but a new bout of agonizing pain shot through her like an impaling rod.

Nan looked up to where her mother's apparition had stood, but was now gone. *She was here, she actually came to help me.* Warmed by the thought, Nan refocused and began taking inventory of her state. She painfully tried to move or raise each individual body part to see what was damaged.

After much strain and anguish, Nan diagnosed based on the pain's sources, that apart from a nasty gash on the back of her head, she quite possibly suffered from bruised or broken ribs, a broken left wrist, dislocated shoulder, and judging from the immobile throb in her lower right leg, a fractured femur as well.

"I guess that's what happens when you fall down eighteen flights of stone stairs," she remarked sourly.

Nan clamped her mouth shut tight in determination and used her good limbs to prop her back up against the wall and then gingerly inched her way up until she was in a standing position. Perspiration dripped down her face as a dizzying vertigo engulfed her head.

Nan sucked in a sharp breath at the pain and surveyed the dungeon chamber to try and form a plan in her throbbing mind of what to do next. Almost too dim to see anything, Nan squinted through the dense light at the ginormous room's hidden horrors. Not present at the time of the gruesome happenings, Nan had heard stories of Ucrane's torturous ways, but as she looked around the room now, it all became bitterly real.

The blood red stones under the Virgin of Nuremberg and Judas Cradle spoke of their victim's pain. The age-old rack and iron shackles on the walls still held the skeletal limbs of poor tormented souls. Heaps of human remains and cloth fragments littered the room's darkened corners and a pile of ash lay under the Brazen Bull.

But what caused Nan's stomach to heave most, were two long wooden tables in the room's centre laid out like a surgeon's prep, containing thumbscrews, a scold's bridle, knee splitters, a heretic's fork, head crushers, breast rippers, a pear of anguish, and many more torturous devices she didn't even want to imagine the purpose for.

Innocent people, witches, had been ripped, spiked, crushed, burned, and genuinely tormented within these unforgiving walls. With no one even able to hear them scream for help. Nan could feel them all, their haunted souls still trapped in their death prison, calling out to her for help.

This is all my fault, she mused remorseful. *They suffered, as did my family, because of my curse. The curse I put on Ucrane that fateful night which started a chain reaction of death and destruction. I have to release them, but first I need to find a way out of here before I become one of them.*

Nan felt the warmth of blood trickle down the back of her neck. She knew her one good limb was too weak to support her weight, so she looked to the rubble on the floor for anything to aid her plight. Nan slid further along the wall with her back pressed firmly against it for support, until she reached a pile of boards and old rags.

Glad for the use of her right arm, Nan leaned to her right, trying not to throw herself off balance, and pulled a propped up board a bit smaller than her shoulder, further up the wall and placed it beside her. Then with a shudder, she grabbed a tattered piece of dirty cloth from the pile (no doubt once belonging to some deceased peasant) and wrapped it awkwardly around her wounded head.

Her chances slightly improved, Nan pushed herself off the wall using the board as a crutch and hobbled through the dungeon in search of a means of escape. A shiver of disgust shook her battered bones as she passed other horrible devices and darkened cells containing the hollow dead eyes of skeletal prisoners. As she rounded a bend just after the staircase, she entered another large chamber full of similar cells and instruments. *Does this place never end,* grumbled Nan as she turned down another hallway of cells.

Nan's gimpy movements ceased as she let out a scream loud enough to wake the dead in their cells. There at the hall's end, staring straight at her was an iron barred coffin in the shape of a human form. The agonizingly distorted, rotting, bug eaten remains of a woman could be discerned locked inside. Her dead red straw-like hair still clinging in patches to her bare exposed scalp and her spring-patterned dress, soiled with bloodstains and excrement.

"Mom," Nan simpered, as she tried to suppress the urge to vomit. Tears streamed down her cheeks as she stared at the horrific sight in front of her. Her mother's obvious suffering was written on her fleshless, contorted face. Abandoned and forgotten to succumb to a paralyzing slow death and then decay in her iron coffin.

Unable to bear the sight of her mother's hollow eyes, Nan turned her gaze to the floor. *I found her, but now I wish I hadn't. It was her ghost who helped me. Trapped here like the rest of Meldun's/Ucrane's victims. No matter how hard she tried in the end she still couldn't escape this family's evil, none of them could. Well I'm going to stop it!*

Nan felt she should do something with her mother's remains, but knew there was no time and she was in no condition to try. She gave the woman she had so yearned to know, a last mournful glance and remorsefully turned back to the mouth of the hall. Nan struggled back into the heart of the dungeon, her strength depleted and hopes lost, replaced by despair and weakness.

She gazed around the ten-foot stonewalls, which surrounded her and sighed, "I'm never getting out of here, just like my mother."

Then, the distinct sound of wings caught Nan's attention and she searched the room for its source. In one of the barred holes at the top of the back wall, she saw the familiar black plumage of her great aunt's raven.

"Hexia?" she uttered in disbelief, as she hobbled closer to the bird's perch. "How did you find me?"

We have been watching you, Gambit and I, a voice explained in Nan's head. *I knew you'd remember our secret passage and all would fall into place, but it seems you have fallen astray.*

"Yes, I was caught off guard, but why didn't you tell me about the tunnel sooner. Why have you been acting like I'm a stranger, old friend?" asked Nan aloud, too tired to communicate with her mind, but knowing the raven could understand her.

You needed to find the memories on your own, the raven replied. *Only you could unlock the truths of the past.*

"But you were once my protector, my family, Hexia. Why watch me struggle? Perhaps you could have prevented this," continued Nan, as she motioned with her head at the dingy chamber she was now a prisoner in.

I am. And I am here to help you. You need to finish your mission, the bird answered.

"And how am I supposed to do that, look where I'm standing. I'm trapped, I'm defeated once again...history repeating itself," retorted Nan bitterly.

No all is not lost, for there is a way out. I was once a prisoner of these very walls after your death, but I escaped, as you will today. There in the far corner the wall is false. Though it appears flush, a small portion is set back leaving a thin crack for one to slide through and will lead you out into the trees.

Amazed, Nan eyed the seemingly normal walled corner and then laboured towards it. "Thank you, my old friend."

But wait, Hexia called out. *There is something you must do first, listen.*

Nan halted and gave the raven a scrutinizing stare. She listened to the soundless dark recesses of the dungeon. Just as Nan was about to turn back and proclaim the bird daff, a faint muffled sound, almost inaudible, was heard in the dimness. Like a mouse moving through the room.

Nan gave it her full attention. She listened and soon heard the distinct sound of movement, of breathing. "There is someone else down here!"

Chapter 27
"You must suffer me to go my own dark way."
Robert Louis Stevenson

Nan pushed her hearing to its limits to try and locate the muffled sounds from within the otherwise deafeningly silent prison. She turned back to the iron barred window to ask Hexia for help, but was surprised to find the raven was gone.

"I guess I'm on my own," she muttered in the gloom. Nan mustered her weakening strength in order to hobble back into the dungeon's belly in search of the breathing's owner.

Nan's head felt woozy and the acute pain attached to her every move was causing a strained bile to rise up her gullet. Even the aiding materials she had found were beginning to falter as she felt a trickle of blood drip down her neck from the soaked rag and the blunt pressure from the thick piece of board had begun to bruise her armpit.

I've got to get out of here and soon, she acknowledged.

Nan searched for any sign of movement. In an uncertain tone, she called out, "Hello, is anyone there?" but got no reply.

Sight lent no aid in the almost impenetrable area as Nan stumbled through the depressing chamber. Frustration caused her to drop her eyes to the floor. *It's hopeless, no one is down here. It was probably just a mouse.* However, just as the thought crossed her mind, Nan noticed the round iron grated top of an oubliette not more than seven feet in front of her.

No way. There's no way someone could be down there, is there?

Nan wobbled forward and looked down the ebony dark pit. "Hello, is anyone down there?" she called, but got no response.

"Please, I'm here to help. Is anyone down there?" she tried again. She was out of options and time was ticking on her body's own state.

Several minutes passed without a sound, but just when Nan was about to give up and press on, a whisper rose from the pit. "I'm here, please help me."

Nan's mind jumped into overdrive at the reply. *O.m.g., there's a real person in there!*

She scrambled to figure out how exactly she was going to pull this rescue off in her current state. Nan whipped her head in all directions trying to form a plan. A bunch of ropes attached to a pulley system fixed to the ceiling caught her attention. Nan forced her exhausted muscles to move across the room to it. "Stay there, I'm going to get you out of there," she said over her shoulder.

What a dumb thing to say! As if they can go anywhere.

Nan grabbed a large blade from one of the disembowelling tables as she passed and cut free a good portion of the aged rope, then returned to the grate. She awkwardly dropped her battered body to the stone floor, hoping she could get back up after. Nan bit her lower lip and winced at the pain as she laced the fingers of her right hand through the grate's bars and heaved upward with all her might.

The rusted iron didn't budge. Worried her depleted strength was going to prove inefficient, Nan took a couple more deep breaths and gave it one last effort. She pulled with all her might. Suddenly the iron surrendered and soon it rested flat beside the open pit.

Nan threw her head back in tired relief. She grabbed the rope, wrapped one end around her waist, held tight to its end with her good arm, and dropped the rest of into the invisible depths of the hole. "Grab hold and try to climb your way up," Nan called down the hole. Without a word, the rope became taut and she felt the tension on her end. Nan braced herself the best she could and hauled the unseen figure out of the darkness.

Nan held strong for what felt like an eternity before she saw a bony hand emerge from the pit and grip the stone edge of the oubliette. Another followed and grabbed the exposed rope to haul its attachment up and soon an emaciated female form appeared out of the person-sized hole. Unable to offer the fragile woman a hand at the risk of letting go of the rope, Nan watched until she was safely free of the pit and then released her supporting hold of the rope with drained pleasure.

"Are you alright?" asked Nan, as she heaved a tired breath from the exertion it took to keep herself from tumbling into the pit as the woman climbed to her freedom.

Nan eyed the victimized woman with sympathy, huddled on the stone floor in soiled rags, which smelled heavily of urine. Her knee length, tangled petrified white hair and ghostly pale almost translucent skin drawn tight over protruding bones, made it hard for Nan to discern her age. However, what was sadder than the rest was the woman's unblinking clouded over unseeing eyes, the years of darkness having robbed her of her sight.

"Yes," the timid, helpless creature replied.

Unable to help herself, Nan blurted out, "How long have you been down there?"

"I'm not certain," the woman replied. "What year is it?"

"2010," answered Nan.

"Oh my," the woman exclaimed, "For many years then." Then, the woman tilted her blind head in Nan's direction and asked, "Who are you?"

"My name is, Nan."

"Mine is, Gwynedd," the woman announced. All the blood drained from Nan's veins.

Could it really be? Could this tattered heap of a woman be my mother's long lost sister? Nan's mind was bursting with questions. *How has she survived? Did she know that only a few feet away her sister was trapped in a coffin left to die?*

"Thank you for helping me, Nan. I've spent so long in the dark. The loneliness was beginning to consume my hope of ever escaping," Gwynedd's soft voice stated.

Nan decided to keep her true identity a secret for the time being to prevent the multitude of questions it would procure and peered at her aunt's morbid face. "You're welcome. Do you think you can walk?"

"I believe so," answered Gwynedd uncertain, having had little use for her legs for some years in her stone well of a forgotten grave.

"Good, I know of a way out, but will need your help. You see I fell and am badly injured."

"I'll do what I can, but need you to be my eyes," assured Gwynedd.

Unsteadily the two harden soldiers got to their feet with each other's help and with Nan's direction and Gwynedd's support, made their way to the far corner of the dungeon where Hexia had indicated the false wall to be.

"Wait!" yelped Gwynedd abruptly, halting their steps. "My sister, Rhiannon, she's trapped down here too, I have to go back for her."

So she did know. Sorrow stricken, Nan gulped back the lump in her throat at Gwynedd's display of sisterly devotion. She thought of her mother's wretched corpse in the iron coffin and a stray tear ran down Nan's cheek. "I'm so sorry, Gwynedd, but she's dead," she regrettably said.

"Oh no," sobbed Gwynedd. "I couldn't help her, though I tried. But what could I do from that pit? I tried to give her hope. I should have assumed the truth. I have not heard her cries now for some time."

Nan's heart felt like it was being ripped from her chest. *Oh, the poor woman, imprisoned herself and then having to listen to her sister suffer as well.*

"I'm so sorry," repeated Nan. She gave Gwynedd's shoulder a consoling squeeze since her arm was draped over her for support. "There was nothing you could have done, now come on, let's get you out of here. She wouldn't have wanted you to die here as she did."

Gwynedd nodded her sorrowful head in agreement and once again braced her scrawny frame to support Nan's surprisingly superior weight. They slid out the crevice in the back wall and vanished down a mason carved passage through the winding entrails of the cliff to freedom.

****

They emerged an hour or so later into the night veiled thick wooded grove. Exhausted Gwynedd and Nan stopped to rest, panting from the exertion of the long trike. "We did it, Gwynedd, we're free," Nan smiled.

Though glad to be free in the world once more, the unfamiliar sounds caused the unseeing Gwynedd to start and shy away. "I owe it all to you," she replied.

Nan was glad for the reprieve, her body's mind numbing pain gnawing at her insides. However, the knowledge they still had far to go made Nan rally the last of her remaining strength and regain Gwynedd's frightened but elated attention to set off again through the trees in search of a road or a way back to civilization and help.

To Nan's surprise, they soon stumbled out of the trees onto the shoulder of a road and almost collided right into the back of a stationed man. Nan gasped, ready to bolt back to cover amongst the trees and drag poor Gwynedd with her. But then she all but shrieked with elation when the man spun around at hearing their clatter and exclaimed, "Nan."

"Parker! Oh am I glad to see you," Nan chirped. She wished she could throw her arms around him.

"What happened to you?" he asked in alarm as he took in Nan's broken state and rushed to her side where he replaced Gwynedd's supporting hold with his own.

"It's a long story. Let's just say I had a little mishap with a staircase, but I'm fine," answered Nan.

"You're far from fine," he rebuked. After a minute he gave Gwynedd a questioning glance and added, "Nan what is going on? How did you get here and why did you leave without telling anyone? And who is this?"

"I know, I know. I'm sorry. I should have told someone where I was going, but it all happened so fast," Nan apologized. Not wanting to waste time talking, but realized she owed him an explanation, she added, "I found Gwynedd in the dungeon and we helped each other escape."

"Dungeon! What dungeon?" Parker bellowed in horror.

"There's no time for that now. I promise you I'll explain everything later, but first we have to get Gwynedd out of here," stated Nan. "How did you get here? And where's Druantia?"

"Druantia," squeaked Gwynedd in uncertain shock.

"Yes, I'll explain later," replied Nan.

"We need to get you to a hospital," interrupted Parker, as he looked at the bloody rag wrapped around Nan's head and then eyed Gwynedd's strange state. "Both of you. Come on, Druantia's just down the road a bit waiting."

"She is, but how did you guys know I was here?" questioned Nan in surprise.

"I don't know, she muttered something about the animals were missing," he answered with a frown. "She is pretty weird sometimes."

Hexia told her. Nan smiled to herself as Parker's bracing arms helped her stiffened frame up the shoulder of the road to where Druantia and Shamus sat waiting in the cart. Gwynedd followed behind with a trembling hand placed on Parker's shoulder for guidance.

Druantia (who had been waiting impatiently while Parker scouted out the forest surrounding the castle for any signs of Nan) perked up at the sight of the party's slow approach, then launched herself out of the parked buggy and rushed towards them.

"Oh, Anabel, thank goodness you're alright, you foolish girl," exclaimed Druantia, as she grabbed her great niece's battered body in a tight hug, unhindered by her British mannerism, almost squeezing all the air out of her. "What were you thinking, coming out here all alone?"

"I'm so sorry, but I figured out the clue, what Hexia was guiding me to and went for it. It was the secret way into the castle. To find my mother," Nan relayed in triumphant exasperation. "I can do it now, I can destroy Meldun."

"Not like this you won't," Parker spat disgruntle, before Druantia had a chance to ask any questions or form a reply.

As Druantia released her great niece and leaned away from her in the process of saying something, her eyes fell on the unimposing silent figure, which skulked behind Parker.

"Can it be, is it really true?" Druantia stammered. She moved towards a timid and confused Gwynedd. "Gwynedd, my dear, is it really you? Oh praise the gods you're safe!" Druantia didn't wait for a reply, she lunged forward and grabbed the unsuspecting woman up in her arms as if to never let her go again.

"Aunt Druantia?" whispered Gwynedd in acknowledgement.

"Oh how I searched for you my dear. I looked, but I couldn't find you. I failed you and I'm so sorry," sobbed Druantia, overwhelmed by it all."But how, how have you survived?"

The bittersweet reunion caused tears to stream down both their cheeks. Filled with regret and tragedy, Gwynedd broke down and the sorrow of her life exploded from her. "I'm sorry, it was my fault. I should have listened to you and stayed close to the house, like you have done all these years. But then he grabbed me and I couldn't escape from the dark. I tried. I tried to use my powers but the grate would not budge. All I could do was bend rainwater to my will and summon rats to sustain me. And then Rhiannon was there...and I heard her screaming night and day...but I couldn't get to her...and now...and now she's dead."

"Shush, shush, my dear. It is alright now, you're safe. Everything will be okay. It's not your fault," cooed Druantia in an attempt to sooth the stricken Gwynedd as she stroked her ivory hair.

Druantia turned her head to look at Nan's sorrowful expression. "I'm so sorry, Anabel," she said mournfully.

"What is she talking about? What is going on?" asked Parker quietly, as not to disturb the distraught women.

"In the dungeon I found my mother's body," whispered Nan, to prevent Gwynedd from hearing her.

"Oh I'm sorry, Nan," Parker sighed.

"It's okay, but right now we need to get out of here. Druantia take Gwynedd back to Magewebb and keep her safe. I'm going to go back to the castle and finish what I started," announced Nan to the stoic audience.

"No you're not," objected Parker, as he held Nan's broken body in his power. "You need a hospital."

"I have to put an end to this Parker. I'm the only one who can," she tried to reason.

"You can't even walk on your own," he argued.

"Parker, he killed my mother. He killed my whole family. He killed me. And look at what he did to Gwynedd. He's got to be stopped," Nan fought back.

"He killed you? Nan what are you talking about? What is going on? See now you're delusional. You need a doctor." He turned to Druantia and pleaded, "Talk some sense into her."

The elder witch looked Nan straight in the eyes, smiled her knowing grin, and said, "I know you can do this, but be careful *mon ami*."

"I will," Nan smiled in return.

"Are you kidding me?" grumbled Parker. "I won't let you," he added steadfast.

"Parker, come on," exclaimed Nan, annoyed. "I don't have time to argue."

"Fine, but I'm coming with you."

"But…," she began to stammer.

"No, I'm coming with you!"

Chapter 28
"Fight on, brave knight! Man dies, glory lives! Fight on; death is better than defeat! Fight on brave knights! For bright eyes behold your deeds!" Walter Scott

"You should have gone with them," grumbled Nan, as they made the slow trike up the long climbing road to Falconhurst. Parker's strong build supported the brunt of her crippled weight, while the pain still gnawed at her mind. Druantia and Shamus had disappeared into the night to ferry Gwynedd back to the safety of Magewebb.

"Yeah okay, because you could have walked this alone," remarked Parker sarcastically. "Now that we're alone and have a long walk ahead of us, why don't you tell me what's going on?"

"There's too much to tell and you'd never believe me if I told you," she fluffed off.

"Try me," groaned Parker in annoyance, as he adjusted his pace to better suit her hampered steps.

"Fine," huffed Nan, too tired to argue.

The rest of the slow march up to the castle, Nan related all the bizarre details of her adventures to a silent Parker. From her arrival in England, to her unusual introduction to Druantia, about the story of Anwen and Ucrane, of how Ucrane was now Meldun, how everyone in her family were witches, that she was in fact a witch, and last but not least how she was Anwen in another life and held all Anwen's memories inside of her.

Once she had finished her tale, Nan waited for Parker to declare she was crazy and say he wanted nothing more to do with her. She closed her eyes in expectation of the unpleasantness to come.

"Is that all?" Parker chuckled.

"What do you mean?" she baulked in disbelief.

"Is that what you've been so afraid to tell me? That your family is messed up, you believe in past lives and weird stuff, and think you're a witch?" he laughed.

Nan was flabbergasted by his unexpected reaction. "Isn't that enough? Don't you think it's totally insane?"

"Of course I do," teased Parker. "You've always been weird Nan....you know, different. But that's what I love about you. You're not like other girls."

"So you don't care that I'm a witch?" she asked, shell-shocked.

"I wouldn't care if you thought you were the queen of the fairies. I still love you," he replied in earnest. He stopped, then turned and gazed deep into Nan's sea grey eyes to press his point.

"But I've changed so much. I'm not the same person I was," she objected.

"I don't care how much you've changed, you're still the same girl to me," he reassured, as he stroked a stay hair off her face with his free hand. He yearned to kiss her again, but was unsure after the silence between them about the events of the prior night if it was wise.

He really does love me. Nan felt herself tear up at Parker's unwavering devotion. *How have I not seen it all these years?* However, in truth Nan knew she hadn't missed it, but had turned a blind eye, unready for what it would create between them.

Nan had almost forgotten their destination and her purpose, absorbed in the pungent chemistry between them, when suddenly the castle's stones assaulted her view. They proceeded on until they came to a stop in front of the siege stopping doors.

"Now what?" inquired Parker.

Nan took a deep breath in anticipation for the reaction she was about to get. "Now I want you to go hide."

"What?" Parker growled indignantly. He scowled at her pleading look.

"Please, just do as I ask," she groaned. "I have to do this alone and I can't go in there thinking you might be in danger."

"I'm not a coward, Nan. I don't go and hide like a little girl," protested Parker.

"I know that and that's why I want you to hide. I don't need you charging in there like a raging bull when I'm trying to fight, Meldun. I have to do this alone. I know what I'm doing," she tried to reason.

"But how are you going to stand, let alone walk in there on your own?" he countered.

"I can do it," answered Nan. She gave him an intense stare.

"Oh fine," huffed Parker reluctantly. "But I'll be close."

"I wouldn't want it any other way," Nan smiled.

Ever so slowly, Parker unwrapped Nan's arm from around his neck. He held his hands on her waist for a couple minutes while she adjusted her weight to stand alone to make sure she was steady and then he gave her an encouraging grin and disappeared into the moonless black night.

****

Nan closed her eyes to block out her body's pain. She reached deep inside herself for the powers of old. She pushed her mind to its furthest limits. *Help me my friend.* Her silent message called out.

Keep ssstrong, Anabel. I am here. Feel my ssstrength in you, she heard the hissing voice reply.

Thank you, Onyx, my friend, Nan smiled. Her body's battery life renewed as if put on charge. But then another spoke in her ear.

Remember his treachery and keep sharp. He is capable of anything as you well know.

Hexia? Nan questioned in astonishment.

Yes, I'm with you my child, as are we all, the raven answered.

With the energizing guidance of the ancestral guardians' coursing through her, Nan focused all her attention and strength into her hands and reached forth with her movable arm. *Well here goes nothing.* Palm raised, Nan commanded the doors to open in her once native tongue, "*Ar agor.*"

As if struck by a wrecking ball the gigantic armour plated doors burst off their hinges. Wood splinters and pieces of iron littered the floor of the entry hall.

Unphased by this miraculous feet, a mere flicker of her true powers, Nan walked into the castle as if no bones had ever been broken. She gazed around the fortress's unusually unlit shadows. "Ucrane!" she bellowed.

All was still, not even a bug crawled on the flagstone floor. "Ucrane," Nan hollered louder.

As if rising from the unholy depths of the netherworld itself, the malicious murderous feign appeared at the top of the stairs. "You have come at last, my sweet. Welcome home," he said into the eerie silence, his fingers laced in a pondering way as if considering a move in a game of chess.

"Let's get this over with once and for all, Ucrane. Or would you rather I call you Meldun?" taunted Nan.

His dark wolfish eyes blazed as his face cracked into a menacing grin. "Ah all pretences aside I see, very well, my love."

"Ha, love! Oh yes and that's why you threw me to my death when I wouldn't do your bidding. Well I am not your wife anymore, you have no power over me," Nan raged.

"You needed to be put in your place, that's all," retorted Ucrane, as he glided down the stairs towards her like a descending spider. "But have it your way, I ridded myself of you once, witch, I can do it again."

Nan felt her power swirl inside her with the rise of her rage. "Come get me then."

Ucrane rushed forward. A red glow suddenly illuminated the room as if from the gates of hell. Nan lowered her head and glowered at the approaching tiger. The Welsh words of the ancient curse filled her soul and she began to chant.

Yr hyn unwaith Dechneuwyd, bellach wedi'i gwblhau
Ni ehaiff unrhyw hud llesteirio cyfiawnder wyf yn gofyn am
Tanau o ddicter, trowch esgyrn i lludw

Nan braced herself for any counter attack Ucrane might try while she recited, but her voice was hushed when Oron's tall handsome figure caught her attention as he stepped out of the shadows.

"Oron get out of here, it's not safe, run," Nan called out, but he stood fast.

His mouth twitched into a wicked smile. "The only monster I see here is you."

Abashed, Nan stared at him transfixed. For the first time she saw a strange dark hatred in his charming features. "What?" she squeaked, "No he's dangerous, Oron, you must leave. He killed my mother."

Oron laughed like a triumphant crow from a treetop. "No he didn't, I did."

"No, it's not true," stammered Nan. She felt dazed. "It couldn't be…he's the one…he's our family's enemy…why would you…but why?"

"To watch her suffer," replied Oron. "To watch as each day the life drained out of her starved putrid form. To hear her scream and plead for life."

"But why? I thought you and I felt...I defended you," she continued puzzled. All of Druantia's warnings sprang to mind. Had she known about Oron's treachery? Why had she not told her?

"You thought what I wanted you to," Oron grinned. He relished in Nan's confusion.

"But why," she repeated, saddened by his unexpected revelations.

"For penance," he answered, "Revenge for the child she tossed away without a thought or care. The son she deemed unworthy of her motherly love."

"Son?" Nan frowned. Then the initials on her mother's locket and the name penned on Druantia's letters flashed in her mind. *Rhiannon Ravenwood. Ravenwood, her first husband's surname,* Nan deciphered as the clues all became clear. Why hadn't she put it together before?

"Oron Ravenwood...you're my mother's son from her first marriage...you're my brother," whispered Nan incredulously.

"Yes, discarded by our mother like a used tissue, while she went off and made a new family," growled Oron, his words dripped with hatred for the corpse below their feet.

"But we can start anew," pleaded Nan. Her sibling revealed, a spark of hope in her heart built at the thought of a new type of intimacy between them, a family blood bond.

"We can..." but she was cut-off when the revelling spectator of the drama, Ucrane, bellowed, "Enough talk, Oron, finish her!"

Still stunned, Nan didn't know what to do next. She wanted so desperately to extend an olive branch to her berated sibling. However, Oron needed no more encouragement. He leaned forward with his arms outstretched towards her and chanted some dark verses.

Nan stiffened in horror. She braced herself as much as possible for the power blow soon to come, but then Oron went soaring across the room. His electrified dark magic orb whizzed inches away from Nan's head as she ducked and watched Parker's broad shoulder plough like a ramming goat into Oron's side, expelling all the air out of his lungs.

The two men collided to the floor where they struggled to achieve the upper hand. However, with his moose-like frame compared to Oron's leanness, Parker had him kissing the floor in no time as he drove his right fist hard into Oron's jaw.

"Hurry," yelled Parker to Nan, which brought her back to her senses.

Nan turned her attention back to Ucrane, who had been caught off guard by Parker's unexpected attack. She summoned her powers once again and continued with the curse, repeating.

Yr hyn unwaith Dechneuwyd, bellach wedi'i gwblhau
Ni ehaiff unrhyw hud llesteirio cyfiawnder wyf yn gofyn am
Tanau o ddicter, trowch esgyrn i lludw

A dark fog grew around Ucrane, an evil sorcery forming into a hideous black shadow. It was the same demonic mass with red laser eyes, which had assaulted Nan in the dungeon.

Boudicca, Nan knew, feeling her former sister's presence.

Not wavering from her spell, Nan watched both man and demon loom in front of her. She felt her enchantment working and relished in her triumph as the souls of the tormented began to rise to freedom from their cells below. Outraged at the sight of his victims' escape, Ucrane thrust his arm in Nan's direction and ordered his wraith to attack. "Boudicca, finish her."

Finally, after a lifetime of delay, it was sister versus sister. Nan lifted her hand to meet the charging spirit and a blue ball of power collided with Boudicca's hell red energy. Nan closed her eyes, focused on the division of her power and continued to chant.

Llawn o lid, dial yn felys
Ar fy gelyn, yr wyf yn bwrw boen hon
Ar gyfer y gweithredoedd efe a gyflawnwyd, a wnaed yn ofer

The power of Nan's words circled Ucrane and he pitched forward in paralyzing pain. The curse's affects possessed his body, while the raging sisters' fight blazed forth in a consuming light wave. The castle's stones shook and flames suddenly sprouted up all around them. Nan drove her spell home.

Rwymo ef, gwasgu arno, dod ag ef i'r llawr
Poenydio ef, llosgi arno, gadewch ei cymalau hylosgi
Gyda hecs hwn gall byth yn dychwelyd

The last of the words surged from her lips and Nan's power embalmed Ucrane full force. An ear-piercing shriek came from the monstrous immortal man as his skin cracked and flaked to the floor. His joints stiffened, his scalp began to smoke, and finally as if a huge boulder had fallen on him, Ucrane's whole form collapsed to the ground in a pile of ashes. He was gone.

With her energy-feeding source gone, Boudicca's spirit dwindled under Nan's purify blue force. Her own ball of power faded as she grew smaller. Then with a haunting screech of rage, Boudicca disappeared. The fight was over.

Nan's power inspired strength left her and she fell to the floor, the pain and weariness of her injuries once again washed over her. Parker had watched the mesmerizing, unbelievable spectacle from the corner where he retained Oron's unconscious body by leaning on him like a pillow. At the sight of Nan's collapse and the alarming speed the consuming flames (which had developed from the battle between good and evil) were devouring the castle's foyer, Parker jumped to his feet and raced heroically across the room. He scooped Nan's limp, tired body up in his arms.

"We have to get out of here," he said and raced out the ruined doors.

Out in the crisp open air, clouds of smoke billowed out of every orifice of the castle and caused the sky to hang heavily grey. Parker headed for the nearest vehicle with Nan tight in his arms. He tried a couple of doors, but found them all locked. Plopping Nan on the hood of a red Austin Martin, Parker walked around to the driver's door. With one punch, he smashed the window out of the car, bloodying his knuckles, and unlocked the door.

Thanks to his less than admirable teen years, he soon hotwired the car, pushed the power lock button to unlock the rest of the doors, grabbed Nan off of the hood, and installed her safely in the passenger-seat.

"Wow, I guess your juvenile hooligan days were worth it," teased Nan weakly, as they raced down the cliff road at top speed, the burning castle monopolizing the mirrors' view.

"Yeah, I have my uses," laughed Parker.

Nan smiled at his jest as she drifted in and out of consciousness. She gave the castle of misery one last fleeting glance in the rear-view mirror and watched how the summit where it stood blazed like a beacon in the night, consumed by the vengeful fires of revenge. Then all went black.

Chapter 29
"I keep turning over new leaves, and spoiling them, as I used to spoil my copybooks; and I make so many beginnings there never will be an end." Louisa May Alcott

Groggy, Nan opened her eyes and looked around the sterile white hospital room; her mind a cloudy haze. *I don't remember coming to the hospital.* Hospitals were her least favourite place.

Not sure of anything, except the desire to get out of there, Nan tried to sit up on the bed and focus, but realized moving wasn't an option. Her left shoulder held fast by a tight sling, which slightly concealed the wrist cast she wore, Nan found she was constricted from escape by a large clump of plaster running from her right thigh to her toes, suspended in the air by another sling.

"Argh," growled Nan. She surveyed a series of tubes and wires entering and exiting her body to an array of machines stationed beside her uncomfortable hospital bed with their flashing lights and beeping noises. Perturbed and sore, Nan struggled against her bonds determined to gain control over her own body.

"If you keep that up, you'll never heal properly. Now sit still and behave," a laughing voice said from the corner. Unbeknownst to Nan, Parker sat watching her power struggle.

Surprised, Nan stopped and squinted through the lingering fog behind her eyes. When Parker's face became visible, she whined like a four year old, "Parker, oh thank goodness. Can you get me out of here? I hate hospitals."

Parker rose from the chair, crossed the room and stood by Nan's side where he stroked her head affectionately. "The doctor said you need to stay here for a few days. You hit your head a lot harder than we figured and they want to observe you."

"Seriously?" bleated Nan. "No, I won't stay, they can't make me."

"And where are you going to go?" he mocked and jiggled the cord, which suspended the sling imprisoning her right leg.

Nan sunk back in the bed with a huff. "It's not fair. I'm not an invalid, I'm a strong witch. You saw what I did. I can take care of myself."

"Yes, I did see," answered Parker, still dumbstruck and slightly unsure about what he had witnessed at the castle. "But even strong witches need help once in a while," he teased and gave her a playful fist nudge on the cheek.

Nan smiled at his toying sweet nature, but made no reply. An awkward silence fell between them, as all other avenues of conversation seemed to evaporate and the unresolved issue of the passionate night they had spent together hung in the air.

Reluctant to bring it up, though she knew it would have to come up sometime, Nan cleared her parched throat and said, "Parker, I...about the other night. I just want you to know..."

Druantia entered the room at that moment much to Nan's relief, cutting off the sensitive conversation. She beamed at her great niece as she approached the other side of the bed. "Splendid, you're awake. How are you feeling, Anabel?"

"Horrible," Nan sulked. "I want to get out of here. Please make the doctors let me go."

"Now, Anabel, you know it's for your own good, stop fussing. Besides you have this charming young man to keep you company. He's a keeper this one, he's been by your side day and night," Druantia smiled coyly at Parker.

"Really?" exclaimed Nan. She looked from her great aunt to Parker, who only shrugged, embarrassed.

"Yes well, you're on the mend now, so I'm sure you won't have to stay much longer," Druantia added. She gave Nan a reassuring pat on the shoulder.

"Fine," huffed Nan, "But I don't have to be pleasant about it."

"Perish the thought," mocked Parker.

Nan scowled at him, then turned her attention back to her great aunt and asked, "How's Gwynedd?"

"Ah, well I am afraid it will take considerable time before the damage of what has happened to her is erased, if it ever is. But she's trying to heal. In fact she's in this very hospital."

"She is?" replied Nan in amazement, having figured the poor woman would never leave the confines of Magewebb again.

"Yes, though she bellyached, like you," Druantia frowned at her niece to get her point across, "Shamus and I took her home in order to clean her up and avoid even more suspicion laced questions then we were already in for, and then brought her here to be checked out. Years in a hole, suffering from starvation and dehydration can do a lot to a body and I may be skilled, as we all are, at healing, but even I have my limits."

A hush fell over the room, each party lost in their own thoughts, until Nan inquired in a sad, bitter-laced tone, "Why didn't you tell me Oron was my brother?"

"Ah," uttered Druantia. She had expected such a question at some point, but still calculated a reply. "I was trying to protect you."

"Protect me!" shrieked Nan incredulously. "You were trying to protect me by not telling me? You knew who he was since we dined at the castle, you probably knew how much he hated our family...his family...and yet you let me lust after him. I actually was tempted to sleep with him and you were going to let me?" Nan stormed, but then thought of her last statement and quickly gave Parker an apologetic glance, the hurt obvious on his face.

"I would never have let it get that far," explained Druantia in desperation. "You had so much to deal with, I didn't want to burden you further and a small part of me hoped he would simply let it be."

"Let it be?" growled Nan. "What the fact that our mother abandoned him too? He's the one who killed her! Did you know that? That's how well he let it be."

"Ha," Druantia breathed in sharply with shock. Then her face fell into a sad remorseful mixture. "It was not his fault."

Now it was Nan's turn for surprise, matched by an equally stunned expression from Parker. "What do you mean?" he asked.

"Oron was the result of your mother's first marriage and at the time we believed he was a weapon manifested by Ucrane's dark magic. No boy has ever been born into the family and I'm afraid your grandmother and I poisoned your mother's mind against the innocent child. It was our misjudgement, which led to his vengeful heart. Your mother never bonded with the boy, staying as far away from him as she could out of fear and when she fled for her life the night Elijah sacrificed himself for her, she left the boy behind. By the time I realized our family's mistake, it was too late. Ucrane had already used the boy's discord to control him and wield his unjust rejection as a weapon against us."

"That's horrible," moaned Nan. "But maybe if you had told me sooner, I could have reached out to him when we were away from the castle and let him know that his family did want him...that I wanted him?"

"He knew who you were, Nan, and he still tried to kill you," protested Parker.

"Yes, I'm afraid you would have failed right from the start. Ucrane's evil worked its way into the boy years ago, if he hadn't indeed masterminded his conception in the first place, which would explain why you have no twin," Druantia added.

"What do you mean, how would that explain it?" Nan frowned, all this information was too much for her pounding head.

"I believe that when your mother gave birth to Oron, it broke the gods' spell on our family, which made us only conceive twin girls, hence your singularity."

"Hmm," Nan mused, she pondered this theory while the room again fell silent. Unable to get the disturbing thought out of her mind that if she had only had more time she could have changed Oron's mind, she inquired quietly, "Do you think he made it out at least? Maybe we should have someone check, call the authorities or something?"

"No," answered Parker adamantly. "I knocked him out when the fire started. He never left the castle as it burnt to the ground. Besides it's not like you can go back and poke around."

"Yeah I guess," she sighed.

"Actually, she could," corrected Druantia, which caused them both to look at her dumbfounded. "You see, as the oldest your mother was the sole inheritor of your grandparent's estate as well as Ucrane's. With both of them dead all the assets now revert to you, including Falconhurst's remains."

"Wow," exclaimed Parker, "You're rich!"

"Quite so," Druantia chuckled in agreement.

"What, really? But I don't want it," fumbled Nan. "It doesn't seem right. Gwynedd should get her parent's property, not me...and I don't want that miserable castle."

"It is kind of a bittersweet irony when you think of it," Druantia continued to laugh. "It was all yours to begin with as Anwen, so in theory you are merely claiming what was robbed from you."

"But I don't want it," assured Nan, growing vehemently annoyed.

"Well we'll talk more about it later shall we? But now you should get some more rest," Druantia smiled down at her grumpy niece. She gave her a parting kiss on the cheek with a reassuring pat on the shoulder and then left the room.

"Wow, you're an heiress," Parker grinned teasingly.

****

Nan had finally fallen into a restless sleep, the weight of her conscience and Druantia's revelations drowning her mind. Unable to pinpoint what exactly disturbed her, Nan suddenly opened her eyes with a start. In a chair beside her bed, mute and unmoving, hauntingly sat Gwynedd with her unseeing eyes.

"I'm sorry if I scared you," said Gwynedd in a hushed tone after hearing Nan's sharp intake of breath, trying not to wake Parker who slumbered in a chair in the far corner.

"No, that's okay. I'm glad to see you," whispered Nan in return. "How did you get here?" she asked, as she gazed around the never truly darkened hospital room for some sign of aid Gwynedd had used.

"My senses are very well defined after so many years in the dark and my strength is slowly returning, so it wasn't hard to make my way to your room. We are on the same floor," replied Gwynedd. "I wanted to talk to you, alone."

"Oh?" uttered Nan questioningly.

"I wanted to thank you again for rescuing me and wanted to ask why you didn't reveal you were my niece back in the dungeon?"

"I'm sorry I deceived you," Nan apologized, regretting her dishonesty. "I guess I was just worried if I told you it would have led to too many questions we didn't really have time to discuss. And at the time I was afraid of you asking about my mother."

"I understand," Gwynedd nodded. "No doubt I would have done the same if circumstances were reversed."

"Thank you for understanding," Nan smiled shyly. Though she had grown accustom to meeting and conversing with newfound family members since her arrival in England, Gwynedd produced a mournful uncertainty Nan couldn't explain, which left her tongue-tied.

A heavy pause hung in the air between them, the only two to survive Meldun's/Ucrane's maliciousness, providing them with an unspoken sense of comradery. Finally Nan cleared her throat in an attempt to remove the apprehensive lump, which had formed inside of it, and commented conversationally, "It must have felt wonderful to be back at Magewebb again after so long...um, away."

Gwynedd gave a little laugh, then smiled at her niece's tact and replied, "You don't have to wash over my imprisonment, Anabel. It is okay. My suffering at Falconhurst is a part of my life, I've accepted it and will not hide it away, nor let it define me. I hope to someday regain what part of me it took and to grow."

"Wow, you are so strong," admired Nan. "I don't know if I could be so positive and philosophic about something like what you have endured."

"You could, I can see it. There is a strength in you, I saw it in the dungeon. But let's hope you never have need again to demonstrate it, shall we," she continued to smile.

"I just wish I had discovered it all sooner. Discovered Magewebb, Druantia, my true path, you...and my mother," Nan sighed.

"As much as we don't understand it, everything in this life and those to come, happens for a reason, Anabel," responded Gwynedd, no longer the frail heap of a woman Nan had found in the dungeon, but an age wise pillar.

"Do you think she will be back? I mean, that my mother will get a chance at another life?" inquired Nan, hopeful.

"I do, but only because of you."

"Me? What did I do?" Nan scowled.

"Much. It was you who released your mother's soul and those of the prisoners from the dungeon when you vanquished Ucrane. Because of that, now your mother is free to live again," answered Gwynedd.

"Oh," exclaimed Nan quietly.

"Your mother talked of you," revealed Gwynedd after another slight pause.

"She did?"

"Oh yes. Before the agonies of her situation ripped her mind with desperate cries and screams of torment, we would talk there in our silent dark prisons. She told me how she had a beautiful little girl and wished she could have watched you grow. She didn't want to leave you or your father, Anabel. She loved you both very much."

"I'm beginning to see that now," acknowledged Nan. "She left to save you and instead it cost her, her life."

"Rhiannon did not leave you to save me," exclaimed Gwynedd, surprised by Nan's mistaken information.

"But she received Druantia's letter about your abduction and soon after left," objected Nan, puzzled.

"It was merely timing my dear. No, soon after receiving our aunt's letter, Rhiannon had a vision of your future if she was to stay. She saw that Ucrane would come for you both and despite her efforts to protect you, she would fail and not only you, but your father would lose his life as well trying to protect you both. As Elijah had done, so many years prior."

"Oh my goodness, I didn't know and neither does Druantia. She received mom's letter stating her return to New Forest, but when she never arrived Druantia didn't know what to think," exclaimed Nan.

"Yes, Ucrane had spies everywhere and learned of Rhiannon's impendent arrival, arranging to have his minions apprehend her before she could ever make it to the safety of Magewebb."

"But Oron said he killed her," Nan frowned at the inconsistencies.

"He did. It was Oron who came up with the method for your mother's demise. It was heartbreaking to be honest. Not hearing Rhiannon's suffering, though that was almost unbearable in itself, but the reunion between mother and child.

When your mother learned Oron's identity, she repented for her sins against him and pleaded for a second chance. She had realized her error many years earlier, but assumed Ucrane had done away with the boy after her flight. How utterly wretched she sounded once she realized he had been alive all this time and she could have claimed him as the son he always should have been to her. But Oron wouldn't listen, the bitterness in his heart from her rejection was too strong."

"How sad," Nan moaned. "Oh how this family has suffered. It is so unfair."

"Yes, but that is all over now, thanks to you," Gwynedd smiled reassuringly. "Your mother would have been proud of you, Anabel."

Nan didn't know what to say and only smiled. Gwynedd rose from her chair and reached out with her hand to identify her surroundings, then said before parting, "You get some sleep now, I'm sure we'll have plenty of time to talk in the future."

"I'd like that very much," replied Nan. "Do you need any help?" she asked worriedly.

"Oh no, my senses will guide me," answered Gwynedd as she disappeared out the door.

Chapter 30
"The owl of Minerva begins its flight only with the coming of the dusk," Georg Wilhelm Friedrich Hegel

A few days later, Nan stood awkwardly on crutches on the terrace and overlooked Magewebb's winter kissed gardens, which she had come to love so much. With Ucrane dead, life had gone back to normal—as normal as it could get for a family of witches—and it was time to start thinking about the future, her future. Nan knew a choice would soon have to be made, a resolution between her soul, head, and heart's desires.

Oh, how I love it here. She let her gaze wander over the property all the way back to the family's graveyard. *Magewebb is my home now.*

Yes, and it always will be, the wise voice of the raven answered in her head.

Nan looked over to Hexia, who was perched by her side on the terrace's wall and asked, *then why am I so conflicted?*

Before the raven had a chance to answer, another guiding light stepped out onto the terrace. "All the problems in the world have been said to be solved with fresh air and a clear head," commented Druantia, as she came to rest at her great niece's side.

"Then why am I still so undecided?" Nan sighed. "What happens now?"

"Now you step forward," she answered wisely."Anabel, I know you are unsure and possibly afraid to leave the security you have found here, with us, your family, but I would hate to see you pass up an opportunity to be happy, because you are too deeply tied to stone and mortar. It is better to have enjoyed a love you could share, even if only briefly, than to shy away from it all together, trust me."

"But I can't stand the thought of leaving here, Magewebb is my home. I've come to love it as much as you, and like you said here I have family," objected Nan.

"Magewebb will always be here for you, as will I and Gwynedd. This is where you belong, but for now your heart belongs with that boy," Druantia smiled coyly. "What you two have shared should not be done so lightly."

Nan started and eyed her ever-knowing great aunt. "How did you know?"

"Oh please dear, I'm old but am not completely unaware of the signs of love or the afterglow of intimacy on a man's face," she laughed, while Nan reddened with embarrassment.

"Oh well, I see," stammered Nan.

Nan changed the uncomfortable subject. "But there is still so much you have to teach me. Plus I have not yet dealt with my inheritance and figured out what to do about Falconhurst."

"There is nothing I can teach you that Anwen's soul within you hasn't already. The rest can be done from overseas. Besides you have the family grimoire to help you. And there's this new device my great niece keeps telling me about, I believe she calls it a telephone," Druantia smirked.

"Oh you heard me mention that did you?" laughed Nan in return. However it would be Druantia, Nan would miss most if she were to leave.

"Yes, maybe someday I will even install one. There is such a thing called a fax machine too, which enables you to sign documents when you're out of the country," Druantia continued to jest.

"Okay, okay, I get your point."

"And as for Falconhurst my dear, it is yours to do with as you wish. It is not going anywhere and can no longer bring harm. It is not but a dark mark on the horizon."

"Yes, and maybe that is where is should remain, as a reminder to any who think to revisit those crimes against our family," thought Nan aloud.

"I couldn't have thought of a better use for it myself," her great aunt seconded.

"As for the rest of it though," continued Nan, "I want Gwynedd to have her parent's London home and any other properties. They belong to her, not me."

"That is very righteous of you dear, I will see to the necessary legal requirements," assured Druantia.

"Thank you, I'm only trying to do what seems right."

"Does this mean we should be preparing to say our adieus?" probed Druantia.

Nan sighed and then said, "I simply don't know what to do. I wish it could all be simple."

"Nothing in life is simple my dear, otherwise what sense of adventure would there be?" replied Druantia. She tapped Nan's hand, which rested on the terrace wall, then turned and walked back into the manor, leaving Nan alone with her immanent decision.

****

Nan cumbersomely made her way up the grand staircase to the second floor in pursuit of her chamber. Cora descended towards her with an armful of linen and said pleasantly, "Ah Miss, it is so lovely to see you walking the halls again. I'm afraid I must admit that I'm going to miss you when you leave us."

Stunned, as she had not yet admitted herself that she planned to leave Magewebb, Nan looked at the old maid's smiling face and replied, "Thank you, Cora, I would miss you too, but I have not yet decided what my plans for the future will be."

"Ah well, when you've lived as long as the rest of us here, my dear, you just seem to have a sense for knowing these things," Cora grinned. She passed Nan's dumbfounded crutched stance and proceeded on with her chores.

Great so everyone in this house knows what I want, except for me. Nan huffed and laboured up the rest of the stairs.

As she made her way to her own room, Nan encountered Parker exiting his room, duffel bag in hand. Nan was about to ask where he was going when he cut her off and blurted out, "I love you Nan, I have since the first day we met, but I can't wait forever. I have a life I have to get back to."

He didn't wait for a reply, his heart pounding in his ears at the thought of losing her but determined to take a stand. He lowered his gaze from hers, stepped around her plaster-covered body, and headed for the stairs.

Nan willed herself to yell for him to wait, her mind going a mile a minute having no more time to doddle over the decision she had been toying with for a week, for years really.

What do I do? What do I do? What do I do?

Buck up girl, it'sss now or never. Ssstop playing the fool, Onyx hissed in exasperation. The serpent wondered if he was going to have to continue spelling everything out for his reunited pupil.

"Well you have to give me time to pack," Nan called out to Parker, before he descended the stairs. "A girl can't be ready to go in a matter of minutes."

His expression was one of astonished elation as Parker stopped and turned back to her. His smile wider than the entrance of the Panama Canal, Parker gave her a fake huff of impatience and teased, "Well hurry up then, I don't have all day."

Nan returned his love infused smile, turned, and gimped down the corridor to her bedroom. *Well there's no turning back now, whatever comes will come. But boy will I miss this place.*

****

About an hour or so later, Nan stood mournfully on the manor's threshold. She thought back to when she had first walked through its oak doors and about how much had changed since then. How much she had changed. This time she would go out them and not come back. The thought made her heart ache.

"Don't look so sad, Anabel, you would think you were going to a funeral, not about to embark on a new chapter of your life," said Druantia, as she stepped forward on the top of the manor's entry steps and reassuringly took Nan's hands in hers.

"I know, but it is just so hard," Nan sighed. She felt the tears of goodbye brimming up in her eyes.

"This is not the end, Anabel, nor is it goodbye," assured Druantia with one of her telltale smiles.

"No it is not," Gwynedd seconded. She stepped cautiously forward with her walking stick to join them, no longer in rags but dressed in a flowing winter festive smock, her white mane pleated beautifully down her back and Beowulf at his rightful place by her side.

"We are your family, you can never truly leave us. We will always be in each other's hearts," she continued, as she felt her blind way up Nan's shoulder to her cheek, which she stroked affectionately.

"And you will write to me, won't you," pleaded Nan, she looked from one woman to the other.

"Of course my dear," Druantia grinned, "Maybe one day I may even install that phone we talked about."

229

"But I wouldn't hold your breath," teased Gwynedd, her years in the dungeon slowly melting off of her to reveal a loving, warm, witty woman.

"Ha-ha," mocked Druantia. "Besides there is always airmail," she added in play, poking the ever-indignant raven perched on her shoulder.

That is what she thinks, grumbled Hexia in reply.

"Nan, are you ready?" Parker called up to Nan amongst the group of woman. He had finished securing their luggage onto the back of the trap, which Shamus had stationed at the ready to transport them to town where they would take a taxi to the airport for their departing flight home to Ontario.

"Yes, I'll be right there," yelled Nan over her shoulder. She turned back to her aunts and seized them in a big reluctant hug goodbye. "Oh how I'll miss you."

Druantia gave Nan's right wrist one last squeeze in farewell. However, Druantia's grip held and she moved her fingers up Nan's arm to examine a slight bulge under the sleeve of Nan's fall coat (pretty much inadequate now that the snow had begun to fall). She eyed her curiously and said, "Anabel, what on earth is wrapped around your wrist?"

A guilty smile spread on Nan's face as she raised the sleeve of her jacket and long sleeve shirt to reveal Onyx coiled around her wrist and part of her lower arm in an attempt to mimic an elaborate bracelet.

"Oh good grief girl, you do tempt fate," Druantia chuckled, as she stared down at the snake. Gwynedd howled with laughter at her side.

"Well how else am I supposed to get him home?" Nan giggled. "He didn't want to have to go through the whole quarantine process and that. This way I can just claim him as a pretty bracelet, a gift."

"I must say that is genius," admired Gwynedd.

"Nan, I'm sorry but we really must go or we'll miss our flight," interjected Parker once more.

"Yes, you best run my dear," said Druantia. Then after one last hug, she watched Nan head down the stairs to the cart. "You take good care of my great niece, young man."

Parker looked up at the regal woman and smiled, "I will, Lady Greenwick."

"Oh none of that now, you may call me Druantia," she grinned back.

"Okay, Druantia, thank you and I hope we see each other again too."

"As do I," she replied with a nod of adieu.

****

"I'm sure gonna miss ye Lassie," said Shamus, as him and Beauty chauffeured them to the village. Nan watched through tear clouded eyes as Magewebb faded into the landscape.

"As will I, Shamus. I will miss all of you," she replied, her voice caught a bit, which caused Parker to reach across from his adjoining seat and grab her hand. He gave it a little reassuring squeeze now and then.

As they boarded the airplane home, Parker and Nan still hadn't come to a verbal agreement on what their future held, but Nan thought it was pretty clear by her consent to accompany him back to Ontario and leave the place she had become so fond of.

Neither one were big fans of heights and as they settled back into their seats they focused on anything but the fading ground outside the plane's oval window. Absorbed in thoughts of the happy conversation she had had with Rory from a pay phone before boarding the plane, Nan didn't even notice when a small piece of folded paper was placed on her lap.

Ahmm, uttered Onyx from her wrist. His head poking casually out from under her shirtsleeve since Nan had removed her jacket once seated on the plane.

What? She stared down at her wrist leisurely placed on her lap.

Do you mind, that note isss ssscratching my nossse, the snake grumbled.

Nan finally noticed the note and picked it up as she rolled her eyes at Onyx's dramatics. She knew that in truth it had been nowhere near his face.

She unfolded the small scrap of paper and read,

So are we dating then?

Nan smiled to herself as she took a pen from her purse and scribbled a reply. She tossed it back on to its author's lap.

Parker reached for the paper, took a deep breath, and read,

Yeah, I guess so.

Translation of Anwen's Spell

Yr hyn unwaith Dechneuwyd, bellach wedi'i gwblhau
Ni ehaiff unrhyw hud llesteirio cyfiawnder wyf yn gofyn am
Tanau o ddicter, trowch esgyrn i lludw

What once was started, now complete
No magic shall hinder the justice I seek
Fires of anger turn bones to dust

Llawn o lid, dial yn felys
Ar fy gelyn, yr wyf yn bwrw boen hon
Ar gyfer y gweithredoedd efe a gyflawnwyd, a wnaed yn ofer

Full of fury, revenge be sweet
Upon my enemy, I cast this pain
For the deeds he committed, done in vain

Rwymo ef, gwasgu arno, dod ag ef i'r llawr
Poenydio ef, llosgi arno, gadewch ei cymalau hylosgi
Gyda hecs hwn gall byth yn dychwelyd

Bind him, crush him, bring him to the ground
Torment him, burn him, let his joints combust
With this hex may he never return.

Other Titles by Siobhan Searle

Tempest of Dreams

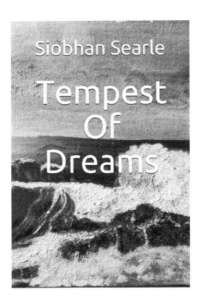

Never taking much stock in her grandmother's Scottish tales of old or her ancestors' pagan faith, Tempest discovers the error of her ways, when she is thrown into one nightmare scenario after another. Has she gone mad or are the gods' trying to tell her something?

Available in paperback or digital form on Amazon and through their associated retailers.

For more information on Siobhan Searle or to keep up to date on new material, check out her website or Facebook page at;
http://siobhansearle.wordpress.com/
https://www.facebook.com/SearleSiobhan/

Manufactured by Amazon.ca
Bolton, ON

14719882R00129